W9-BLJ-737

Acclaim for
Georgia Bockoven

"Bockoven's well-charted heartwrencher is sensitively depicted and thought-provoking."

—*Publishers Weekly*,
on *An Unspoken Promise*

"With compassion, understanding, and page-turning suspense, Georgia Bockoven explores the powerful bond between two strong and determined sisters."

—Diane Chamberlain,
on *An Unspoken Promise*

"The sensational Georgia Bockoven has written a stunning and heart-wrenching novel guaranteed to touch the soul. *Far From Home* is her greatest triumph yet."

—*Romantic Times*,
on *Far From Home*

Books by Georgia Bockoven

A Marriage of Convenience
The Way It Should Have Been
Moments
Alone in a Crowd
Far from Home
An Unspoken Promise
The Beach House

Published by HarperPaperbacks

THE
BEACH
HOUSE

GEORGIA BOCKOVEN

HarperPaperbacks
A Division of HarperCollinsPublishers

HarperPaperbacks

A Division of HarperCollins*Publishers*
10 East 53rd Street, New York, N.Y. 10022-5299

This is a work of fiction. The characters, incidents, and
dialogues are products of the author's imagination and are not to
be construed as real. Any resemblance to actual events or
persons, living or dead, is entirely coincidental.

ISBN: 0-06-108440-9

HarperCollins®, 📖 ®, and HarperPaperbacks™
are trademarks of HarperCollins*Publishers*.

Cover illustration by Rick Johnson

First printing: August 1997

Printed in the United States of America

Visit HarperPaperbacks on the World Wide Web at
http://www.harpercollins.com

❖ 10 9 8 7 6 5 4 3 2 1

PART ONE

MAY

CHAPTER

1

Julia dug in her pocket for the key and opened the front door to the beach house. Instead of going in, she stood at the threshold and stared inside. Light from the evening sun spilled into the room, gaining entry from a missing slat on the shuttered window. Dust hung suspended in the stagnant air, silent and waiting.

She'd expected the inside of the house to look as abandoned as the outside. But it didn't. It was as if she and Ken had been there just that past weekend. Her sweater still hung on the back of the chair where she'd left it all those months ago; the book Ken had been reading lay open and waiting on the end table.

They'd left late that Sunday evening last September, reluctant to end what had been a wonderfully intimate weekend, where they'd wandered through the booths at the Capitola Art Wine Festival, taken long walks on the beach, and talked about everything from where they would go on their next anniversary to finally starting their family, and then, for the first time in their married life, having sex without protection.

It had been the beginning of their season at the beach house, the nine months that they kept for themselves each year when most of the tourists were gone and the area returned to the artists, musicians, and radically liberal populace who called the half dozen towns that made up the Santa Cruz area their home.

Planning to come back the next Friday, they'd simply gotten in the car and driven away. Now there were nights Julia put herself to sleep wondering if they would have done anything differently had they known what was ahead. An unanswerable question, an anchor to slow her as she navigated the waters of being alone.

Unable to postpone going inside any longer, she crossed the threshold and closed the door behind her. How long would it take to shake the feeling that being there without Ken was wrong? There was no place Ken had loved more than this small, familiar cottage, no house that felt more like home, no other refuge that gave him the freedom just to be himself.

In her mind, Ken was as much a part of this place as the walls and foundation. How could she convince herself that she was stronger than the memories if she stayed where they were the most powerful? At thirty-two, she had decades ahead of her, all of them without Ken. No one had loved life more. He would be furious if he knew she'd ever questioned being able to go on without him.

She hung her sweater in the closet, closed the book, and put it away, then went into the kitchen for a drink of water, pausing to look out the one unshuttered window in the house.

The view was one she'd shared up until now, Ken teaching her the nuances of the tides, the patterns of the birds, and how to spot the wandering otter in the rolling waves. Binoculars were an essential part of every rear-facing room in the nearly century-old clapboard house. Perched on top of a fifteen-foot cliff and located in almost the exact middle of a milewide cove, they had a panoramic view of not only their small section of the California coast, but much of the Monterey Bay.

They were part of an island of twenty-five houses surrounded by a forest of pine, redwood, and eucalyptus that was kept from further development by the state of California. Ken was convinced there was no more beautiful place on earth. He'd once told her his fondest dream was to live out his life in this house with her at his side.

It was one dream too many.

Perhaps if he hadn't experienced the unbelievable meteoric rise from college dropout to owner of one of the largest computer software companies in the world. Maybe if they'd been a little less in love . . .

Julia reached for a glass and noticed a lone ant wandering across the cupboard door. Out of the corner of her eye she saw another and then three more. Following their path to the corner of the windowsill, she watched as one disappeared through what appeared to be a surface crack in the wood.

In the eight years she'd been coming to the beach house, this was the first time she'd found ants inside. She began opening cupboards and was about to congratulate herself that she'd caught the invasion early when she discovered an inchwide trail of two-way traffic leading to an open bag of sugar. Ants with empty mandibles moved up the wall while those with full loads moved down.

Like the stressed-out executive who snaps when her shoelace breaks, Julia was almost undone at the sight of the entrenched insects. After all these years, why had the damn ants chosen now to invade? She felt overwhelmed, beaten down, and sorely tempted to simply turn around and walk away.

But walking away wasn't her style. She faced things head on. Which was why she'd come down herself to get the house ready instead of turning the job over to someone else. Ken would have been proud of her.

A half hour later, reasonably sure she'd won the battle, Julia scrubbed the cupboard and counters. Giving the sink a final wash down, she reached up to turn off the water and was dumfounded when the knob came off in her hand. She tried putting the knob back by carefully fitting the broken pieces together but she couldn't get the handle to turn enough to even slow the stream of water.

She didn't have a clue what to do next. With two brothers, a doting father, and a husband who'd prided himself on being able to repair anything, Julia had never had to fix so much as a clogged sink. She'd never even taken her car in for service herself. How could she ever hope to become independent if she couldn't take care of a simple broken faucet?

She'd never sought independence and hated that it had become the focus of her life. Even more, she hated that it had become a necessity. She'd never kept it a secret that she loved being taken care of by Ken. She gladly let him do things for her that she could easily have done for herself.

Some of their friends thought her spoiled, some of her friends were jealous. Both sets predicted sagely that she wouldn't be able to survive without Ken. They were closer to the truth than they imagined, but not for the reasons they believed.

The sound of water rushing down the drain in a county as drought conscious as Santa Cruz triggered her practical side. She'd work on being independent tomorrow when there was a plumber available. For now she would throw herself on the mercy of her next-door neighbor, Andrew.

The door to Andrew's bungalow opened before Julia had brought her hand down from knocking. A tall man with prematurely gray hair and dark blue eyes—someone she'd never seen before—answered. He had a kitchen towel draped over his left shoulder, a glass of wine in his right hand, and an openly curious look on his face. "Yes?"

An enticing smell of peppers and onion and other things she couldn't identify wafted around him, reminding Julia she hadn't eaten since lunch. "Is Andrew here?"

He smiled. The effect was startling. A face that had seemed ordinary became enormously appealing. "I'm afraid not. Last I heard he was leaving Hawaii and headed for New Zealand."

"Andrew?" He'd talked about sailing around the world, but never without the word "someday" thrown in, and certainly not before he was sure his business would survive without him. "Who's running the nursery?"

"The guy who bought it."

She'd been away only eight months and it suddenly felt like years. "Andrew sold the nursery?" she repeated, convinced she'd heard him wrong.

"Completed the deal on Christmas Eve and took off in his boat on New Year's Day. He said he just woke up one morning and decided it was time he stopped putting things off."

"You're a friend of his?"

"Since college. We were fraternity brothers."

There were several other neighbors she could ask for help. Imposing on one she didn't know wasn't necessary. "I'm sorry I interrupted your dinner. Next time you hear from Andrew please tell him I said hi and that I'd love to see him when he gets home."

"And you are?"

"Julia Huntington."

"You're Julia?" He shifted his glass to his left hand and reached for hers. "Andrew told me to keep an eye out for you."

"He did? Why?"

"No particular reason, just that you were a friend of his."

"Uh-huh." Andrew and Ken had known each other fifteen years. With Ken gone, it was only natural that Andrew would feel an obligation to look after her, if only by proxy.

"All right. He said you might need some help around the place getting it ready for summer and that part of my rent would be to see that you got it."

Her hand still in his, she said, "I didn't catch your name."

"Eric Lawson."

"You have no idea how much I hate to admit this, Eric Lawson, but Andrew was right. I could use your help. Do you know anything about faucets?"

"Some."

She took the chrome knob out of her pocket and handed it to him. "Any ideas?"

He studied it for several seconds. "Besides tossing it?"

"That's okay by me, as long as you can tell me how to turn the water off without it."

"The shut-off valve doesn't work?"

She had no idea what a shut-off valve was. "I don't know. I didn't try it."

"Hang on a minute." He started back inside. "I have to check the stove, and then I'll come over and give it a try."

"That's not necessary. If you just tell me where—" But he was already gone. While she waited, she looked around the living room, noting the changes Eric had made since moving in. Andrew's beaten-up recliner was gone, replaced by a computer desk. The normally empty bookshelves were filled to overflowing with what appeared to be old, leather-bound volumes of important literature. There were a few paperbacks and hardbound popular fiction titles scattered here and there as if to point out the owner wasn't a complete intellectual snob. The coffee table held stacks of magazines with *JAMA* written on the top—medical journals.

Eric came back, minus the towel and wine. "Ready?"

"I'm sorry about taking you away from your dinner."

"It'll keep. Besides, this shouldn't take long."

The tone of voice was as familiar as the self-assured confidence. Ken had been the same way, supremely secure he could handle anything tossed his way. And he'd never been wrong, right up until the end.

As they headed toward Julia's house, Eric said, "Andrew mentioned you live in Atherton. How do you like it?"

"Fine." There was no need to act like a reluctant guest on a talk show. He was making an effort at conversation, not prying. "Actually it's very nice."

"My wife's father has his practice near there. He wanted me to go in with him and his partners when I completed my residency, but Sacramento seemed more my style."

She'd never heard anyone give Sacramento credit for style. Even the legislators left what many still privately called a farm town every opportunity they got. "You're a doctor?"

"Nonpracticing at the moment."

Her curiosity piqued, she asked, "On hiatus?"

"Of a sort." He held the garden gate for her. As they made their way through the tangle of overgrown flowers that grew alongside the brick pathway, Eric asked, "Would you like me to take down the shutters tomorrow?"

"I'm not completely inept." It would be a first, but how hard could it be?

"I didn't mean to imply you were. It's the rent thing. I take my obligations seriously."

She opened the door and led him inside. "Andrew is a sweet guy, but he had no right to dump me on you."

"He's not the only one around here who's been concerned."

"Oh?"

"You're a real favorite in this neighborhood."

"Thank you. That's nice to hear." She didn't take the compliment personally. She'd been the beneficiary of the goodwill Ken engendered from the day they met. His loving her had been all the recommendation his friends and family had needed, a wondrous gift to someone as shy as she'd been her entire life.

When they reached the kitchen, Eric went straight to the cupboard under the sink and reached inside. Seconds later the water stopped.

"How did you do that?" she asked.

"Come here, I'll show you." She moved next to him and lowered herself to her haunches. "See that handle?" He waited for her to nod. "It's called a shut-off valve. Every sink and toilet in the house has one. There's one outside that will turn the water off to everything in the house."

She stood. "Please tell me I'm not the first person you've met who didn't know this."

"Not the first." He rose from his haunches and stood beside her.

"How did you find out?"

"My uncle was a contractor. I spent my summers working for him."

She was abruptly and acutely aware how close they were. If either of them moved even an inch toward each other, they would be touching. The situation became claustrophobic. Julia took a quick step backward and caught her foot on the rug.

Eric reached out to steady her. "Are you okay?"

"I'm fine." She forced a smile as she freed herself from his hand. "With Grace for a middle name, it was almost a given that I'd be clumsy."

He returned her smile. "Julia Grace Huntington . . . it has a nice ring to it."

She'd been around a lot of men since Ken's death, had even had several come on to her in the past couple of months, but this was the first time she'd felt anything close to a response. The feeling was so unexpected, she didn't know what to think. "Thanks for fixing the water." She moved back into the living room. "When I see Andrew again, I'll be sure and tell him that you kept your part of the bargain."

"I didn't fix anything. Shutting the water off was a temporary solution. You still need—"

"I know—a plumber. I'll call one first thing in the morning." She could see that he was aware he was being dismissed but that he didn't understand why. How could he know the effect he'd had on her when he'd done nothing to precipitate it? She held the door for him. "You should get back to your dinner while it's still salvageable."

He stood on the small brick landing, his hands propped on the door frame. "Why don't you join me? I always make too much."

"I'm not hungry," she said, dismissing his invitation. "I already ate." That was every bit as bad. She sounded like the homecoming queen turning down a date with the fourth-string quarterback. She might as well have told him she had to wash her hair. "I appreciate the offer, Eric. Maybe another time."

He didn't say anything right away, just looked deeply into her eyes. And then, softly and with a depth of understanding that left him exposed, he said, "It's hard, isn't it?"

The question caught her off guard. "What?"

"Learning to live again."

He was a stranger, someone she would likely see once, maybe twice, more in the time she was there and then never again. There would be no long-term consequences to revealing the feelings she'd kept hidden from even her closest friends. The answer created a lump in her throat. "Almost too hard sometimes."

"It gets better."

"When?"

"First it's only five or ten minutes at a time, and then it's whole days."

"Did your wife die?"

"No, she found someone else before I learned how to stop loving her."

"I'm sorry."

"Yeah, me too. But I'm past it now."

"Really?"

"Maybe not completely. I'm still working on the guilt thing. But I think I've just about got that licked, too."

"Is the offer for dinner still open?" she asked impulsively.

The question brought a smile. "You don't even have to help with the dishes."

"Give me a couple of minutes to unload the car and change out of these clothes."

"I hope you like eel."

She was too surprised to hide her reaction. "Eel?"

He laughed. "Sorry, I couldn't resist. Actually it's just plain old spaghetti."

"I don't know. . . ." At one time she'd been capable of giving as good as she got; it had just been a long time since anyone had allowed her the opportunity. "I'm not sure I can trust you now. Maybe I should send out for something."

He started down the walkway toward his house. "Make it a sausage-and-pepperoni pizza and you're on."

"You're not even going to try to talk me into tasting your spaghetti?"

"I'm easy, Julia—didn't used to be, but I've learned."

"I wish you'd tell me how you did it," she said, not realizing how much she was unwittingly revealing about herself until the words were out.

He turned and walked backward as he talked to her. "I don't know if I could, but I'd be willing to try."

CHAPTER

2

Julia waited until Eric was inside his house before she took her suitcase out of the car and went inside to change. She started to put on a pair of linen slacks and then discarded them in favor of chinos and a knit top. It wasn't a date she'd agreed to, simply a shared meal.

On impulse, as she passed through the garden, she stopped to pick a bouquet. During the desolate eight months a timer had kept the small lawn watered and a gardener had come by to mow, but no one had tended the flowers. The bleeding hearts, foxglove, cosmos, plume poppy, and alum-root had long ago spilled from their tidy beds, collapsing from the weight of their flowers onto the brick walkways.

After picking only a few blooms from each plant, she presented the colorful assortment to Eric as he opened the door.

"For me?" He seemed genuinely surprised at the casual offering. "This is a first."

"No one has ever given you flowers?" She'd always sent them to Ken, everything from single roses to wildly extravagant arrangements.

"Friends sent plants when I started my practice, but nothing that bloomed."

She followed him into the kitchen, where he took a glass out of the cupboard and filled it with water. "It smells wonderful in here," she said. Her stomach growled in anticipation.

"It's amazing what you can put together with cans and packages." He put the bouquet in the glass and the glass on the table, letting the flowers arrange themselves. The effect was in keeping with the casual dishes, paper napkins, and multicolored candles already there.

"What can I do to help?" Julia asked when he went back to the stove to stir the sauce. Over the years she'd been in Andrew's kitchen a hundred times and felt almost as comfortable in it as she did in her own.

"The garlic bread should be ready." He handed her an oven mitt. "There's a knife in the drawer by the sink."

They worked together, completing the meal in an easy, companionable silence, as if they were old friends who'd shared the ritual a dozen times before. When everything was on the table, Eric poured the wine, lit the candles, and held Julia's chair.

"Thank you," she said, sliding into place.

When he was seated across from her, he

held his glass up in a toast. "To broken faucets and new friendships."

She touched her glass to his. "And successful publishing ventures."

His thick eyebrows, several shades darker than his hair, drew together in a questioning look. "How did you know?"

"It was simple deduction, Dr. Lawson. I asked myself what a physician on hiatus would be doing with a computer."

"And from that you concluded I was writing a book?"

"That . . ." She smiled and reached for something on the counter behind him. Holding it up, she added, "And this—*Ten Steps to Writing the Best-Selling Novel.*"

"You had me there for a minute."

She put the book back. "Have you always wanted to write?"

"Since I was in high school. I could never see myself actually making a living at it, though. Medicine seemed a more promising way to feed myself, at least in the beginning."

"What happened?"

He reached for a piece of bread and laid it on the edge of his plate. "I got tired of some twenty-year-old sitting behind a desk in an insurance office telling me what tests I could order for my patients."

Her father was a doctor, the complaint a familiar one. "I thought the problem was getting better."

"Not fast enough for me. I figured out that

my staff was spending as much time on the phone getting permission to treat people as I was treating them."

"So you just up and quit?"

"Not until I'd taken my frustration out on all the wrong people, including my wife. Shelly tried to get me to see what I was doing, but by the time I did, it was too late."

Julia took a sip of wine before commenting. "Don't you hate hindsight?"

"You sound as if you've been there."

"Ken had his heart attack on the way to work. He was on the freeway at the time—the fast lane." Which lane he was in, the temperature, the clothes she'd worn, were only a few of the meaningless things about that morning she couldn't put aside. She speared a mushroom and absently pushed it around the plate, focusing on the path it made through the red sauce to keep the image of Ken behind the wheel of his car from filling her mind. "There was a chain reaction, as people tried to avoid hitting him, that tied up traffic for hours."

The accident had made the national news that night. The local stations and newspapers carried the story for days. Weeks and months later came the magazine articles. Half a year went by before she felt safe looking at any of the business journals that came to the house.

One detail, however, had escaped all of the media sources; it was something she'd never told anyone. For eight long months she'd kept her painful secret. It was time she let go. "I was on the freeway that morning. I left the house a half hour after Ken and got caught in the backup from his accident." The rest was harder, something she hated admitting even to herself. "All I could think about . . . my only feeling was frustration that the wreck was going to make me late for my hair appointment."

She chanced looking at him. He appeared neither shocked nor repulsed at her self-damning revelation. "I got to the accident a few minutes after the ambulance arrived, but I was so busy watching the clock, I didn't even look over to see what kind of car it was. The doctor told me later that Ken was still alive when they got him out of his Range Rover. I could have been with him if I hadn't been so damn—"

"Even if you had stopped, it wouldn't have changed anything. Beating yourself up about it is useless." He reached across the table and put his hand over hers. "The hardest thing any of us has to do when someone close to us dies is accept that there are times when shit just happens. Nothing we could have done or said would have made any difference."

"I could have told him good-bye."

"You're imagining something that wouldn't have happened even if you had stopped. The rescue workers had to get Ken out of there as fast as they could. There's no way they would have stopped to let you talk to him. At best, you would have been in the front seat of the ambulance when he died."

They were the words she needed to hear, not absolution but reality. "You must have been one hell of a doctor. I'll bet your patients miss you."

"I left them in good hands."

"Have you always had a fatalistic attitude, or did it come with being a doctor?"

"I suppose a part of me has. However, I've never taken it so far as to think your faucet was predestined to break tonight so we could meet." His eyes lit with a spark of amusement. "Some things in life I chalk up to blind luck."

He was flirting with her. The thought left her disconcerted. She quickly changed the subject. "Do you like being a writer?"

"Some days."

She twirled her fork against her spoon, capturing a round of spaghetti. "And the others?"

"It just seems like plain old work."

"Have you given yourself a deadline?" she asked.

"For finishing or succeeding?"

"Either—both."

"The end of the year to finish. After that it's out of my hands for the most part." He reached for another piece of bread. "How about you? Are you working on any deadlines?"

"Meaning?"

"Oh, you know . . . three months to get the finances in order, six months to grieve, a year to figure out what you want to do with the rest of your life, that kind of thing."

She shook her head. "I've never been that organized. Things just kind of happen with me."

"I've always admired people like you."

"You're kidding." She took a bite and licked the sauce from the corner of her mouth. "I was under the impression I drove your kind crazy."

"My kind?"

"People who are driven to succeed. Overachievers."

He winced.

She had her wineglass halfway to her mouth and put it down again. "What did I say?"

"Nothing."

"Come on . . . I thought we were being honest with each other."

"You sounded just like my wife—my ex-wife. She used words like those when I tried to talk her into giving me another chance."

"I'm sorry."

"Yeah, me too." He put his napkin on the table and leaned forward on his elbows. "I see my kids every other weekend now."

"That must be hard on all of you."

He made a disparaging sound. "I hate like hell to say it, but it's more time than I spent with them when we were living together."

She could see the admission had cost him and offered a commiserating smile. "There's that damn hindsight again."

"Time for a change of subject." He put his hands against the table and pushed back his chair. "More wine?"

"No thanks. I think I've had enough." It was

easier to blame the wine for her talkativeness than to acknowledge the need that prompted it.

He brought the bottle to the table and poured himself a healthy splash. "Before Andrew left he started telling me about an old couple who spend July here, but we got interrupted and he never got around to finishing the story."

"Joe and Maggie." Just thinking about them brought a smile. "They're the ones who sold the house to Ken. They kind of adopted him in the process."

"Andrew said there was a special connection."

"They really didn't want to sell, but Joe had had a stroke that used up his and Maggie's savings, and they really needed the money. Ken was renting the place at the time and told them that if they would carry the note themselves so that he wouldn't have to look for outside financing, he would give them the summer months to do with as they pleased for as long as he owned the house."

"I wondered how the place had become a summer rental—Joe and Maggie used it to supplement their income. Now it makes sense."

"Actually, Joe gave the money to Ken." Again she smiled. "He was so proud of himself for figuring out a way to help Ken financially that Ken didn't have the heart to tell him he didn't need it." Every September for eighteen years Joe and Maggie and Ken had gotten together for dinner. Joe would give Ken the rental check, and Ken would give a toast to their friendship. When Ken and Julia were married, Joe and Maggie came as honored guests. At the end of summer the September dinner reservation went from three to four. It was as if Julia had always been a part of their little group.

"They sound like special people."

"They are. But then so are the others. Joe was very selective in whom he chose as renters."

"It will be nice to see someone there. The place was getting pretty desolate looking." It took half a second for what he'd said to hit. "Jesus, I'm sorry, Julia. I shouldn't have—"

"It's all right. The same thought hit me when I drove up."

"How about some coffee? It would only take a minute to fix."

She shook her head. "I should probably call it a night. I've got a big day ahead of me tomorrow."

"I'll walk you home."

Deciding that protesting would take more effort than giving in, she let him see her to her front door.

"Thank you for dinner." She stepped inside and turned to face him. "It was wonderful. You really know your cans and packages."

"Someday I'll have to show you what I can do with bakeries. There isn't one within a five-mile radius I haven't tried."

"Now you're stepping on my territory."

"Restaurants?" he asked.

"I have a drawer full of menus."

"Delis?"

"Kosher or non?"

He held his hands up in defeat. "I yield to your time and experience."

She smiled. "Thanks again for the plumbing lesson."

"Anytime." He stepped up to the landing, leaned forward, and gave her a quick kiss on the cheek.

Julia waited until she saw him cross the road, then went inside and closed the door. The thought hit that she was as alone as she had been that afternoon, but not as lonely. Progress could be a funny thing sometimes, coming not only when one least expected it, but from a direction never imagined.

CHAPTER

3

Eric zipped his jacket against the early morning fog as he stopped to examine a sand dollar that had washed up on a wave. The last time Jason and Susan spent their weekend with him at the beach, Eric had blithely promised Jason he would collect the fragile shells for him so that he could surprise his mother with a homemade wreath for her birthday, never suspecting how hard it would be to find them unbroken. In three days he'd be in Sacramento for their twice-a-month visit, and the box Jason had left to be filled held less than half a dozen shells.

Susan had requested he bring her a starfish, orange like the ones she'd seen in San Francisco with her mother and her mother's new "friend," Roger. He'd already found a nice big one for her in a shop near the boardwalk in Santa Cruz.

Even after being divorced almost two years, Eric had still felt a moment of possessiveness when he heard about one of Shelly's dates, especially if that date involved the kids. Now she was engaged and about to be married, and he'd been forced to accept that they were never going to get back together. Still, he couldn't picture her with someone else. Just as he couldn't imagine himself ever loving another woman.

Some people were meant for each other.

He turned over the sand dollar, saw a large hole on the crown, and returned the shell to the sea.

And sometimes one of them was too blind, or too stupid, or too preoccupied, to realize that even something predestined needed nurturing to survive.

Behind him a lone gull landed in the cream-colored foam left by a wave. For several seconds it explored the popping bubbles, then shook its head and flew away, disappearing in the fog. Before he'd moved into Andrew's house, Eric had never considered himself an ocean person, preferring to spend his free weekends in the mountains, his vacations in Europe. But in the months he'd walked the beach and listened to the waves, he'd come to understand the lure and, finally, to be taken in by it.

Selfishly he liked having the beach to himself, which was why he came there in the early morning when it was him and one or two fishermen. He also came late at night, when he would happen upon the occasional lovers, but they were as oblivious of him as of their surroundings. Neighbors had told him how dramatically things changed in the summer, how the tourists filled every campground, hotel, and rental house in the cluster of small cities between their small cove and Santa Cruz, how they would come to the beach to stake out a section of sand for their day-long homage to sun and surf. He'd been forewarned about music that blared from untended radios and how often free-flowing beer led to strutting and puffing and the occasional fight between young men seeking to impress.

Eric always listened with what he hoped was a properly concerned expression. Although summer would mean the loss of privacy and his solitary walks, in a strange way he found he was looking forward to the change. In reality, he wasn't so far removed from those years himself that he'd forgotten their sweet misery or felt the need to condemn their excesses. Perhaps when his own children neared that age his fear would make him less tolerant and he would feel compelled to bluster and warn. Until then he would bask in the memories.

A wave lapped at his feet, reminding him why he was there. He toed aside a tangle of kelp and went back to searching for sand dollars.

Julia came to the previous night's high-water mark and stopped to roll up the pant legs to her khaki slacks before she stepped onto the cold, wet sand. She wasn't normally out and about this early, but the fog and the empty beach had been such a welcome sight when she'd looked outside that morning that she'd been lured to go for a walk even before she'd had her first cup of coffee.

Shoving her hands into the pockets of her sweatshirt, she moved forward to let the waves wash over her feet. As the water retreated, it stole sand from beneath her feet and forced her to readjust to keep her balance. It reminded her of the way her life had been since Ken's death. Every time she felt herself on sure footing again, something happened that left her scrambling to stay upright.

The Wednesday of the first week in December, when she'd actually begun to believe she would make it through Christmas without him, a package had arrived that Ken had ordered a month before he died. It was a Fabergé piece he'd bought at auction, a lily of the valley spray made out of diamonds and pearls propped in a glass made out of clear topaz. Without question the miniature had cost a fortune, but for her the value came from the care he'd taken to find the gift, knowing how the flower would please her.

She'd waited until their anniversary in March to scatter his ashes at sea, believing the symbolism would help her say the good-bye she'd missed on the roadside. Instead she'd gone home that night with the quiet conviction she and Ken were bound by ties that could never be broken. Only in death had she come to realize how truly perfect a match they had been, fulfilling each other's needs with a joy that made the giving seem a gift. From the day they met they had inhabited a world of their own making, where understanding was expressed with a look and love with a smile.

It was her luck and her misfortune that they had found each other. Had they never met, she might have been able to settle for something less in another man. But now, having known the love of a lifetime, she realized more clearly with each passing day that she was destined to live the rest of her life alone.

Sometimes in the middle of the night when she couldn't sleep, an irrational anger would steal into her feelings of loss. She would question how Ken could abandon her after spoiling her for any other man. Why hadn't he told her that he had a grandfather and uncle who had both died of heart attacks before they were fifty? She would have forced him to take better care of himself, made him go to the doctor for more frequent checkups. Hadn't he known that it wasn't just his life he'd held in his hands, but hers, too?

She dug her toes into the sand to reclaim her position. The receding wave snatched the grains she'd disturbed, leaving her toes exposed again. Somewhere in the battle was a lesson, but she couldn't summon the energy to figure out what it was.

Something solid washed over her foot. She reached down and captured a plastic top from a six-pack of soda as it made a second pass. Before stuffing it in her pocket, she automatically tore the loops to keep some seagull or curious otter from inadvertently choking itself to death.

Was this something Ken had taught her, or had she always known?

She had no idea anymore where she began and he left off.

Her gaze fixed on the fog-shrouded sea, she froze when she heard her name being called, seemingly carried on an incoming wave. Rigid with anticipation, she waited to see if she would hear it again. When it came a third time, she realized with a stab of disappointment that the voice was coming not from the sea, but from somewhere to her left. She looked and saw a man heading toward her. For the length of a heartbeat she let herself believe it was Ken.

But it wasn't.

"I thought it was you," Eric said as he drew closer. "Beautiful morning, huh?"

She studied his face to see if he was serious. "My favorite kind."

"Me too." He stopped beside her and brushed back hair the same color as the fog from his forehead. "I love mornings like this almost as much as a good storm."

"I understand you had plenty of both last winter."

"I missed most of the really good stuff. Things had settled down by the time I moved in. I was on my way up for some breakfast. Would you like to join me?"

She shook her head. She'd wanted to be

alone this first morning at the beach without Ken, but she didn't know how to tell Eric.

He didn't push. "Guess I'll see you later, then."

Oddly, now that he was going, she wanted him to stay. "What's that in your hand?"

He held up a lone sand dollar. "I promised my son I'd collect them for him, but I'm not having much luck."

"Have you tried Sunset State Beach?" His puzzled expression told her that he didn't know what she was talking about. "It's the beach near Watsonville . . . where the Pajaro River empties into the ocean." She still hadn't placed it for him. "Anyway, you should check it out. I've been there when you couldn't walk on the shoreline without stepping on sand dollar shells."

"Thanks. Maybe I'll give it a try this afternoon." He smiled and started to leave. Turning back, he said, "Would you like to come with me?"

She answered before she even considered the invitation. "No—I have a hundred things to do and not much time." She was doing the same thing to him she had the night before. "And there's the plumber. I'm not sure what time he's coming."

"Have you called one yet?"

He knew she hadn't. It had been barely six o'clock when she'd left the house. It couldn't be much past that now. "No, but I looked in the phone book and there are several listed. I figured I'd just keep trying until I found someone who could come out today."

He flashed an intriguing smile. "I'll make you a deal."

She had no choice but to respond. "What is it?"

"Come with me to find Jason's shells and I'll fix your faucet."

Why was she resisting him? It was only a couple of hours he wanted from her, not the entire day. "I haven't even brushed my teeth yet."

"You're going to have to help me out here. Does that statement mean you're going to come with me as soon as you do, or is it supposed to be a reason for not going?"

"I'll go. But I can't be gone long. I really do have a lot of work to get the house ready before next week." She spotted a piece of glass in the sand and reached down to pick it up.

Eric opened his jacket pocket. "You might as well put it in here with the rest of this stuff."

She looked inside and saw that he, too, collected litter on his walks. "One more thing."

"Yes?"

"Coffee . . . I can't last the morning without it."

He slipped his arm around her shoulder and gave her a quick, friendly hug before starting across the sand toward the stairs. "We'll stop on the way. I know just the place."

Panic gripped her. Before she could reason it out, she came to an abrupt stop and asked, "What place?"

He frowned. Slowly a look of understanding appeared. "In Soquel, down the street from Carpos."

"I don't remember a coffee shop there."

"It's only been open a couple of months."

"Oh."

"I take it you and Ken used to go out for coffee."

"He had this thing for mochas."

"With me it's vanilla latte."

She shuddered. "Real coffee should be strong and have a bite."

"Could we talk about this on the way?" He motioned for her to get moving. "My last trip to Watsonville I got caught in a traffic tie-up because of that movie they're filming over there."

"They're shooting a movie in Watsonville? What kind?"

"I think it has to do with migrant farm workers. Several of the people involved are renting houses around here, but they pretty much keep to themselves."

"My brother is head of security for Kramer Studios. I wonder if this is one of theirs."

"I've never heard of the people making this movie." He considered what he'd said. "But then I'm not sure I could name half a dozen production companies if I tried."

"Seems to me you'd better start doing your research. You don't want your book sold to some second-rate outfit."

He chuckled. "I'll put it on my list of things

to do—right after the laundry." As he turned to leave her at her driveway, he said, "Bring your checkbook. We'll stop by the hardware store on the way back."

"You mean the faucet isn't part of the deal?" Was this really her? She couldn't remember the last time she'd actually teased someone.

He grinned. "I'm just a poor struggling writer, remember?"

"Who just happens to drink expensive vintage wine for every day." She liked that he gave as good as he got and that he wasn't intimidated or impressed by the empire Ken had built and left her. So many people were. When that happened, it created a barrier that obviated friendship.

"On the contrary, having you over for dinner was far from 'every day.'"

"I'd be more impressed if you hadn't opened the bottle before I knocked on the door."

"Ouch." He put his hand to his chest as if she'd wounded him. "I'll pick you up in five minutes."

"Make it ten."

"Eight."

Laughing for the second time that morning, she left without countering further. With the shutters still in place, the house was dark, the feeling oppressive. Yesterday she might have welcomed it as a respite from the ceaseless smiles and optimistic attitudes that assailed her everywhere she went at home. Today she felt a flash of irritation that the house didn't share her newfound enthusiasm for the day ahead.

That afternoon the sun came at them from a dozen directions, off windows, and water, and the chrome strips on the Mercedes, as if trying to make up for the gray morning. Reluctant to be inside on such a glorious day, Julia worked on the flower beds while Eric took down the shutters. She'd picked up several new plants at the hardware store, ignoring the voice that questioned her reasoning. Not only wouldn't she be there to enjoy the fruits of her labor, she'd be putting the house up for sale in September. Still, by the time she was through in the nursery, she'd filled the back of Eric's car with flats of dianthus, snapdragons, zinnias, and dahlias, forgetting the other work she'd planned to get done in favor of being outside and digging in the dirt.

"That looks great," Eric said as he came out of the garage.

She rocked back on her heels and looked up at him. "I've talked about replanting this walkway for ages. The nasturtiums were past their prime years ago."

"Is that what I've got growing at my place—nasturtiums?"

"Andrew keeps them because they're low maintenance." She smiled. "And he likes to use them in salads when he has company."

"That reminds me, I'm starved. How about you?"

"Yeah, now that you mention it, I could eat something."

"Sandwiches okay? I know a great deli in Aptos." Before she could say anything he added, "It's the one in the shopping center at—"

"Sandwiches are fine. And I know which one you mean. There's a take-out place down the road from there that's even better." She stood and brushed the dirt from her slacks. "My treat."

He hooked his thumbs in the front pockets of his jeans and studied her. "This is none of my business—"

"I hear a 'but' coming." She sent him a look she hoped would relay how weary she was of well-meaning advice.

He either didn't pick up on her look or chose to ignore it. "From everything I've heard about you and Ken, he left you with hundreds of wonderful memories. Turning every place you went together into some kind of shrine could really be self-destructive."

Her anger left her speechless. She'd known him less than twenty-four hours. What made him think he had a right to comment on the way she chose to mourn her husband?

"I can see that went over well," Eric said. "I'm sorry. I shouldn't have said anything."

"What is it about me? Do I have a sign taped to my back saying 'Will work for advice'?"

"You make people care. And when they care, they want to help."

"So it's all my doing?"

"You don't think I'm going to accept blame, do you?"

At the same time the idiocy of the argument hit, her anger dissipated. How could she expect anyone, let alone someone who hadn't even known Ken, to understand what he'd meant to her or what it had meant for her to lose him? Despite a concentrated effort not to, she smiled. "If you think it's fun to be around me now, you should see me when I'm really trying to be charming."

Eric was caught off guard at the abrupt change. For an instant it was as if her abandonment of the battlefield had given him a glimpse into her mind. The depth of her loneliness shook him. She touched the "vanquishing hero" part of his mind, the childhood fantasy hero who told him all he had to do was wrap her tightly in his protective cape and she would be shielded from pain. Only the man he'd become knew there was no shelter from pain that came from inside. "Pickles?"

She frowned. "What?"

"Do you want pickles on your sandwich? I figured I'd go alone so you could stay here and finish the flowers."

"Yes."

"Yes what? The pickles or me going alone?"

"Both," she said. "But not in the sandwich. On the side."

"What kind?"

"Dill."

"I meant what kind of sandwich."

"Ham and cheese."

"On rye?"

She nodded. "With lots of mayonnaise but no mustard."

"Chips?"

"Barbecue."

He made a face. "Anything else?"

"Macaroni salad."

"What about dessert?"

She thought a minute. "Carrot cake. I'm willing to share, if you'd like."

"No thanks. I'm having humble pie."

She didn't say anything for several seconds. "What happened was my fault. You got hit with something that's been building inside me for months. It wasn't fair, and I apologize."

"Don't. You were absolutely right to do what you did. I had no business interfering."

"But you were right about what you said. The strange thing is that at home I've almost made it a mission to go back to all the places Ken and I frequented. I knew if I didn't, they would wind up holding power over me, and I refused to let that happen." She turned away from him, put her hand up to shield her eyes, and looked at the ocean. "Then I came here and it's as if I'm starting all over again."

"As busy as you must have been, you probably forgot all about this place."

"No, I didn't," she said softly.

Finally he understood. It hadn't been business or friends or family that had kept her away from the beach house. This was the one place she could not face without Ken.

Yet she had.

While Julia was looking away from him, Eric took the opportunity to study her. He tried to imagine the way she had been with Ken, before the sadness had stolen even the small joys that made up a day. He'd seen traces of what he'd assumed was the old Julia as they'd searched for sand dollars, both in her smile and in the way she'd accepted his challenge over who could collect the most unbroken shells. At times the looks she'd given him held questions; at others, mischief. But they were fleeting moments, gone before he could respond.

He wondered about the woman Ken had known. Was she hiding somewhere inside, or had that part of her died when Ken did?

CHAPTER

4

Julia heard a sound behind her and, thinking it was Eric back from the deli, said, "It's about time."

"I would have come sooner, but I didn't notice your car until just a few minutes ago."

She let out a squeal of delight as she dropped her spade and got up. "Peter—how wonderful to see you."

He took her in his arms in a hug that lifted her off the ground. "I've been worried about you," he said, putting her down again and looking directly into her eyes. "I haven't heard from you in weeks."

"I kept telling myself I should call, but it's been crazy at work lately. You wouldn't believe what I had to go through just to get away this week."

"Well, no matter. You're here now and you look wonderful."

Peter Wylie was Ken's oldest friend in

California. Tall and fit with a square jaw and intense blue eyes, his black hair untouched by gray, he looked more like a construction worker than an artist. He'd been the one she'd called to clean out the refrigerator and close the beach house that past winter, knowing he would understand why she couldn't do it herself. Born and reared in the area, he'd taught Ken to surf and sail and helped instill a California attitude that left him sounding and thinking like a native. They'd been drinking buddies back when they had to scrounge through car ashtrays and sofa cushions to come up with the price of a six-pack. Peter had sold his first watercolor the day Ken sold his first computer program. Their celebration had lasted for days.

Now Peter's watercolors were handled by some of the finest galleries in the country and collected by as many investors as fans. He could afford to live anywhere, but for ten months every year he resided in the small five-room house he'd been living in when he and Ken first met. The other two months he escaped the summer crush of tourists by going on the road to visit galleries and friends.

A couple of years ago Julia had asked him why he left for June and July and then returned in August every year in the height of the summer season. His only reply had been a shrug, as if it were a mystery to him, too. She had looked to Ken for an answer, and his response had been as inexplicable. In the end, she'd put it off as one of those "guy" things.

"Are you packed and ready to go?" Julia asked.

"Just about."

An unfamiliar awkwardness overcame her. She didn't know what to say. For as long as she and Peter had known each other, Ken had been a part of their friendship. Since his death they'd been like two legs of a three-legged stool. "I'm thinking about selling the house," she blurted out.

He nodded. "I figured you might. When?"

"Not until after the summer. I wanted everyone to have this last year." She still hadn't decided how to break it to the families that had been coming there twice as long as she had. Telling Joe and Maggie would be especially hard. Ken had promised they would have their summer at the beach for as long as he owned the house. At the time he'd honestly believed his promise was good for as long as they lived. Somehow she would make it up to them.

"Let me know before you put the place on the market, would you?"

Julia gave him a questioning look. "Why?"

"I don't know. . . ." He rubbed his hand across the back of his neck. "After all this time I can't imagine having strangers living here."

"You're not thinking about buying it yourself, are you?"

When he didn't answer, she pushed a little harder. "You couldn't paint here. The lighting is terrible. You've told me so a hundred times."

"I was thinking I could live over here and

turn my place into a studio. They're only two houses apart. I think I might like having some distance between where I work and live."

The idea appealed to her, too much so. Had she told Peter about selling the house because she wanted him to come up with a solution that would make it easier for her to let go? "When are you leaving?"

"I have to be out by the first of next week. I told a friend of mine that his daughter-in-law could use the place while he's in town working on that movie they're shooting in Watsonville."

"I heard that one of the actors was staying in the house up on the hill."

"Rumor has it they're all over the place. If it's true, they're keeping a low profile. The first I saw of any of them was a couple of days ago on the beach. There were five guys—they told me only one of them was actually in the movie, and that the others were crew—playing volley-ball and drinking designer water."

"You sound disappointed."

"Designer water? I'd always heard it got pretty wild on location."

"Like the parties they throw for you at the galleries?"

He laughed. "An insomniac could sleep through the best of them."

"When will you be back?"

"The last week in July."

It was always the same. Peter might leave early, but he never came home late.

"We'll talk about selling the house when

you get back," Julia said. It occurred to her then that Peter might not want to stop by to see her before going home now that Ken was gone. "Unless—"

"I'll be there," Peter said. "When did you ever know me to pass up a home-cooked meal?"

"I just thought it would be a good time to talk things over. Who knows, we could have both changed our minds by then."

She wouldn't, but the summer would give Peter time to get used to the idea. "God knows I do that often enough. There are days I hardly know what I want anymore."

"You look good," he repeated. "Better than the last time I saw you."

"Thanks." She smiled. "I think." He'd last seen her at Christmas, catching her by surprise an hour after Ken's present had arrived. Even though he'd had other plans for the rest of the day, he'd canceled them and stayed with her. Not once did he utter one of the standard empty platitudes she'd come to know by heart. He hadn't even flinched at her free-flowing tears.

She heard a car door slam and looked up to see Eric headed their way. Judging by the size of the bags he carried, he'd bought enough to feed the neighborhood.

"Hey, Peter," Eric called out, "where have you been keeping yourself?"

When it became obvious Eric was there because of Julia, Peter looked from one to the other, his expression going from surprise to confusion to questioning. Guilt washed over Julia, leaving her feeling as if she'd been caught doing something wrong.

"You know each other, I take it," she said, fighting an irrational urge to escape inside the house.

"Eric found me on the beach and took me to the hospital after some asshole fisherman shot me when I was out on my board. The fisherman said he thought I looked like the seal that had been eating *his* salmon."

Julia's jaw dropped. "When did this happen?"

"A couple of months ago."

"Are you all right?"

"It was just a flesh wound," Peter said dismissively.

"Another half inch and he could have lost his arm," Eric added.

Julia searched Peter's arms for scars. She found one just above his left elbow. "My God, you're left-handed . . . your painting . . ."

"That was the first thing I thought about, too," Peter admitted.

She touched his arm as if to confirm the scar was real. "I take it they caught him?"

Peter smiled. "I repeated that boat number to myself all the way to shore. The cops were waiting for him when he docked in Monterey later that night."

"Have you had lunch?" Eric asked Peter as he shifted the bags to keep them from slipping.

Again Peter looked from Julia to Eric and

back again. He answered as if Julia had been the one who'd issued the invitation. "I'm meeting someone later."

"How about a beer?" she said.

"I don't think so."

She fought the urge to tell him what he was thinking was wrong, that there was nothing between her and Eric, that there never could be. He knew she would never look at another man. She loved Ken. He was her husband.

He had been her husband.

Ken was no more. Her loyalty was tied to a memory.

"I'm going to take these in," Eric said.

It was everything she could do to keep from physically reaching out to stop him. "Why don't we eat outside—on the back deck."

His eyebrow rose in question. "Do you want me to get a couple of chairs out of the garage?"

"No." She was only making it worse. "I forgot they were still in there. I guess we'll have to go inside after all." There was no mistaking the lack of enthusiasm in her voice.

"Would you rather we went to my place?" he asked.

What was wrong with her? Eric had done nothing to deserve being treated like a door-to-door salesman. She turned her attention to Peter. "Are you sure you won't join us?"

"I really have to get going," he said.

"I'd like to see you before you leave town."

He leaned forward to give her a kiss. "Are you free for dinner tomorrow?"

"Of course I'm free. Why wouldn't I be?"

The silence that followed hung heavy in the air. Finally Eric saved her. "I'm going to put this stuff away while you and Peter work things out." He headed for his house.

Five minutes later she was at his front door.

"What? No flowers?" He held the screen for her to come inside.

"I'm sorry."

"It's okay. The ones you brought last night still look terrific."

She looked up at him. "That's not what I mean."

"I know." He brushed a leaf from her hair. "Don't worry about it. I've done worse."

"Peter and Ken go way back."

"He told me."

"You've talked to him about Ken?"

He nodded. "About you, too."

Yet another surprise that day. "What did he say?"

"That you were the most beautiful woman he'd ever met and that you and Ken were the perfect couple. I think 'made for each other' was the way he put it. I don't know about the perfect couple part, but he was sure right about the other."

People had told her she was beautiful all her life. To her the words were as meaningless as saying the ocean was blue. What possible difference did it make how others saw her? Had her looks been a bargaining chip, she would have gladly traded them away to have Ken back, if only for an hour.

"I never know how to respond to something like that," she said.

A teasing twinkle lit his eyes. "If it bothers you, you could always dissuade them of the idea. Picking your nose while they were telling you about your beautiful eyes would probably do the trick."

She laughed, deep and full throated. It made her feel better than she had in a long time. "Will you be my friend?"

He put his arm around her and led her into the kitchen. "I already am. I think it happened last night sometime between shutting the water off and seeing you drip spaghetti sauce on your shirt."

"I did not."

"Gotcha."

He had, and she didn't mind one bit. Actually, she rather liked it.

CHAPTER

5

The next two days Eric worked on his book while Julia worked off pent-up energy in a flurry of housecleaning, dusting, polishing, and scrubbing between visits from her neighbors. This particular type of physical activity, so different from her workouts at the gym, was something she did only at the beach house. At home every room sparkled, every piece of silver shone, and every flower knew its place because of the people Ken had hired to free her from mundane chores.

She had a degree in advertising with exactly three months' experience at an ad agency. Ken had never asked her to give up her job, he'd simply offered to take her with him to meetings in London and Paris and Munich and left the decision whether to go or not up to her.

Their courtship had lasted three months, the engagement two. Ken was known for his uncanny, unerring ability to pick people who would be with him forever, whether it was his wife, his friends, or his employees. Even in death their loyalty survived. Not one friend had stopped talking about him, not one executive had left the company.

Since she'd stepped in to run things, the entire company, from board member to clerical assistant, had shown her the same loyalty they had shown Ken. It should have made her job easier, but it seemed nothing could do that. The more she learned about the business, the more she discovered she didn't know. Perhaps if she had just a little of Ken's drive and enthusiasm, she could pull it off. But no matter how hard she tried, going to work each day was just that. She continued because she felt she owed it to Ken to try.

She stood back to admire the change her efforts had made in the living room, to breathe in the traces of lemon oil, glass cleaner, and rug shampoo, and to take pleasure in knowing every book had been taken down and dusted. She could have called the service she normally used—her friends would think her crazy that she hadn't—but she wanted to be the one who removed these last traces of Ken's presence, no matter how small or inconsequential. As it was, the work had been cathartic, even satisfying in a way she hadn't expected.

A knock on the front door drew her attention. It was Eric. She smiled and stood aside to let him enter. "You're just in time to join me for a cup of coffee."

He declined. "I'm on my way to the grocery

store and thought I'd see if you needed anything."

"Milk—a quart, nonfat."

"Is that all?"

"You've probably been too busy to notice, but the neighbors have been plying me with food the last couple of days."

"Several of them told me they'd regretted not being able to help when Ken died and wanted to do something when you came down again."

"I don't understand. . . . I made a point of telling everyone at the funeral that they were welcome to stop by the house to see me anytime they were in the area, but no one ever took me up on it."

"You honestly expected someone from this neighborhood to show up on your doorstep in Atherton to see how you were doing?"

"Why not?"

Eric shook his head. "That's pretty rare air up there where you live, lady. You have to know how to breathe that stuff to feel comfortable in it."

"I'm the same person there as I am here."

"Are you?"

"What do you think I do, stop by someplace in San Jose to shed the Armani and put on sweats?"

"Hey, I'm not trying to pick a fight with you."

"I'm not a snob."

He grinned. "I never said you were."

"Just because I have a little money—"

"Maybe a little to Bill Gates and the Catholic Church. To the rest of the world, it's a hell of a lot."

"Why are you baiting me?"

"Because you need a friend who isn't afraid of you."

He'd done it. She was at a loss for words.

"Now that we have that behind us," he said, "is there anything you need besides milk?"

"No—I'll be leaving day after tomorrow."

It was his turn to feel the ladder tip. "So soon?"

"The Sadlers and McCormicks will be here on Friday."

"I thought they weren't due until June."

His reaction was more than simple surprise. "I told them they could come a little early."

"When did you do that?"

It seemed an odd question, but she answered anyway. "Weeks ago." She decided she wanted to know what had prompted the query. "Why?"

"No reason," he answered cryptically.

"Don't do that."

"I was wondering whether your leaving early had something to do with me."

She considered his statement. The obvious conclusion didn't make sense. "I don't understand what you mean."

"Whether being around me made you uncomfortable."

"Why would it? I thought we decided we were friends."

He stared at her for agonizingly long seconds, his gaze locked on her. "Never mind," he said softly. "It isn't important."

This time she didn't ask him to explain. "If you'll wait just a minute, I'll get my purse."

"What for?"

"To pay you for the milk."

He brought his hand up. "I think I can handle it."

She closed the door. Burdened with the feeling that something lay unfinished between them, she went to the window to watch him leave. The way he walked with long, sure strides and the way he moved to keep his shoulders from brushing the roses on the arbor suggested he'd been an athlete, probably a runner or swimmer, something nonviolent, a sport that required discipline and a solitary commitment. Eric didn't need people, he liked them, a difference she hadn't understood until she'd met Ken.

Would Eric's book provide clues to the man he was inside, hint at his dreams, or reveal the type of woman he admired? Julia considered the single women she knew and tried to imagine Eric with one of them. Perhaps Anne . . . No, Anne couldn't handle a man who sat still long enough to read a book, let alone write one. Judy refused to date a man whose portfolio wasn't as large as her own, and Eileen wanted someone so blinded by her beauty that he would never notice how much it cost to keep her that way.

From what she knew of Eric, he appreciated beauty but wasn't overly impressed by it, had enough money to support himself and his children while he pursued a dream, but not so much he could buy a house at the beach rather than stay at a friend's. From things he'd said she'd reached the conclusion he was someone who would as soon listen to the rain as attend opening night at the opera—definitely not Anne's idea of fun.

Not a sterling accounting of her friends, but an interesting analysis of Eric. She had a feeling he and Ken would have liked each other.

But then everyone had liked Ken.

When Eric delivered the milk later that afternoon, Julia asked him in for a drink, but he declined, telling her he'd already taken off too much time that day and needed to get back to work. She didn't see him at all the next day and had begun to wonder if he was avoiding her when he showed up at her front door early Friday morning and asked if she wanted to go for a walk on the beach.

"I'm glad you came over," she told him as they descended the stairs to the beach. She stopped to zip her jacket when she reached the bottom. "I wanted to talk to you before I left, but didn't want to disturb your work."

He made a disparaging sound. "There wasn't anything to disturb. When I turned on the computer this morning I wound up deleting everything I wrote yesterday."

She shoved her hands in her jacket pockets and looked up at him. "Does that happen a lot?"

"No—thank God. There are a lot of times I don't like what I've done, but I usually find something salvageable." He moved toward the harder sand near the water's edge. "You said you wanted to talk to me?"

"I have a favor to ask."

"Ask away."

"First I want you to know it's okay to refuse. I know it's an imposition, but—"

"That isn't necessary, Julia. Just tell me what it is you want."

"Andrew kept a key to the house in case something happened that needed attention right away. I don't expect anything to go wrong, but it would be nice to know I could count on you if something did."

"That's it?"

"It's a lot," she insisted. "At least it is to me."

"Consider it done."

She saw a large wave building and moved to get out of its way. "I'll let the summer people know that you've got the extra key. They all have their own, but Margaret's been known to lock herself out occasionally." She moved back to the packed sand as soon as the wave receded. "You'll like her—and her son, Chris. They're really nice people. I'm not as crazy about the McCormicks. Actually, it's their daughter I don't like. She's—" Julia stopped herself before she could say any more. "I'm sorry. I don't usually gossip this way. I don't know what got into me."

Eric froze. His eyes narrowed as he studied something floating in the water. After several seconds, he took her arm and turned her toward the sea. "Look," he said, and pointed.

"Where?"

He pulled her to him so that she was standing in his line of vision. "Right there. Do you see it?"

"No. . . ." But then she did. It was an otter, floating on his back and cracking a shell with a rock as he rode the swells. "Yes, I do," she exclaimed. And then, her voice filled with wonder, "Oh, isn't he beautiful?"

She leaned her back into his chest, the contact as natural as if they'd stood that way a hundred times before. Eric put his arms around her waist and she laid her own on top of them. "What a nice going-away present," she said.

Before he could reply, a wave broke and came racing toward them. He grabbed Julia's elbow and backpedaled as cold water licked at his running shoes. As soon as they were clear of the wave, he let her go. Through it all her gaze remained fixed on the sea.

"He's gone," she announced. "You look that way"—she pointed to the left—"and I'll watch over here."

They followed the otter's path for over half an hour, until he'd moved past the cove and out of their sight.

"Thank you for asking me to come with

you this morning," Julia said as they headed back. The beach had begun to fill with fishermen and couples out for an early morning stroll. Soon the sanderlings and gulls would move on to a stretch of sand less populated where they could hunt in peace for their breakfast.

"You're welcome," he said simply.

"It seems as if I've been thanking you for one thing or another all week. It wouldn't begin to pay you back for all you've done, but how about letting me take you out to lunch before I leave? I know a really great place in Aptos."

"Are you sure?"

She understood what he was asking: was she sure she wanted to take him someplace where she and Ken had gone. "I'm very sure," she said. "Is twelve-thirty okay?"

"I'll be ready."

After lunch they stopped by a hardware store to get a new hinge for Julia's garden gate. She insisted on installing it herself but allowed Eric to oversee the operation.

"Well done," he told her when she'd finished and was picking up her tools.

The simple task had given her an incredible sense of accomplishment. "I think I might like this handyman stuff," she said.

"Next time you're here, I'll show you how to fix that cupboard door that's sticking."

There likely wouldn't be a next time, but she didn't want to remind him now. The moment was too good to spoil. "Now all I have left to do is pick a bouquet for Margaret and get on the road before the traffic starts."

"Margaret?" he asked. Before she could answer, he remembered. "Ah, yes, the June renter. I take it the flowers are some sort of tradition?"

She picked up the clippers she'd brought out with her and started snipping pink cosmos. "It's just my way of saying welcome." On impulse, she handed him the flowers she'd just picked. "And good-bye."

He took them and held them upside-down at his side. "I'll put them next to my computer. Maybe they'll inspire me."

"Consider the garden yours. Pick as many flowers as you want." She moved on to the daisies. "The plants actually do better if they're thinned once in a while."

Eric stayed with her as she gathered more flowers, periodically adding to the ones she'd already given him. Finally, both bouquets complete, she moved to go inside.

Eric caught her arm. "Take care of yourself, Julia."

She looked into his eyes and saw that it wasn't a meaningless platitude, but said with genuine concern. "I will," she assured him.

He kissed her then, their lips touching longer than if he'd intended it to be purely platonic, but less than a lover's. Somewhere in her mind, or maybe it was her body, she felt a stir of response and was bemused by it.

He let go of her arm and held up the flowers

she'd given him. "I'm going to put these in water."

She nodded. "Thanks again, Eric—for everything."

He didn't say anything, just smiled, gave her a quick wave, and left.

Watching him walk away, Julia was once again aware of how alone she was. The feeling had become as familiar as the road she would take back to Atherton. The odd part, what she hadn't realized until that moment, was how often the past week she'd forgotten.

PART TWO

JUNE

CHAPTER

1

Margaret Sadler parked her ten-year-old Volvo in the driveway of the beach house and popped the trunk lid. She turned to her son and said, "Help me unload and then you can take that run on the beach."

Chris opened the door, got out, and stretched. "Feel that?" Salt-laden air swirled around them, riffling his hair and the narrow leaves of the eucalyptus overhead. "I swear I'm going live on the ocean someday."

She started to make an automatic, flippant statement about the price of beachfront property but caught herself in time. Since her and Kevin's divorce three years ago, Chris had assumed a role she'd never asked of him and could do nothing to stop.

With the loss of his college savings and her income less than half what it was when she'd been married, Chris no longer talked about going to the University of Southern California or Stanford or

Yale. He'd accepted that if he was ever to have a car of his own, he would have to pay for it himself. He had even taken a job in his uncle's restaurant to pay his own way to wrestling camp despite her rule about working during school. He rarely talked about the dreams that had once been as much a part of him as his wheat-colored hair and lanky, muscular build.

Margaret opened her own door and got out. The drive up from Fresno had left the car a bug-encrusted mess. She'd have to see what she could do to bribe Chris into washing it for her later. "Just remember when you get that house on the ocean . . ."

"Yeah?"

"Be sure it has an extra bedroom. You're going to have to put up with me visiting—a lot."

"That's okay, you just have to remember to give me plenty of warning so I can clear out the beer and babes."

Margaret laughed. "How thoughtful."

"Hey, I'm a thoughtful kind of guy." Chris waited for Margaret to open the trunk and then started unloading.

Ten minutes later he made his final trip. "What do you want me to do with this box?" he called out to her as he nudged the front door closed with his foot.

"What does it say on the side?" Margaret answered from the kitchen.

"C.S."

"Cleaning supplies—bring it in here."

Chris waited for his mother to move the flowers before he slid the box on the table, cut the tape, and peered inside. "I don't understand why you need all this stuff. The house always looks clean to me."

"Which is precisely the way I want to leave it." She took his arm and moved him out of the way.

"I'll bet everything you need is already here."

"What's here belongs to Julia and K—" She stopped and waited for the quick stab of indignation to leave. Why was it the world was filled with cruel, unproductive people who would live to a hundred and a man like Ken died when he still had so much to give? "It's still hard to believe Ken's really gone. He was so young." She handed Chris the cleanser and dishwashing soap and pointed to the cupboard under the sink.

"Yeah, five years younger than you and Dad." He lowered himself to his haunches and popped up again with effortless grace. "How's Julia doing?"

She motioned for him to stay where he was and passed him the pine cleaner and bleach. "I thought about asking her, but it's such a dumb question."

"I don't think so."

"She's undoubtedly heard it a thousand times by now."

"That doesn't make it dumb."

"It's a rhetorical question, Chris, like saying

'How are you?' when you're introduced to someone. I wanted her to know I cared more than that, but didn't know how to tell her."

"Is that how you felt after you and Dad got divorced and people asked you how you were doing?"

When was she going to stop being surprised that he was no longer her little boy but a near adult with uncanny powers of observation? Had she done this to him? Had she made him a misfit in his own generation by letting him assume too much responsibility? "It's how everyone feels who's gone through a big change in their life."

"You're not answering me."

"What I felt is over and done with. When you spend all your time looking back—"

"You miss the opportunities ahead," he finished for her.

She laughed. "I must have used that one before."

"About a hundred times."

"That doesn't mean—"

"It isn't true," he again finished for her.

She handed him the last of the cleaning supplies and closed the box. "Put those away and get out of here before I unleash my entire repertoire of clichés on you."

He made a movement as if to ward off impending blows. Finishing his task, he asked, "What are you going to do?"

She sighed in pleasure at the prospect of two whole hours with absolutely no demands on her.

At home, between full-time school and part-time job with mother and homemaker thrown into the mix, she rarely had five minutes to call her own. "I should wash the car . . . but I'll probably read a book or, if the urge strikes, take a nap."

Chris shook his head. "You really are getting old."

"Watch yourself, young man. You're not too big to take—"

"I'm ready for you, Mom," he challenged, a mischievous twinkle in his eyes. "I'll even make it easy on you, two out of three falls with one arm tied behind my back."

"Don't you think for a minute I couldn't win. I just don't feel like taking you on right now." She swatted him on the rear with a folded paper bag.

Of all the sports Chris could have chosen, he'd settled on the one Margaret liked the least. For three years she'd watched him wrestle the state's best on his way to the championship and had yet to comprehend how he could leave a match bruised and bloodied and smiling.

He put his arm around her shoulders and gave her a hug. "I'm always telling the guys what a macho mom you are."

She handed him the empty box. "Here, take this to the garage on your way out."

He started to leave, but before he'd reached the living room, he turned and asked, "What time are they coming?"

Margaret glanced at the clock over the

stove. "Beverly said their plane got in at three-thirty. Figure three hours to pick up the rental car and get through rush-hour traffic. That should put them here between six-thirty and seven—assuming they don't stop for dinner."

She'd tried to sound as casual with her answer as Chris had with the question. She knew Chris wanted her to think he was over his near lifelong crush on Tracy. For the last ten of the sixteen years that the two families had spent each June together at the beach house, Chris had arrived with his heart on his sleeve, hoping, believing, that in the eleven months since he'd last seen Tracy she'd become the girl he desperately wanted her to be, that she would finally realize how he felt about her and maybe even reciprocate that feeling.

It was Margaret's hope that at the very least, Tracy had matured enough to let Chris down easily this time. His ego was like a newly sprouted seed, easy to nourish with a little encouragement and kindness, just as easy to destroy with the cold of indifference. At home he was completely oblivious of the girls who turned to watch him as he passed. The muscles he worked so hard to develop were for his sport. It never occurred to him to show them off. He was unfailingly polite, gentle, and caring. The kinds of qualities a woman looked for in a man, but that a girl thought boring in a boy.

"I don't understand why Beverly always insists on flying into San Francisco. San Jose is a lot closer."

"It's a direct flight from St. Louis. She hates changing planes."

"Beverly hates a lot of things."

"*Chris.*"

"Well, it's true."

"She has a lot of strong opinions," Margaret admitted. "And she doesn't hesitate to express them. I suppose you could say she's a lot like Tracy that way." She knew she was on dangerous ground even hinting that Tracy might be less than perfect.

Chris chose not to offer a defense. "Whatever."

"If you don't get out of here, I'm going to find something for you to do."

He held up his free hand in surrender and backed out the door. "See ya later."

Margaret returned to the kitchen to put away the few groceries she'd brought from home—basic things for them to get by with until she and Beverly went shopping the next day. Chris tapped on the window as he rounded the house on his way to the beach. She smiled and waved and took a minute to watch him. After hitting the stairs, he disappeared for several seconds, then reappeared again, running through the soft sand on his way to the water's edge. He headed north toward the rocky outcropping that cut them off from the neighboring beaches, running with effortless strides.

As soon as she lost sight of Chris, Margaret left the window. She picked up the bouquet to return it to the table, adjusting a yellow rose that had fallen to the side. The mingled fragrances sparked a memory of the first time eight years ago when she'd arrived and found flowers on the kitchen table. For one glorious second she'd set aside logic and let herself believe Kevin had sent them to apologize for the fight they'd had before she and Chris took off to meet the McCormicks in Santa Cruz.

Kevin had been defensive and angry that she had dared to question him about a lipstick-marked cigarette butt she'd found in the ashtray of his car. When the argument escalated to her desire to go back to work and then to how she handled the household money, he abruptly announced that he was not going on their vacation that year. She and Chris could go alone.

Margaret had realized the flowers weren't from a florist at the same time Chris had stated the obvious—someone had picked them from the profusion of blooms that had been planted around the house.

Every summer since, unfailingly, there had been flowers to greet them, always accompanied by a note of welcome. This year, there were only flowers. She missed the note.

Chris made the turn at the outcropping and headed back down the beach. He ran a zigzag pattern, veering to step on kelp pods and broken sand dollars to hear them pop and crunch beneath his feet, stopping to watch a novice surfer take a header, and searching the faces of those he passed for one of the locals he'd come to know over the years.

He glanced up as he passed the house again, looking to see if his mother had come out on the deck. He worried about her—what she would do when he went off to college next year, if she'd ever find someone she liked, if the Volvo would last until she could afford a new car. She hated it when he told her she should get out more, that she was never going to find someone unless she put some effort into it.

He had to give her credit for leaving him alone about when he went out and who it was with. She never said anything, but it was obvious she knew about him and Tracy.

Him and Tracy? What a joke. There was no more "him and Tracy" than there was him and Stanford or Yale or USC. All his life he'd figured both were a given eventually. For as long as he could remember, his dad had talked about the savings account he'd started the day his son was born to pay for Chris's college.

Although community property, at his mother's insistence, the account was not divided in the divorce but left intact for Chris's use later. Her only mistake was in trusting his dad to take care of the money. When his father remarried—a woman with three children of her own—the funds slowly began to disappear. Believing his father an honorable man, neither Chris nor his mother thought to check the account. Not until Chris went to make a deposit of the tips he'd saved from working at the restaurant did he learn the money was almost gone.

When he'd confronted his father at his office later that day, Kevin had asked Chris to try to understand how hard it was to deny his new family basic necessities. Besides, it wasn't as if there had been any formal agreement about the savings account.

Sure, Kevin had agreed the money should go to Chris for college, but at the time there'd been no way for him to foresee the financial circumstances he'd be faced with in the future.

Chris left through the company garage and did something he had never done before or since. He took the key to his mother's old, beaten-up Volvo, dug it into the front fender of his father's new red BMW, and walked the full length, trailing the key behind him.

It took Chris months to realize it wasn't the money he cared about, it was being burdened with a dream his father had instilled and then abandoned.

Now, with only a year to go before graduation, he still had no idea where he wanted to go to college or what he wanted to study. At seventeen how was he supposed to know what he wanted to do for the rest of his life? He wasn't even sure what he wanted to do tomorrow.

Lost in what had become depressingly familiar thoughts, Chris almost missed seeing a volleyball headed his way. More on reflex than intent, he lunged and hit it back. A guy with shoulder-length black hair, wraparound sunglasses, and a baseball cap with the bill facing backward received the ball and made a perfect spike over the net. The ball came back, to the server this time. He passed it to Chris, and without anyone saying a word, Chris was in the game.

The rally lasted until the other team miscalculated an out-of-bounds ball. The guy with long hair rotated to server, holding his hand up for a high five from Chris as he moved into position. Chris figured him to be in his early twenties, younger than the others, but not by much. He wore faded swim trunks, a torn T-shirt, and small gold earrings in both ears.

"You in?" he said to Chris.

The score had been the same as the players on the teams, three to two, before Chris arrived and evened both. "What the hell—I've got nothing better to do."

Both sides were good and fought hard for every point, screaming in outrage when they didn't agree with a call, but too caught up in the game to stop the action to argue. From the coarse language and rough teasing it was obvious they all knew each other and that they played together often.

When they rotated again, the guy with the long hair called out introductions, ending with himself. "Antonio Gallardo—but call me Tony."

A flicker of recognition came and was gone again before it registered. "Chris Sadler."

"You're up, Chris," Tony said.

Chris hit a perfect serve, the ball landing dead center, where all three opponents believed one of the others would get it.

Tony let out a shout of triumph and pumped the air. "That was beautiful. Do it again."

Unbelievably, Chris did. This time everyone howled.

It took almost forty-five minutes, but they won the game.

Their opponents cried foul, insisting Chris was a ringer Tony had flown in from Los Angeles. At first Chris thought they were kidding, then realized that underneath the good-natured protests the guys on the other team actually believed what they were saying, that in their minds it was exactly the kind of thing Tony would do.

When they changed sides, Chris took the opportunity to check Tony out more closely. He didn't give the impression he was someone who had the money to pull off a stunt that involved a cab ride, let alone an airline ticket.

During the next game Chris paid more attention to the interaction among the five men. It soon became clear from tone and reference that they not only worked together, but spent a lot of off hours in each other's company. Each of them paid Tony a peculiar deference, as if he were on a slightly higher level than the rest of them—the foreman on a construction crew, the corporal among privates.

Whatever their jobs, they were plainly temporary. A lot of the talk centered around missing girlfriends and homes they couldn't wait to get back to.

The second game was closer, with Chris's side winning by a single, disputed point. As they moved to change sides again, Chris asked for the time.

The tall African American on the opposite team dug in his pocket and pulled out a watch. "It's six twenty-five."

"I gotta go," Chris said.

Tony came over, the ball tucked under his arm. "Same time, same place, tomorrow?"

Chris picked up the T-shirt he'd taken off after the first game and pulled it over his head. "I'm not sure."

The third member of Chris's team, a guy who looked like a refugee from the American Gladiators, spoke up. "Hey, man, you don't want us to have to play these three—"

"Leave the kid alone," their blond opponent said. "If he's not sure, he's not sure."

"Fuck off, Mason," Tony said, laughing as he threw the ball at him. "You're just afraid you'll get your sorry ass beaten again."

"I'll try," Chris said. He'd enjoyed the game as much as they had and wouldn't mind playing again if and when he had the time. But Tracy came first.

Tony nodded and moved back into position. Chris took off running, headed toward the road that paralleled the highway and led to the beach house. He arrived in time to see a glimpse of Tracy's blond hair as her mother's rental car made the curve that would put them at the house ahead of him.

Now he either arrived on their heels, sucking air from the run, or found something to do to kill time until he could come in looking composed and surprised to find them there.

CHAPTER

2

I sn't that Margaret?" Tracy said as they drove by the gray shingled house next door to their rental.

"Yes," Beverly said, turning to take a second look. "But I don't think that's Andrew. At least it doesn't look like him."

Margaret spotted their car and waved. She said something to the man she'd been talking to, then came over to greet them. "You look wonderful," she said to Beverly, giving her a hug when she got out of the car. "You, too, Tracy."

Still standing with her arm around Beverly, Margaret smiled at the third person who emerged from the car. "And who's this?"

"This is Tracy's friend, Janice Carlson," Beverly said. "Clyde couldn't make it this year, so she'll be spending the month with us instead."

"Oh." Margaret obviously tried but couldn't hide her surprise at the news. "It's nice to meet you, Janice," she said graciously.

"It's nice to meet you, too," Janice said.

Margaret turned back to Beverly. "Is Clyde all right?"

"He's fine—at least he was when he dropped us off at the airport." She responded to Margaret's concerned expression by adding, "It's nothing like that. He's been working around the clock on some new project. You know how wrapped up Clyde can get in his work." Beverly went to the back of the Town Car. "Where's Chris?"

"He went for a run on the beach."

"I was hoping he'd be here to help. You won't believe the luggage these girls brought." She opened the trunk and stood aside for Margaret to see for herself.

Out of earshot, Tracy exchanged looks with Janice. "I told you," she whispered.

"What's wrong with running on the beach?"

"He's always doing things like that. Most guys would be down at the boardwalk checking out the action, but not good old Chris."

"How do you know he's not checking out the action around here?"

"Just wait," Tracy said. "You'll see what I mean when you meet him." She'd had her doubts about bringing Janice on the trip. They'd never been really close the way she and the rest of the cheerleaders were, but no one else she asked could get away for the entire month. In April when her mom had started making plans for the trip, Tracy had gone to her father and told him there was no way she was going to spend one more June stuck all the way out in California without a friend for company. He'd made all kinds of promises of things they could do together, even telling her he would teach her how to play golf, but she'd held out for taking someone with her instead.

She might not have been so stubborn if she'd known her father couldn't afford another airline ticket for himself. But she hadn't found out about that until she'd already asked Janice and she'd accepted the invitation.

Besides, her dad was always saying how he wished he had more time to work on the yard. Now he had a whole month to do whatever he wanted.

Beverly handed Tracy and Janice their suitcases. "This is so exciting," Janice said. "I can't wait to get on the beach."

"Is this your first time in California?" Margaret asked.

"It's practically my first time anywhere. We went to Disney World when I was ten, but we never left the grounds, so I only got to see the ocean from the plane."

"I told you not to tell anyone about that. The people out here will think you're some kind of weirdo." Tracy let out a long-suffering sigh. Janice was all right in a midwest kind of way, but she was a hick by California standards.

"That's not true," Beverly said, fingering her overprocessed blond hair as if checking to make sure it was still there. "I think it's charming that Janice is excited about being here."

Tracy looked at Janice. *"Charming,"* she said in a singsong voice. "See what I mean?"

Margaret grabbed a garment bag from the trunk. "As soon as we get this unloaded why don't we all go down to the beach? Dinner won't be ready for another hour."

"You shouldn't have made dinner," Beverly said. "We could have—"

"It's only pot roast, potatoes, and carrots."

"I told Janice we could have Mexican," Tracy said. "She's never had *real* Mexican food." She might as well let everyone know how things were going to be this year right from the start. No way was she going to let the others push her into doing things she didn't want to do or make her go places she didn't want to go. This was her vacation, too. And for once she was going to spend it the way she wanted.

"Tomorrow," Beverly said, giving Tracy a silencing look.

"Sorry," Tracy said to Janice. "It looks like you'll just have to wait." An idea struck. "But then I don't see why we couldn't go by ourselves." Even though she was still pissed about the car her mother had rented—it was as big as a goddamned boat and was like having a sign that said "Old People on Board"—it was her only way out of there.

"That's okay," Janice said quickly. "I don't mind. I told you I'm not all that crazy about Mexican food anyway."

Instantly furious that even Janice had let her down, Tracy picked up her suitcases and headed for the house. She was going to have to talk to Janice—again. If they didn't stick together, she didn't have a prayer making her plan work. Worst of all, if Janice seemed the least bit willing, they'd be stuck taking Chris with them everywhere they went.

"I thought you said the house was a dump," Janice said when they were inside. "It's beautiful."

"Wait till you've been here a while."

"Why don't you and Janice take the room where Dad and I usually stay," Beverly said.

"Why?" Tracy liked her usual room. It was at the back of the house and stayed dark in the morning. It also had a window she could get in and out of at night without anyone knowing.

"So Chris doesn't have to sleep on the sofa again this year."

"Where will you and Margaret sleep?"

"In your old room." She looked at Margaret. "You don't mind sharing, do you?"

"It'll be just like old times, Beverly. You were the best roommate I ever had. And, yes, that includes Kevin."

Tracy couldn't believe what she was hearing. She'd never shared a bedroom with anyone in her life. "You expect me and Janice to sleep together in the same bed?"

"It's a king-size bed, Tracy," Beverly said.

"I don't care. I won't do it."

Janice broke in. "My sister and I sleep together all the time. We have—"

Tracy shut her down with a look. "If you

don't think it's a big deal," she said to Beverly, "then you and Margaret can take that room."

"It doesn't matter to me which room we take," Margaret said.

Beverly glared at her daughter as she asked Margaret, "Are you sure you don't mind?"

"Positive."

Tracy smiled, satisfied that finally something was going her way. "Now that we have that settled, Janice and I are going to dump this stuff and head down to the beach. We'll be back in time for dinner."

Janice sent a helpless look in Beverly's direction. "Is there anything you'd like us to do first?"

"There's nothing that won't wait," Beverly told her.

"Why don't you come with us? We don't have to go right now. We can wait until you're ready."

It was everything Tracy could do to keep from groaning out loud. She'd had no idea Janice was such a suck-up. "Mom never does anything until she gets unpacked. If we wait for her, it will be dark before you get to see the beach."

"You go ahead," Beverly said. "Margaret and I will be down later."

Beverly and Margaret dropped the suitcases they were carrying and headed back out to the car for another load. Tracy and Janice were gone by the time they got back in the house.

"I'm sorry," Beverly said. "Tracy has just

been impossible lately. Nothing I do seems to satisfy her anymore."

The only part Margaret would question was the "lately." As far as she was concerned, Tracy had been a monster in the making from the day she screamed her way into the world. "Maybe it's just a case of teenage angst."

"Clyde thought it might be the way she's been raised."

Margaret had sense enough to let that one go without comment.

"You know—the constant moving around," Beverly went on. "Three years is the longest we've ever lived in one house, and that was just after Tracy was born. The longest poor Tracy has ever gone to one school is two years. She's always the new kid, always having to prove herself. Something like that is bound to be upsetting." Beverly laid Tracy's garment bag across the bed. "Don't you think?"

"I know it was hard on me." Margaret's father had been in the air force, a master sergeant determined to see as much of the world as possible at the government's expense.

"How did you do it?"

"It wasn't as if I had any choice." Margaret dug a little deeper in her memories, looking for something that would help Beverly. "I think it's probably why I'm still in Fresno today, letting Kevin rub my nose in his new, incredibly happy family life every time I see him. If I hadn't set down such deep roots when I finally could, I would have packed up and moved away after the divorce. Especially if I'd known how little time Kevin would spend with Chris."

"I wonder if Tracy will be like that." She unzipped the garment bag, took out the clothes, and laid them on the bed. "Have you been having trouble with Chris?" The note of hopefulness was pathetically obvious.

The only thing Margaret worried about with Chris was that he was too perfect. He never stayed out late, always called to let her know where he was, and helped out around the house without being asked. If she feared anything where he was concerned, it was that the divorce had cost Chris the freedom to be a kid and experience the rebellion that brought its own brand of wisdom as an adult. She wanted him to do at least a few of the things that were confessed years later when he had children of his own.

"Not yet," Margaret admitted. "But I figure it's bound to happen any day now." She took a duffel bag with Tracy's initials into the room with the twin beds.

"You know I always hoped Tracy and Chris would wind up together. Tracy doesn't know this, but the real reason Clyde gave up his ticket was that he was afraid if he didn't, she wouldn't come at all. With both of them getting ready to go off to college next year, this might be her and Chris's last chance to connect."

"I wouldn't be too disappointed if that doesn't happen," Margaret said carefully. "They only see each other one month out of twelve,

and to people their ages, that's an eternity."
Thank God, Margaret added to herself. Even
knowing how Chris felt about Tracy, she
couldn't imagine a worse pairing.

Beverly systematically began going through
Tracy's pockets before she put the clothes away,
as if it were a long-established habit. "Clyde
just thinks the world of Chris."

The action surprised Margaret. It would
never occur to her to search Chris's things at
all, let alone under the guise of being helpful.
Was Beverly looking for something specific or
simply snooping? Neither possibility held much
appeal.

"Chris likes Clyde, too," Margaret said
automatically. She turned at the sound of the
front door opening.

"I'm back," Chris said.

Margaret went to the door. "We're in here."

The glow of anticipation dulled when Chris
saw Tracy was not with them. He looked at his
mother over Beverly's shoulder as Beverly gave
him a hug. Margaret pointed to the beach.
"Wow, look at all this stuff," he said, reaching
up to run his hand through his hair. "She must
have cleaned out her closet."

"Tracy brought a friend," Margaret said.

He shot her a questioning look.

"Janice Carlson," Beverly filled in. "She's
on the cheerleading squad with Tracy."

"Tracy's a cheerleader? When did this happen?"

Beverly's smile was somewhere between

beaming and smug. "I'm sure I told your mother. She must have forgotten to pass the news on to you."

No, she hadn't, but Margaret was wondering now if she wouldn't have been better off doing so, especially considering how Chris felt about the cheerleaders he knew at school. His favorite word for them was airheads, but there were other, less flattering, words, too. "Clyde couldn't come, so he let Janice use his ticket. This is her first time at the ocean."

"Cool," he said without much enthusiasm.

"Best of all," Beverly said, "you get your own room. No more sleeping on the sofa."

"I'll move my things after dinner," Margaret told him.

"Where will you sleep?"

"With Beverly."

"You don't have to do that, Mom. The sofa's fine with me."

The contrast between Chris's and Tracy's reactions to the sleeping arrangements was too obvious to ignore. "Would you like to come home with me?" Beverly said. "Just long enough for some of your behavior to rub off on Tracy."

He looked to Margaret to interpret. "It's not important." She purposely changed the subject. "Where have you been? You look as if you ran to Monterey and back."

"I probably smell that way, too." He lifted the sleeve of his T-shirt and sniffed. "I'm going to take a shower. What time's dinner?"

"I told the girls an hour"—she checked her watch—"and that was thirty minutes ago."

An hour and a half later, Tracy and Janice still hadn't returned. Chris was on his way to find them just as they started up the stairs from the beach.

"Damn," Tracy said. "He's come to get us."

Janice looked up. She stopped in midstep. "*That's* Chris Sadler?"

"For cryin' out loud, Janice, shut your mouth before he sees you looking at him like that. I never said he was ugly." Tracy checked Chris out again to see what had gotten to Janice that she might have missed. He was dressed in cutoffs and a blue tank top, and for once his hair looked decent. Obviously he'd stopped letting his mother cut it for him.

"He's *gorgeous,*" Janice said under her breath.

"Just wait till he says something. Then you'll understand." Tracy gave him the dismissive smile she used on guys at school who actually thought she could be interested in talking to them. "Chris—hi."

"Everyone's been wondering what happened to you."

"I told Mom we were going for a walk." She waited for him to move out of the way before she started up the stairs again.

"Dinner's ready," he said. When Janice

reached the top of landing, he held out his
hand. "Hi, I'm Chris."

She seemed surprised at the formality but
shook his hand without comment. "Janice
Carlson."

"I was hoping you'd eaten without us,"
Tracy said. "Janice really wanted to have
Mexican food tonight."

Chris looked to Janice for confirmation.

"We talked about it on the plane," she conceded.

"Maybe we could go tomorrow. . . ." Chris
didn't know what else to say.

"Or even the next day," Janice said. "We
have a whole month."

Chris waited for Tracy to start up the path
to the house and then followed. "So, what do
you think of the ocean?" he asked Janice.
"Beverly said it was your first time."

She and Tracy both giggled at his unin-
tended double entendre. "I love it. But the
water's a lot colder than I thought it would be."

"It's the Alaska current. You wouldn't think
it would be an influence this far south, but it is.
It's also one of the reasons there are more great
white sharks in the triangle between here, San
Francisco, and the Farallon Islands than anywhere else in the world."

"Jesus, Chris," Tracy said. "She tells you
the water's cold and you give her a marine bio-
logy lesson."

Janice ignored her. "I thought great whites
were all on the East Coast, like in *Jaws.*"

Chris could have told her a hundred things about the movie and about the ocean around Monterey Bay, but Tracy would only think he was some geek trying to impress Janice with how much he knew because she thought it was all he had to offer.

The worst part was that she'd be right. He could make small talk with people he'd just met if they didn't count. But when the people were girls who looked like Tracy and Janice, he always wound up saying something dumb.

"We're going to the Monterey aquarium tomorrow," Chris said. "They've got a lot of stuff there about sharks."

"Not me," Tracy said, shaking her head for emphasis. "I swore last time we went that I was never going back to that place again. It's soooo boring."

"They have a new exhibit." The minute it was out, he knew he'd made a mistake. Tracy never changed her mind about anything.

"I don't care if they've started feeding little kids to the sharks. Janice and I came here to have fun."

CHAPTER

3

The next day Margaret and Beverly went grocery shopping while Tracy and Janice worked on their tans. Chris joined them, but not even having Tracy lying next to him in a thong suit could keep him from getting restless after the first hour.

"I'm going for a swim to cool off," he said. Both Tracy and Janice reacted with giggles.

Tracy turned to her side and propped her head up with her hand, her long blond hair curling around her wrist like a golden bracelet. The small triangle of bright red material designed to cover no more than half her breast slipped to the side. Another half inch and her nipple would be exposed. "Before you go would you do me a favor?"

He waited, his gaze locked on her face because he knew if he dared look anywhere else, he'd make a fool of himself. He expected her to ask him to go back to the house and get her and Janice something to drink, or to eat, or to listen to. Instead she handed him a tube of lotion.

"Rub this on my back?" She smiled sweetly and lay down again. "You'll have to untie the straps first. I don't want them to get oily."

Chris could hardly breathe. He'd dreamed about taking Tracy's clothes off, about running his hands over her body, but not like this. In his dreams they were alone and she was kissing him. And she always responded to his touch with deep-throated moans, then by pressing her body against his.

A flush burned his chest and neck and face. He was dead sure his thoughts were obvious to anyone who looked at him. It was everything he could do to stay where he was.

Jesus, he was getting a boner.

"Is something wrong?" Tracy asked. She started to roll to her side again.

"The cap's stuck." Chris put his hand on her shoulder and pushed her back down.

"It snaps open."

His hands shaking, he untied the string that circled her chest. "Do you want the one around your neck undone, too?"

"Please." She brought her hand up, caught her hair, and pulled it out of the way.

A gentle tug on the end of one string was all it took. He pictured her sitting up and turning to him, her eyes filled with desire.

"For crying out loud, Chris, what's taking so long?"

Chris filled his hand with enough lotion for

Tracy and Janice and half a dozen other people. He tried to put some back and wound up with the stuff coating the tube and dripping on his suit. Janice put her hand over her mouth to stifle a laugh and turned to face the opposite direction.

He was such a loser. No wonder Tracy didn't want to have anything to do with him.

Determined to get one thing right, Chris spread the lotion with strong, firm strokes, stopping just below her waist. She could reach the rest herself. He tossed the tube on the towel beside her and, with great effort, announced casually, "I'm going for a swim."

Thankful he'd worn baggy trunks that day, Chris headed for the water. He was halfway there when he heard the sound of female laughter coming from behind him. His first instinct was to turn around, but at the same instant he understood something that was as pathetic as it was cowardly. If he didn't look, he wouldn't know if Tracy and Janice were laughing at him or at something else.

Tracy and Janice were gone when Chris came back from his swim. He halfheartedly looked for them before he picked up his towel and went back to the house to fix a roast beef sandwich.

Afterward he stood at the top of the stairs and scanned the beach for a long time, trying to convince himself he'd simply missed them when he'd looked before. But they were either gone or hiding.

He killed a couple of hours talking to a lifeguard he'd met that past summer. The lifeguard told Chris that he'd spent the year traveling up and down the state, putting in applications for work as a firefighter, and it looked as if he would have to leave the state to find work. Chris said he couldn't imagine living anywhere else.

When the lifeguard changed shift and there was still no sign of Tracy or Janice, Chris took off to see if the volleyball game had started.

The following day turned out to be almost identical to the first except that Tracy asked Janice to put on her lotion and Janice went swimming with Chris. She lasted less than fifteen minutes in the cold water—as long as it took her to make an attempt at body surfing and to wind up with a mouth full of sand. This time the two of them disappeared when Chris went back to the house to use the bathroom.

That evening he stayed at the volleyball game until it ended. When he arrived back at the house he found a note from his mother on the kitchen table, telling him they'd gone out for Mexican food and that she had left his dinner in the refrigerator. She ended with the promise to bring him chips and salsa from the restaurant.

Chris warmed his dinner in the microwave and went outside on the deck to eat and watch the sunset. The wind and sea were calm, the beach nearly deserted. During the night the waves would erase the signs of human trespass, leaving the sand unmarked save for the early morning creatures that came to eat and to be eaten.

When Chris thought about what he wanted to do with his life it wasn't the job that mattered, it was the money. He'd looked at one of those free real estate magazines that were all over the place, and an oceanfront bungalow not nearly as nice as the one they were renting cost close to half a million dollars. What was it going to be like in ten years when he'd be looking to buy a place of his own?

Unlike Tracy, he couldn't imagine spending June anywhere but at the beach house. Harder yet was imagining a time when she wouldn't be there with him. She was as much a part of what he loved about being here as the waves and sand.

Every year he told himself she couldn't possibly be as beautiful as he remembered, that she couldn't wear jeans and a sweatshirt and look better than his prom date had in a three-hundred-dollar dress. She was perfect—her skin, her hair, her eyes, her mouth, everything. Even her breasts were just the right size, not so big they hung over the top of her suit or so small they needed to be pushed and lifted into being something they weren't.

He was out of his league with her. A part of him saw that as clearly and instinctively as he saw the weaknesses of his opponents on the wrestling mat. Why couldn't he make the rest of him see it, too?

A man's voice broke the silence. "Pretty spectacular, huh?"

Chris turned at the sound, spilling his iced tea.

"I'm sorry," Eric said. "I didn't mean to startle you."

"I wasn't expecting anyone." He righted the glass and wiped the chair with a napkin. "Hey—aren't you the guy staying at Andrew's house?"

"Eric Lawson."

"You want some iced tea?" Tossing the napkin in his empty plate, he added, "I think there's some beer in the refrigerator."

"No thanks. I was just on my way back from a walk and saw you sitting here. I figured it was time I stopped by to introduce myself."

"My mom said you're a writer."

He leaned his shoulder against the pole that held the bird feeder. "I'm working at it."

"What do you write?"

"Fiction."

"What kind?"

"A medical thriller. At least that's what my agent calls it." Eric smiled. "Something tells me you're a science fiction fan."

"Yeah, but I like lots of other stuff, too." Eric wasn't what Chris had expected. For some reason he'd always pictured people who wrote for a living as a bit on the strange side. He was a little disappointed that Eric seemed so normal. "You a doctor?"

"Congratulations. You're the first person to make the connection."

"Seems to me it would be pretty hard to write about that kind of stuff and not know what you were talking about." Doctors made a ton of money. Why would anyone give up something like that to write books?

"Actually I've discovered it's just plain hard. If I hadn't given up my medical practice, I'd probably be back there by now."

Chris was beginning to like this Eric guy. He was straightforward and didn't talk down to him the way a lot of adults automatically did because of his age. "You here for the summer?"

"I'm here for as long as it takes Andrew to sail around the world. Which he figured was about a year, or possibly two if he found places he wanted to stay a while."

"I wish it was me."

"Sailing?"

"Huh-uh, staying at the house. You can have the boat. It's always been my dream to spend a winter here."

"You wouldn't recognize the place," Eric said. "The beach is usually deserted except for a couple of crazy surfers and a few people like me. Us diehards are out here every day—fog, rain, sun, wind—nothing keeps us away." He smiled. "Which is undoubtedly why I'm no farther along on my book than I am."

"Does it matter when you finish?"

He shifted position. "There's nobody except my agent waiting for it, if that's what you mean."

"Still, I'll bet you can't wait to find out what other people think." He sometimes felt that way when he'd worked especially hard on something for class, but that was nothing like writing a whole book.

"Occasionally," he admitted. "Most of the time just thinking about it scares the hell out of me."

"I'll bet it's great."

Car lights swept past them. "Looks like your mom is back," Eric said.

"They went out to dinner without me." He considered what he'd said and how it must sound and added, "I got caught up in a volleyball game and came home late."

Eric straightened and stretched. "I saw you play."

He was surprised—and oddly pleased. "You did?"

"You're really good. Is it your sport in school?"

"I'm on the wrestling team. I lettered in cross country, too, but the only reason I went out was to stay in shape for wrestling."

"Are you any good? At wrestling, I mean."

He was proud of the medals and championships he'd won but rarely talked about them. "I'm okay."

"I have a feeling you're better than just okay," Eric said. "You going to be around next week?"

The question caught Chris by surprise. "Yeah, we're here till the end of the month."

"I have a friend stopping by for dinner. I think you might get a kick out of meeting him if you're not doing anything else that night. His name is Charlie Stephens."

It took a second for the name to register. "*The* Charlie Stephens?" He'd won more Olympic gold medals than any other American wrestler.

"I'll call and ask him to bring his medals so you can see them. They're really something. He normally hates that kind of thing, but I think I can talk him into it."

The sliding glass door opened behind Chris. "There you are," Margaret said. "I see you found your dinner."

She smiled when she saw Eric. "How's the book coming?"

"I'm four pages further along than this time yesterday."

"Is that good?"

"Not as good as I'd like, but I've had worse days."

"You haven't met the rest of our group yet," Margaret said. "We picked up a cake while we were out. I was just about to make a pot of coffee to go with it. Why don't you join us?"

Eric held up his hand. "Maybe next time. I've already used up my break time. If I go back now, I might be able to get in another page or two before I call it a night."

Margaret took the plate and glass from

Chris. "Stop by anytime. I know the girls would love to meet a real writer."

Eric chuckled. "Thanks. I appreciate the offer." He waved to Chris. "I'll let you know when Charlie gets here."

"See ya later," Chris said. When Eric was gone, Chris grabbed his mother's arm. "You're not going to believe what just happened."

She gave him a wary look. "Please tell me it's something good. I've just spent a miserable two hours listening to Tracy and Beverly fight about everything from whether tacos are real Mexican food to the effects of tanning booths."

Chris took his mother's other arm and made her sit down. When he finished telling her his news, he was convinced all over again that he had the coolest mother in the world. Not only was she excited about his getting a chance to meet Charlie Stephens, she actually knew who he was.

CHAPTER

4

Saturday morning during breakfast, Chris let it drop that he'd been invited to a party that night. While he waited for the news to sink in, he added a couple of pancakes to the stack already on his plate. For almost the first time ever, he could give Tracy something she wanted—some fun. For the entire week she'd done nothing but complain about how bored she was.

Fighting to keep his voice casual, he glanced at Tracy and said, "I asked, and the guys said it would be all right if you and Janice wanted to come, too."

Tracy abruptly brightened, sat up straight, and pushed her plate away. "If you're going out, that means Janice and I can go to the boardwalk—" She caught herself, gave Janice a "Did you hear what I almost said?" look, and put her hand to her mouth to hold in a grin.

The missing end to the sentence was obvious. She'd been about to add, "alone." Chris wanted to die. Right there at the table. Tracy could have stuck her knife in his chest and it would have been a favor.

"I don't know, a party might be kind of fun," Janice said lamely. "Whose is it?"

"Just some guys I met." He cut a wedge of pancake but left it on the plate. There was no way he could get anything down without having it come right back up again.

Margaret came out of the kitchen with a fresh supply of bacon at the same time Beverly came out of the bedroom. She was still wearing her bathrobe. "Morning." She stifled a yawn. "I can't remember the last time I slept this late."

"You're on vacation," Margaret said. "You can—"

"Don't plan on using the car tonight," Tracy broke in. "Janice and I are going to need it."

"What's up?" Beverly asked.

"We're going to the boardwalk." She dipped her finger in her orange juice, then popped it in her mouth, as if the amount were the precise called for on her special diet. "I'm going to need money. Did you go by the ATM?"

Beverly looked at Chris. "Are you going, too?"

"He's been invited to a party," Tracy answered for him.

Margaret put the bacon on the table and sat down opposite Chris. "You have?"

"It's no big deal," Chris said. "A couple of the guys I play volleyball with have their girlfriends coming up for the weekend. Tony's throwing a party for them at his place."

Beverly poured herself a cup of coffee. "That sounds like fun," she said to Tracy. "Maybe you could talk Chris into letting you come along."

"*Mother.*"

"I'm sure he wouldn't mind. Would you, Chris?"

There wasn't a hint of doubt in her voice. She automatically assumed he would do whatever she asked. He felt like some goddamned mongrel dog—fetch, carry, sit, stay, but don't expect to come in the house with the purebreds. He pushed his chair back and stood. "It's up to Tracy."

"Tracy?" Beverly prompted.

"I told you, we already made plans."

"I'm sure it's nothing that—"

Chris went outside. He didn't want to hear the rest.

He headed for the beach, saw how crowded it was, and took off down the road. He was almost to the corner when he heard his mother calling him. She'd seen and heard everything and would know what he was thinking. Undoubtedly she believed she could say something that would make him feel better, but he didn't want to hear it. He looked up and waved. After several seconds she waved back, letting him go.

He broke into a loping jog, bypassing the parking lot for the public entrance to the beach, then cutting through a eucalyptus grove. Ten minutes later he was on the frontage road that led to the highway. He heard a car come up behind him and veered off the asphalt to the shoulder to let it pass. It was a Jeep, one of the fancy kind, painted black with gold trim. The driver went about fifty yards past Chris, stopped, and shifted into reverse.

Chris slowed as he came up to the Jeep, figuring the driver was lost and needed directions.

Tony leaned out the window and hollered, "Hey, kid, can't you move any faster?"

Reaching the driver's window, Chris said, "I thought you were working today."

"I'm on my way there now. Wanna come?"

"You want me to go to work with you?" It seemed an odd invitation.

Tony shook his head in amazement. "You don't have a clue who I am, do you?"

"Should I?"

He laughed. "My press agent thinks so."

Finally Chris made the connection. "You're an actor. You know, I thought I recognized you that first day on the beach. What are you doing here?"

"We're on location—in Watsonville." He looked at his watch. "And I'm running late. You coming or not?"

Since his father walked out, Chris rarely did things on impulse. Out of necessity his life had become structured, his responsibilities habitual. His first thought was that his mother might need him. But she'd made a point of insisting that this was his vacation, too. His second thought was that it would be rude to abandon Tracy and Janice, but they'd probably think he was doing them a favor.

"Yeah, sure. Why not?" He went around the Jeep and got in the passenger side.

The movie set was nothing like Chris had thought it would be. With lights, cameras, wires, scaffolding, and people all over the place, the filmmaking process seemed chaotic and unfocused one minute and like a perfectly organized and orchestrated machine the next. While everyone was friendly, they were dead serious about what they were doing, showing low tolerance for mistakes or excuses. Chris was mesmerized by everything from the man who rushed in to repair makeup between takes to the woman who seemingly effortlessly operated a camera almost as big as she was. In one scene, shot over and over again for reasons Chris never understood, a man's sole job was to refill a beer bottle and supply a half-smoked cigarette to one of the actors.

He was disappointed when they broke for lunch.

"So, what do you think?" Tony asked, strolling over to him.

Chris had been so caught up in the character Tony was playing—a hostile sixties farm laborer frustrated with the peaceful ideology of

Cesar Chavez—that he was taken aback when Tony smiled and turned into the guy Chris knew from the beach.

"I love it," he said with unabashed enthusiasm. He felt the way he had after his first state wrestling championship, lightheaded with excitement.

"Me too." Tony nodded toward a tent set up at the end of the street. "Let's get something to eat before it's all gone."

"Are you sure it's all right? If I come, I mean. I'm not part of—"

"Yeah, I'm sure."

Chris expected something along the lines of bologna sandwiches and chips. What he found was a buffet even fancier than the one at the reception after his father's fancy second marriage. "Wow, this is really something. Do you guys eat like this all the time?"

"It's one of the perks." Tony indicated Chris should get in line in front of him. "We don't have a lot of time."

Chris grabbed a plate and started dishing up, aware that he was an unexpected guest and taking small portions to be sure there was plenty for everyone. When he held himself to two shrimp, Tony took the ladle and added half a dozen more. After that, Chris dished up what he wanted, ending with a plate loaded to overflowing.

They ate in Tony's air-conditioned trailer, joined by two of the other volleyball players. The talk drifted from gossip about people Chris didn't know to the party taking place later that night, but mostly the conversation centered around the business. Chris got so caught up in listening, he had to be reminded to eat.

When lunch was over and he and Tony were on their way back to the set, Tony commented, "You really dig all this stuff."

"It's a world I didn't know anything about," Chris admitted. "I don't get the chance to go to many movies anymore. When I did, I just never gave much thought to how they were made."

"Think you might like to act?"

"*Me?*"

"Why not?"

"I could never do what you do. There for a while you actually had me believing you were that guy you were playing. It was really weird."

Tony grinned. "Thanks."

When they were on the set again, Chris climbed back up on the stool that one of the grips had given him while Tony went over to have his makeup checked. Chris watched the lighting technicians working overhead for several minutes, then looked back to where Tony had been. But he was gone.

A woman carrying a clipboard came up and asked Chris to move his stool to another location. In the process, Chris caught sight of Tony standing alone in a doorway. He was very still and had a faraway look in his eyes. As Chris watched he saw an incredible transformation take place. The Tony Chris knew was gone, the angry farm worker in his place.

Later that afternoon, on the way home, Chris asked Tony about what he'd seen and received a quick lesson on acting.

"I didn't know it was something you could learn," Chris said. "I thought you either had it or you didn't."

"My teacher used to tell us that a successful actor was ten percent talent and ninety percent tenacity, that you need one as much as the other."

"Do you believe that?"

"Which part?" Tony asked, rolling down the window and letting the warm moist air mix with the air-conditioning.

"Either one."

"Luck and timing are important, too. In this business you can't get anywhere without them."

"You consider yourself lucky?" Chris asked.

"Hell, yes. I wouldn't be where I am now if I hadn't gotten sick and stayed home from a cruise that I'd won on a game show. As soon as I started feeling better, one of my friends called and asked if I wanted to earn some extra money bartending for a party in Malibu. I had no idea whose house it was until we got there. It was an agent from William Morris I'd been trying to get in to see for months. The rest, as they say, is history."

Chris shook his head. "I love stories like that."

Tony chuckled. "Me too, especially when they're about me."

CHAPTER

5

Disappointment tugged at the tail of Chris's kite of excitement when he got home and found Beverly's rental car gone and the house empty. He'd called his mother from the movie set to tell her he would be late getting back, but he'd saved the news about where he was to tell her in person.

And now she wasn't there.

Frustrated, he checked the house for a clue to where she might have gone, then walked around the outside to make sure she hadn't stayed behind to work in the garden. Finally, accepting that his news was going to have to wait, he got a soda from the refrigerator and went out on the deck. But he was too excited to sit still long.

It wasn't just his mother he wanted to tell about the movie. He could hardly wait to see Tracy's reaction. She'd try to be cool about it, but there was no way she wouldn't be impressed.

The thought brought him up short. His mind

was working like a little kid's whose only defense against the school bully was to say, "Someday you'll be sorry." Well, his day had come, sooner than he'd believed possible. How many times did *that* happen in a lifetime?

When Tracy heard whose party it was, she would beg him to take her. He closed his eyes to picture them walking in together. When the image came, it left him with an odd, empty feeling. Confused that his fantasy had let him down, he went back in the house.

After the enormous lunch he'd eaten, he wasn't hungry, but he strayed to the kitchen and started going through the cupboards. He found a bag of Oreos and was in the process of twisting one apart when his mother came in the front door.

"You're home," she said as he came out of the kitchen.

"I got here about ten minutes ago. Where is everybody?" She had on a pair of shorts over her swimming suit but didn't look as if she'd been in the water.

"You mean everyone else?" she chided gently. "They went shopping. Tracy wanted to get something new to wear tonight."

Chris caught a note of disapproval, unusual for his mother. "I'm glad they're not here," he said, surprised that he meant it. "Wait till you hear where I've been today. It's so cool, Mom. You're not going to believe it."

She smiled at his enthusiasm. "So tell me."

He did, and just as he knew she would, she

asked the right questions and showed the right amount of excitement.

"You had no idea who he was?" Margaret asked when he'd finished.

"None. I had the whole bunch of them pegged for construction workers."

"Eric told me they were shooting a movie in Watsonville. But who would have thought a movie star would be out on the beach playing volleyball like everyone else."

"You wouldn't recognize him if you saw him. He's got long hair and always has on sunglasses and a hat."

She reached up and affectionately lifted his hair off his forehead and combed it back with her fingers. "Antonio Gallardo could look the exact way he did in his last movie and you still wouldn't have recognized him."

"What's that supposed to mean?"

"You're the least starstruck person I know."

On impulse he asked, "You want to come to the party with me tonight?"

"Thanks, but I have a date."

"With Eric?"

Her eyes widened in genuine surprise. "Whatever made you think that?"

"I dunno, he's single, you're single. You're both about the same age. He seems like a nice guy, and you're not bad yourself."

"How could he resist, with all that going for me?"

"Well?"

"No, I'm not going out with Eric. After we

drop Tracy and Janice off at the boardwalk, Beverly and I are going to a movie."

"Does Tracy know you're taking the car?"

"I figure that's Beverly's problem."

He nodded sagely. "Which is why you didn't go shopping with them."

She laughed. "Sometimes you're too smart for your own good."

"Hey, do me a favor?"

"Yes?" Margaret said.

"Don't tell anyone about the movie thing, okay?"

"Want to spring it on Tracy and Janice yourself?"

Actually, he'd begun to wonder if he wanted to tell them about it at all. "I don't like the idea of Tracy . . ." He shrugged. "I don't know. I just don't feel right about it."

"She'd be impressed," Margaret said. "She might even want to go with you tonight after all."

"I know—that's what I mean."

"I'm impressed."

"Don't be. I could always change my mind."

The battle over the car was still going on when Beverly and Tracy walked in the door an hour later. Janice slipped in behind them, passed through the living room with her head down, and disappeared into her and Tracy's room. She came out a short time later carrying a towel and announced she was going for a swim.

Margaret looked at Chris and said softly, "Why don't you go with her?"

He changed into his trunks and left. Tracy's and Beverly's raised voices followed him out the door. The beach was crowded, and it took Chris several minutes to find Janice. She was standing in the surf, her hands open at her sides as if trying to stop the incoming waves. In the week and a half she'd been there, Janice had picked up a tan—which wasn't surprising, considering the hours she and Tracy had lain in the sun. While her skin had darkened, her hair seemed lighter, as if some gold were now mixed in with the brown.

Chris supposed she was pretty in a cheerleader kind of way. Not the sort that usually appealed to him—in anyone but Tracy, of course. Tracy was the exception to every rule he lived by, someone so special that she wasn't held to any standards.

In the ordinary world, Chris liked girls who didn't worry what the wind would do to their hair if someone rolled down the window in the car, a girl who wore makeup to a party but didn't worry about it at the beach. He scanned Janice's near naked body and added mentally—a girl who wore suits they actually could swim in. Most important, he wanted a girl who could beat him at something besides television trivia.

Chris came up to stand beside Janice. "So now that you've been here a while, have you changed your mind?"

Janice didn't show surprise at finding him there. "About the ocean?"

The question puzzled him. What else could he have been talking about? "Yeah."

"I love it more every day." She rocked up on her toes when a late-breaking wave sent the water rushing up her thighs. "I'm starting to feel pretty selfish about it, though. I resent the other people hanging around *my* beach." She gave him a sheepish grin. "I want this place all to myself."

With Tracy he would have figured it was her way of telling him to get lost. He didn't get the same feeling with Janice. "You have to get up pretty early to—"

"I know."

He eyed her. "You do?"

"Just before sunrise is the best time. No one is up yet, or if they are, they aren't on the beach. There isn't any music or kids screaming, or parents hollering, just the sound of the birds and waves." She scooped up a handful of water and let it drain through her fingers.

"Do you come alone?"

She laughed. "Get serious. Tom Cruise couldn't get Tracy out of bed at that hour."

"You shouldn't, you know."

"Why?"

"It just doesn't seem like a very smart thing to take off alone that way." He was automatically repeating a warning he'd heard given to every girl and woman he knew.

"I refuse to live my life being afraid," she

said. "That doesn't mean I'm going to be stupid. There are a whole lot of places in St. Louis I wouldn't go by myself at night, but they're places my brothers wouldn't go, either."

"Still, I'd go with you if—"

"I don't need a bodyguard, Chris. I'm perfectly capable of taking care of myself."

"That's not what I meant. I like the beach when it's empty, too."

She turned to look at him. "Then how come I never see you here?"

"I go at night. After everyone else is in bed."

"Does your mother know?"

"No."

"I didn't think so."

"What's that supposed to mean?"

"Tracy said Margaret keeps a really tight rein on you since your dad left."

He didn't like knowing he was being talked about, even if it was Tracy doing the talking. "Well, she's wrong."

"Come on, Chris. I've seen how your mother controls you. All it takes is a look and you're right there doing the dishes or going to the store. I'll bet she's the one who sent you down here after me."

"So what?" What right did she have to judge him or his mother? "She cares what happens to you, that's all. What's the big deal in that?"

"If she cares so much, why didn't she come herself?"

He couldn't believe he had actually thought he might be starting to like Janice. "What's your point?"

"She needs to let go of you and get herself a man."

The statement left Chris speechless. When he recovered, he spat out, "You're such a bitch." He threw his arms wide in a disgusted gesture and backed away. "Drown, for all I care."

Janice watched him start to jog toward the stairs and then veer off and head down the beach instead. She couldn't believe she'd said what she had to him. She'd opened her mouth, but it was Tracy's words that had come out. What in the hell had she been thinking? The worst part was she didn't even believe what she'd said. She'd give anything if her own mother were more like Margaret.

For weeks she'd heard what a loser Chris was; then she'd seen him for herself, and nothing Tracy had said made sense. It was obvious he had a thing for Tracy and that Tracy would rather make it with Quasimodo. At home Tracy loved it when guys fell all over themselves chasing her. With Chris it was as if it were an insult.

She waited for the next wave and dove in, not caring what it would do to her hair or how much longer it would take to get ready that night. At least she wouldn't have to listen to Tracy complain about her mother or Chris or the car while the blow dryer was running.

* * *

After trying on the one pair of slacks he'd
brought with him, Chris put on a new white T-
shirt and a clean pair of jeans. It was just a barbecue, after all, not a sit-down formal dinner.
His run-in with Janice had dampened his party
mood, but he'd be damned if he was going to
let her or Tracy ruin the entire night.

The party was at the house Tony was renting. Rather, the house the movie people had
rented for him. Chris had recognized which one
it was as soon as Tony started giving directions.
Everyone who lived in the neighborhood knew
about the place, but Chris had never found anyone who'd actually been there. The rock-and-
brick house sat on the southernmost point of the
cove, its height atop the cliff and prominent
location providing what had to be an uninter-
rupted view of the entire Monterey Bay from
Santa Cruz all the way down to Pacific Grove.
Curious who could afford such a place, Chris
had imagined everything from Silicon Valley
royalty to Mob bosses.

Once he'd tried to get a better look by taking the inland route, but an eight-foot-high
fence and acres of dense forest prevented even a
glimpse.

Tonight the ornate wrought-iron gate was
open, but a man in uniform stood guard outside, checking names against a list attached to a
clipboard. Cars were lined up on both sides of

the road a good hundred yards before Chris caught sight of the house. Plainly the party was not the small gathering he had believed.

Chris parked behind a cobalt blue Viper, the first he'd seen outside a magazine. He spent a good five minutes looking it over before heading up the hill. Wait till the guys at school heard about this night. They'd never believe him. Not in a million years.

The house itself wasn't as big as he'd expected—more the size of the rich people's places in Fresno than those in Bel Air. But he'd take it. In a heartbeat. The thought brought the now familiar itch to one day own his own piece of the coast. Only he'd never dreamed of anything like this. Better to forget about it. Put it out of his mind right now. Something like that just wasn't possible.

He was just being reasonable, keeping himself from going after impossible dreams. Then why the voice that insisted, *Why not?*

A woman with a cigarette in one hand and a drink in the other spotted him, smiled, and when he approached, handed him her empty glass. She was wearing four-inch heels and a dress made out of a material that shimmered the way peacock feathers did in the sunlight.

"Another of the same," she said. "Vodka straight."

"Okay," Chris said, returning her smile. "Just point me in the direction of the bar."

She gave him a quick once-over. "My God, you're a guest. How embarrassing." Hooking her arm through his, she dropped her cigarette and ground it out with her foot. "Come with me. I'll introduce you to everyone." She laughed. "Everyone you haven't already met, that is. Wait, I need to know your name first."

"Chris Sadler."

"Pleased to meet you, Mr. Chris Sadler." She stood to the side to let him open the massive carved mahogany door, then swept through to the marble foyer and waited for him to follow. "Dolores Langtry."

Chris couldn't decide whether she was drunk, eccentric, just plain strange, or a mixture of all three. Whatever—she seemed the kind of woman accustomed to forging heedlessly into the river and having others follow in her wake. She led him through the living room and out onto the flagstone patio, where she paused expectantly.

"Everyone. . . ," she said when she had their attention. "I want you to meet Chris Sadler. Be nice to him, he's a very dear friend of mine."

Her announcement was met with polite smiles, a few acknowledging nods, and a chorus of varied greetings. Tony left the couple he'd been talking to and came up to Chris, a warm smile in his eyes for Dolores. "I see you've met my mother," he said to Chris.

Chris took a closer look at Dolores and then at Tony. They looked nothing alike. "Dolores is your *mother?*"

"What a *dear* boy," Dolores said, lovingly touching his cheek, obviously misinterpreting his meaning.

"Score one for the kid," Tony said.

"Now that you're in good hands," Dolores said to Chris, "I can get my drink. What can I bring you?"

How could he let Tony's mother wait on him? How could he refuse? "Uh, water would be fine."

"Sparkling or bottled?"

"Sparkling." Chris wanted to make it as easy as possible.

"With a twist of lime?"

"Yeah, sure—that would be great."

"She likes you," Tony said when his mother had gone.

"She just met me." He looked around and saw with relief that he wasn't the only one wearing jeans.

"According to Dolores, snap judgments are the only ones that count."

"You call your mother Dolores?"

Tony eyed him. "How old are you?"

Chris's first impulse was to add a couple of years, an action so alien that it left him tongue-tied.

"It's okay," Tony said. "You don't have to answer."

"Seventeen."

Tony nodded. "That's what I figured. Come on, I'll introduce you around."

Chris had an irrational urge to ask if being seventeen was okay. He had no idea why it mattered, only that it did. "I'll be eighteen in September."

"Really? September what?"

"Twenty-third."

"Mine's the thirteenth."

"No kidding. How old will you be?"

"Twenty-seven."

God, Tony was old. A lot older than Chris had thought. Now that he knew he was hanging around with a kid, would he want to have anything to do with him anymore? "This is really some house."

"It belongs to a friend of mine. I've been trying to talk him into selling it to me." He stopped at a small group of people sitting around a glass-topped rattan table. "Robert, this is the guy I've been telling you about."

Robert wore wire-rimmed glasses, a golf shirt with a shark on the pocket, and a baseball cap from the Sundance Film Festival. He looked to be around fifty and someone you didn't want to mess with. After giving Chris a quick once-over, he shifted his cigar to the corner of his mouth and said to Tony, "You're right, he does look like David."

"I suppose that's enough for now," Tony said, pleased with himself.

Robert laughed. "You SOB. Do you always get what you want?"

"Just when I'm right."

Chris looked around at the other people seated at the table. It was obvious they had no more idea what was going on than he did. "Who's David?"

"I'll explain later," Tony said.

A woman Chris believed to be hands down the most beautiful he'd ever seen patted the empty chair beside her, inviting him to sit down. When he did, she introduced herself. "Gloria Sinclair." She moved her chair to give him more room. "Whatever they're doing, Chris, there's no way you're going to get it out of them until they're ready to tell you. But don't worry, I'm sure it's something good."

Tony bent and gave her an intimate kiss, leaving her lips wet and glistening. "Will you marry me?"

"I'll think about it."

Chris looked down at her finger and saw a diamond the size of his thumbnail.

She smiled and brought her hand up to give him a closer look. "Nice, huh?"

"I've never seen anything like it," Chris said. It was on the tip of his tongue to ask if it was real, but luckily he caught himself in time.

Tony kissed her again. "Now all I have to do is get her to slow down long enough to set the date."

"Me slow down?" she said. "What about you?"

"Are you an actor, too?" Chris asked. Dead silence reigned where only moments before fifty people had been engaged in two dozen conversations. Even those on the other side of the patio who couldn't possibly have heard what he'd said stopped to listen to her answer.

"You don't go to many movies, do you?" Robert said, removing his cigar.

Chris could feel people staring at him. "Not in the past couple of years. I've been kinda busy."

"Leave the kid alone," Gloria said. "I like knowing there are people who've never seen me. It makes me work harder."

Tony stood behind her and put his hands on her shoulders. "I sure as hell hope not. We hardly see each other as it is."

She reached up to touch him. "No way that's going to happen."

Dolores came up and handed Chris his drink. In a slowly widening circle, conversations began again. Chris learned that Gloria had a movie coming out that fall that everyone was sure would win her an Academy Award nomination and that she was on her way to being one of the hottest new actors in Los Angeles.

Best of all, Chris was pleased to discover later that she was also an extraordinarily nice person.

CHAPTER

6

hris left the party at a quarter after two, not realizing it was so late until he went inside to use the bathroom and found the house empty and Gloria curled up, asleep on the sofa. He'd had a great time. Better than great—fantastic.

And he had news. Wonderful, exciting news. He hoped his mother hadn't kept her promise not to wait up. Something like this had to be shared. He'd go crazy if he had to wait until morning to talk about it.

He was going to be in a movie. It was just a crowd scene, but Tony said it should take at least a couple of days to shoot. He had to cut his hair, a flattop, one of the guys had told him, but he didn't care. He always cut his hair for wrestling season anyway.

It was so friggin' cool.

A week ago, if someone had told him they were filming a movie in Watsonville, he wouldn't have taken the time to pull off the highway to watch. Now, after spending the day on the set with Tony, he would have traded his next state wrestling championship to be involved. Only he didn't have to. The director had actually *asked* him if he wanted to go to work on Monday.

God, it was just so cool.

Chris neared the bottom of the hill and slowed to make the turn for home when he noticed Beverly's rental car parked on the side of the road. He pulled the wheel of the Volvo to the right to shine his headlights inside. Someone turned to look but put a hand over their eyes before he could tell who it was.

Chris pulled in behind the car and got out, leaving the engine of his own car running and the lights on. Janice leaned out the window. "Tracy? Is that you?"

"It's Chris."

"Oh, great," she said, and rolled her eyes. "Just what I need."

"What are you doing here?" He came up to the window and bent over to look inside. "Where's Tracy?"

"What business is it of yours?"

"Forget I asked," he said wearily. "I just thought you might need some help."

"Wait." Janice got out and leaned against the car door. "You're right. I do need your help—but not the kind you mean. I don't know what to do," she admitted. "Tracy said she would meet me here two hours ago."

"Where'd she go?"

"Out—with a guy she met on the boardwalk."

It took a second for the information to sink in. "She just took off and left you there?"

"I said it was okay," she said defensively.

"Was he a local?"

"I don't know. What difference does that make?"

"If he lives here, we could look him up. What's his name?"

"I don't know that, either."

"Jesus, you let her go with some guy you knew nothing about?"

"What was I supposed to do? I'm not her keeper."

"No, but you're her friend."

"No, I'm not," Janice said with impassioned denial. "Tracy and I barely knew each other before she went out for cheerleader. She asked me on this trip because she couldn't get anyone else to go with her and she didn't want to spend the whole month here alone with you."

As soon as the words were out Janice covered her mouth with the ends of her fingers as if to keep the rest inside. As she looked at him, her eyes pooled with tears.

She'd only confirmed something Chris had suspected, but that didn't make it hurt any less. "Did she tell you that?"

"I'm sorry. That was so mean. None of it is true. I made it all up."

Chris could hide behind her apology and pretend he believed it, but what was the point? "No, you didn't."

"I really am sorry," she said between her fingers.

To his amazement, Chris saw that she was crying. "You didn't do anything but tell the truth."

"Honestly, I'm not the bitch you think I am. Everyone at home says I'm one of the nicest people they know. I don't know why I've been so mean to you. Your mom has been terrific . . . so have you . . . and all I've done . . ." She let out a hiccuped sob. "I'm so sorry."

Chris hated it when someone cried around him. He had no idea what to say or do, and whenever possible he got away as fast as he could. But he couldn't just take off and leave her standing there. "You're probably homesick." It was something his mother would have said.

She ran her hands over her cheeks and then wiped them on her shorts. "Do you really think that's it?"

"Yeah, I'm sure it is. I was yelling at everyone when I had to stay at my cousin's last summer." It wasn't true, but he'd do or say anything to stop the tears.

She considered what he'd said. "I think it's more than being homesick. I didn't feel this way when I was at cheerleading camp."

"Was Tracy with you?"

"Not that time." The hint of a smile formed. "I see what you mean."

Realizing he was going to be there a while, Chris went back to turn off the Volvo and get the Kleenex his mother kept under the seat. Janice took one and blew her nose, softly at first and then hard enough to make a weird honking noise.

When she looked up and saw his smile, she smiled back. "I feel better. Thanks."

Because he didn't know what else to say, he asked, "How long have you been a cheerleader?"

"Three years."

"Do you like it?"

"Of course. It's great. We get to go . . ." She hesitated, as if considering her answer. "Not always. Sometimes when we're out there yelling and no one is paying attention, or when we get the cheer all screwed up because the other team got the ball, I feel really stupid."

"No one notices."

"The hell they don't. I look up in the stands and see guys like you looking back at me all the time."

"What do you mean, guys like me?"

"You think all I care about is how I look and who I run around with."

She had him. "You're saying I'm wrong?"

"Prejudice is always wrong."

He laughed. "Some answer."

"I care about a lot of things that have nothing to do with being a cheerleader."

"Such as?"

"Why should I have to explain myself to you?"

"You don't."

They were right back where they'd started, at each other's throats. "Want to try again?"

"I do a lot of work at Al-Anon, helping other kids."

It took a second for the name to register.
"Isn't that the place—"

"It isn't a place, it's an organization . . . for
kids with alcoholic parents."

"Your dad's an alcoholic?"

"My mother." She didn't say anything for a
long time and then added, "None of my friends
know."

"Not even Tracy?"

"I told you, Tracy and I aren't friends. I
don't even like her."

"Does your dad know? About your mom, I
mean." Could he have come up with a dumber
question?

"He's the one who got me and my brothers
involved in Al-Anon."

"Wow. . . that's got to be hard." The only
alcoholic Chris knew was a friend of his
father's. They used to go to parties at his
house, and when he got drunk he always started
hitting on his daughter's girlfriends. Chris
hated going there, but his dad said the guy
wasn't serious, that he was just having a little
fun.

"Sometimes I hate her, and then I feel so
guilty."

"Sometimes I hate my dad, too," Chris said.

"Because he divorced your mom?"

"Not that so much as the way he did it. He
was screwing around and let her catch him at
it—right in their own bed. Less than three years
later he got married again and she hasn't even
gone out on a date."

"Your mom is great. Your dad must be a real jerk."

"That's what I keep telling her, but she says that what he did to her is between them, that it has nothing to do with him and me." He never talked to anyone about his father. As far as his friends knew, they got along fine.

"As if that were possible. When I see what my mom's drinking does to my dad, there are times I can hardly stand to be around her. She thinks she's so sly, that we can't smell the stuff on her, or that we don't know when she's drunk. My brothers leave when she gets really bad, but I can't. She passed out one time when she was cooking bacon and almost burned down the house."

"How old are your brothers?"

"Fourteen and fifteen."

"Where do they go?"

"To my grandmother's house. She only lives a couple of blocks away and lets them stay whenever they want."

"I won't say anything." It was important she knew she could trust him.

"Thanks. I won't say anything about your dad, either." She slapped a mosquito that had drilled into her wrist. "Do you think we should do something about Tracy?"

"Like what?"

"I don't know, but I'm getting worried about her."

Chris didn't know whether to be worried or pissed off. He had a feeling that if Tracy was having a good time, she wouldn't think twice about staying out all night. "What kind of car did the guy have?"

"A blue Mustang, one of the real old ones. Why?"

"I know some of the hangout spots," Chris said. "I could try looking for them there."

"I'll come with you."

"What if she comes back while we're gone?"

"Then she can just wait for us." Janice took the keys and her purse out of the car. "I'm ready."

Chris pulled around the Town Car, made a U-turn, and started back the way he'd come. "This isn't the first time Tracy has done something like this," he said. "If she's pulling one of her usual stunts, I feel sorry for the guy."

"I feel sorry for her boyfriend."

Chris's hands tightened on the steering wheel. "What boyfriend?"

"The one who's waiting for her back home. Haven't you noticed how much she's on the phone? And how many postcards she's been sending?"

"She said she was calling her dad." He'd wondered about it at the time but saw no reason to doubt her. "How long has she been going with this guy?"

"Since last summer."

"A whole year? But Tracy never said anything . . . neither did her mom."

"I think it's because Beverly hopes you two will get together eventually."

"That's crazy." Still, the possibility had

appeal, or at least it should have. "She's never said anything about it to me." Had she said something to his mom? The thought didn't sit well.

"Because she knows if Tracy ever found out, she would do just the opposite."

"Like that's not what she's already doing. She treats me like I'm something she stepped in and can't get off her shoe."

"I don't understand it," Janice said. "Did something happen between you two?"

"Yeah—every summer I make an ass out of myself trying to get her to notice me and she falls all over herself getting out of my way." It was something he'd never admitted to anyone, not even himself.

They were passing the road to Tony's house. Chris glanced at Janice, then back at the road again. Would she tell Tracy what he'd said, giving Tracy yet another reason to laugh at him?

There was no reason he should trust Janice.

But he did.

As they neared the highway he realized it was Janice, not his mother, he wanted to tell about the party. "Have you ever heard of—"

"There they are," Janice said, pointing at a passing car. She swung around to get a better look. "Damn her. Now that I know she's all right, I could kill her myself."

Chris made a U-turn and followed the rapidly disappearing taillights. He would tell Janice about the party later.

CHAPTER

7

Chris pulled in behind the Mustang just as Tracy got out. She ignored them as she waited for the guy who'd been driving to come around to her side of the car. When he got there she wrapped her arms around his neck, gave him tongue that must have cleaned his back teeth, and ground her hips into his.

"Some show, huh?" Janice said. She looked at Chris. "You know she's doing this for you."

It should have bothered him. He waited to see if it would. But he felt nothing. "Like I said, I feel sorry for the guy."

"Really?"

"Why don't you give her the keys so we can get out of here?"

"Great idea." Janice rolled down the window as Chris drove by. "Tracy—catch." She tossed the keys before Tracy had a chance to react, hitting her on the rear end.

"Good throw," Chris said.

She grinned. "Thanks."

Normally Chris would have parked on the street in front of the house, leaving the driveway free for Tracy. But not tonight. He and Janice had been inconvenienced enough.

He glanced at the clock on the nightstand as he climbed in bed. It was going on four and he was wide awake. When the early morning sun hit his blinds, casting a weird geometric shadow on the opposite wall, he was still wide-eyed. Giving up on sleep, he'd switched to waiting for sounds that would tell him his mother was up. So much had happened in the past twenty-four hours that he needed to talk to her about. His mind kept racing from one thing to the next, never settling long enough to let him think anything through.

In less than twenty-four hours, he'd gone from being as ordinary as hamburger and fries to a guest at a movie star's party where he couldn't identify half the food on the buffet table. He had no illusions. The ride he was on would be short, a week or two at the most, and then everybody would pack up and go home and forget all about the kid they'd met that summer. But Chris would remember. For the rest of his life he would remember.

Somewhere between thinking about the rock on Gloria's finger and the way he'd felt being on the set with Tony, it had come to Chris that it might be fun to try out for a school play that fall. Not a big role, of course. He'd start out with a small part, and if he liked it, he'd try out for something bigger in the spring, or maybe in college.

When he got home he was going to have to do some research on colleges that had drama departments. Not that he was considering majoring in acting or anything like that. He'd have to have some gigantic ego to think anyone would pay to see him on a stage or in a movie.

But then he didn't care about being a star. He'd be happy doing crowd scenes for the rest of his life. They didn't have to pay him, just being a part of the action was enough—even if it meant he'd never get to buy his own beach house.

He was never going to make it through the weekend and wished he could just sleep until Monday morning.

He heard the door open to the bedroom next to his and softly close again. It had to be his mother. Beverly never got up before nine. After jumping out of bed and into his jeans, he caught up with her before she reached the kitchen.

"You're up early," she said. "How was the party?"

He put his hands on her shoulders, looked down into her eyes, and grinned. *"Un-be-lie-vable."*

She stood patiently in his arm-length embrace. "I take it you had a good time."

"The best ever. Wait till you hear."

"Can you tell me while I make coffee?"

"I don't know if it can wait that long."

"Goodness—this must really be something."
She eyed him for several seconds and then said,
"You met a girl."

"I met lots of them, but no one special." He
had no sooner finished the sentence than an
image of Janice flashed through his mind.

"Well? I'm waiting."

He dropped his arms and affected a casual
air. "I don't know, I suppose it could wait until
after you've had your coffee."

"You rat." She started toward the kitchen.
"I've a good mind to take you up on that."

He went after her. "I'm going to be in
Tony's movie."

When she turned to look at him she seemed
more stunned than happy. "I don't know what
to say."

Her reaction confused him. "It's nothing
big, just a crowd scene. I think Tony arranged
it as a favor because he saw how much I liked
being on the set." When she didn't comment,
he asked, "Is something wrong? I thought you'd
be really excited for me."

"You just surprised me." She struggled to
find a better answer. "I thought I knew everything about you, but never in a million years
would I have guessed that you'd feel this way
about being in a movie."

"Me either," he admitted.

"I think it's great." She opened the refrigerator to get the coffee. "We'll have a party when
the movie comes out and invite all your
friends."

He didn't know whether he was more disappointed at her lack of enthusiasm or her attempt to make up for it. No way would he have a party. He decided not to tell her the rest. If she didn't understand about the movie, she wouldn't understand about his decision to try out for the school play.

"How was the show?" he asked, changing the subject.

"I'm not sure. The subtitles were so long, it took forever to read them and I didn't get to see a lot of the movie." She filled the pot with water and grounds and plugged it in. "We did have a good dinner, though. We went to an East Indian restaurant that Eric recommended. Beverly thought the shrimp had a little too much curry, but I . . . "

Chris stopped listening. His mind drifted to Janice and what she'd told him about her mother. He understood about her not wanting to tell anyone. Chris hadn't even told his best friend, Paul, about his college money being gone. The coach was checking into scholarships for him, and it looked as if some schools might come through with offers, but none of them were Chris's first choice. He loved wrestling, and thought he'd do okay at the college level, but he'd begun to have doubts about the dedication it would take.

"Chris?"

He looked up and realized his mother was talking to him. "What?"

"Do you have any other plans?"

He had no idea what she was talking about. Admitting he hadn't been listening, he asked, "Plans for what?"

"Tonight."

She wasn't going to let him off that easily. "Okay, I give up. What are we talking about?"

"Eric dropped by last night and said his friend was coming sooner then he'd thought and if you weren't doing anything, you were invited for dessert around eight."

"You know, I'm sure it would be all right if you came, too," he said.

"Give it up, Chris. I told you I'm not interested in Eric Lawson, so would you please stop trying to get us together?" She stepped around him to get bowls down for cereal. "Besides, Beverly and I are going to a concert in Monterey tonight."

"What's wrong with Eric?"

"Nothing."

"Then why—"

"I told you, I'm not ready for a relationship."

"Dad got married again. I don't see why you can't at least go out once in a while."

"Sit down, Chris." He did while she got them both a cup of coffee and then joined him at the table. "As hard as this may be for you to understand, I like being on my own. I went from living at home to living in a dorm in college to living with your father. This is the first time in my life that no one is setting rules for me or telling me what to do. Why would I want to give that up?"

"Don't you ever get lonely?"

"Sometimes. But then I think how high a price I would have to pay for company." She added milk to her coffee and passed the carton to Chris. "I'm not saying I won't change my mind someday. As a matter of fact, I'm almost certain I will. But for now, I like things the way they are."

"Have you looked around, Mom? You're getting old—older," he corrected. "There aren't that many guys for you to pick from. What if the right one comes along while you're stuck in this freedom thing?"

"If it happens, it happens. There are worse things in life than living alone." She picked up her mug and took a drink. "Like marrying the wrong man."

"You mean Dad."

She shook her head. "He was only wrong in the end. I'll never regret marrying your father, Chris. If I hadn't, I wouldn't have you."

"You know, I'm going to be gone pretty soon, too."

"Is that what this is all about?"

"What do you mean?"

"The reason you're trying to fix me up. Are you worried what I'm going to do when you leave for school?"

"I've thought about it," he acknowledged.

"Well, stop." She reached across the table, took his hand, and gave it a squeeze. "I don't want to hurt your feelings, but I'm actually looking forward to having the house all to myself."

He didn't believe her but knew it was important that he at least pretend he did. "Is this your way of telling me you want me to move out sooner?"

She smiled. "I think I can put up with you for one more year."

Chris put his arms over his head and stretched. "I'm going running before breakfast. You want to come?"

She considered his invitation. "I'll go down to the beach with you, but walking is more my speed this morning." She topped off her coffee. "You never said what time you got in last night."

"Late."

"Hmmm . . . and you got up early this morning. You really are excited about this movie thing."

"I'm going to change. I'll meet you outside."

She picked up a magazine, glanced at the cover, and stretched lazily. "Too late. I've been distracted. I'll be out on the deck if you need me."

He laughed. "Like I said, you're starting to get old, Mom. Next thing you know, you'll need a cane and then one of those walkers. And then who knows what's next?"

"I prefer to think I'm conserving energy."

When Chris returned an hour later he walked in on the middle of a screaming match between Tracy and Beverly over who would take the car that afternoon. Janice was at the table, eating cereal.

"I don't see why you can't take Margaret's car." Tracy slammed the puffed-rice box onto the table. "She doesn't need it. She never goes anywhere."

Beverly dumped a packet of sugar substitute into her coffee. "I told you—"

"I'm using the Volvo this afternoon," Chris said. "Janice and I are going to Big Sur."

Janice brought her head up, gave him a sidelong glance, and silently mouthed, "Thank you."

"Since when?" challenged Tracy.

"Since last night." He met her hostile gaze without flinching, something he would have been incapable of doing even a day ago. "You're welcome to come along if you like." The invitation rang with the same sincerity as telling the wrestler whose pin cost the team their match that it didn't matter.

"I have a date," she said with an almost laughable superiority.

"Then I don't see the problem." Chris used the bottom of his tank top to wipe the sweat from his forehead. "Have him pick you up here."

Tracy sent a quick look in her mother's direction. "I can't. He doesn't know where I live."

"What time are you supposed to meet him? We could drop you off." Chris smiled at Janice. "You wouldn't mind, would you?"

Janice flinched at being brought into the conversation. "No . . . that's fine with me."

Tracy turned on Janice. "How could you do this to me?"

"That's enough," Beverly said.

"You promised that if I came with you this summer, it would be different," Tracy shouted at her mother, tears welling in her eyes. "You said I could do whatever I wanted, that this was my vacation, too."

Chris and Janice exchanged looks, both dumbfounded at Tracy's emotional outburst.

Beverly tried to put her arm around Tracy, but she backed away, refusing to be placated. "I want to go home," she said. "Today. Right now."

"Be reasonable, Tracy," Beverly pleaded. "You know how much I look forward to this trip every year. It's the only time Margaret and I get to see each other anymore."

"Why is it always what you want? What about me?"

Chris had witnessed a hundred arguments between Tracy and her mother and had automatically taken Tracy's side, choosing to believe it was her strong will and ability to stick up for herself that got under Beverly's skin.

Had he been blind or just plain stupid?

"I'm serious, Mother," Tracy went on. "I want to go home."

"What if I got you a car?" Beverly asked. "Would you change your mind?"

The tears disappeared with a blink. "My own car?" she asked suspiciously.

"We could look into what the difference

would be if I turned in the Town Car and rented a couple of compacts."

Tracy's eyes lit up at the suggestion. "Will they let you do that—rent two cars at once?"

"I don't see why not."

"But if they won't, you could put one of them under Margaret's name," she said, closing a possible escape route for her mother.

"Margaret might not want to do that," Beverly said. "We'll have to ask her first."

"You can talk her into it," Tracy said.

Janice got up to clear her dishes. "I'm ready when you are," she said to Chris.

"Give me five minutes." One to let his mother know what was going on and four for a shower.

"I'll pack a lunch. You did say we were going to be gone all day, didn't you?"

He nodded. To Beverly he said, "I don't know for sure when we'll be back, so don't count on us for dinner."

Tracy looked at Janice. "I was going to ask you to come with me. Jimmy said he could probably fix you up with one of his friends. But if you're going to be gone all day . . ." She let out a sigh, plainly waiting for Janice to jump in and tell her that she could arrange to be back in time.

Janice made a face. "I can't imagine anything worse than a blind date with a biker."

Beverly gasped, almost choking on her coffee. "You're going out with a biker?"

Tracy glared at Janice. "Just because Jimmy

said you were stuck-up is no reason to say something like that about him."

"If he's not a biker," Janice said, "how do you explain all the Harley-Davidson tattoos?"

"He has tattoos?" Beverly said, her voice rising a level.

"Everybody has tattoos out here," Tracy said. "I've been thinking about getting one myself."

It was the wrong thing to say. Beverly's reaction was swift and firm. "I have no control over what you do when you move out of your father's and my house, but as long as you are living with us, you will not disfigure yourself with tattoos. And—"

"It's my body. I'll do what I want to it," Tracy challenged. "And there's no way you can stop me."

"No, but I don't have to look at them. You seem to forget the application we sent to St. Michael's Academy was approved last month. All we have to do is—"

"How could you?" Tracy looked at Chris and then Janice as angry tears came to her eyes. "You promised you wouldn't say anything."

Beverly also glanced in Chris and Janice's direction as if to gauge their reaction. "I'm sorry," she said to Tracy. "I wasn't thinking."

"That's the excuse you always use." Tracy got up and ran into her room. Seconds later Beverly followed.

Silence hung heavy in the air between Chris and Janice. Finally it was Chris who asked, "Do you know what that was all about?"

Janice hesitated. "I'm only guessing, but I'll bet sending her away has something to do with the time Tracy's folks came home early from one of their trips and found her doing drugs with her boyfriend."

He looked at Janice and realized that he probably knew more about what she thought and felt than he'd ever known about Tracy. Who was the girl he'd been in love with all this time? Had he simply imagined her?

"I've known Tracy all my life," he said. "And I have no idea who she really is."

"Are you okay?" Janice asked.

"I'm going to get ready so we can get out of here."

"I'll make the sandwiches."

"Don't bother." He wanted to get away as fast as he could, wishing selfishly now that he could be alone. He had a lot of thinking to do. "We'll stop for something."

On the way to his room, Chris spotted his mother on the deck. He stopped to tell his plans.

She looked up from her magazine as he opened the screen. "You don't have to say anything. I heard."

"Did you know about the private school?"

She shook her head. "I suppose if I'd tried, I could have pieced the story together from little things in Beverly's letters, but I never cared enough to try."

"You don't mind my taking the car?"

She closed the magazine and laid it on her lap. "I don't want you to get the idea I approve of you telling lies, but it's hard to be upset with someone and feel proud of them at the same time."

He didn't know how to answer her.

"Go. Forget what happened here this morning and have a good time with Janice. Just don't forget you're expected at Eric's tonight."

"What time are you and Beverly leaving?"

"I don't know."

"Where are you going?"

"I don't know that, either."

He gave her answer some thought. "What you're saying is that I wasn't the only one in there lying about needing the car."

She smiled.

CHAPTER

8

Chris and Janice didn't make it to Big Sur. As they neared Monterey, Janice remembered him telling her about the aquarium on Cannery Row and asked to stop. They had to park half a mile away and stand in lines to see the exhibits with an overflow Sunday crowd, but nothing dampened Janice's enthusiasm. She stopped and craned her neck to see the life-size whale models suspended overhead in the main hall, becoming a rock in the constantly flowing river of visitors.

"Move it, lady." Chris put his hand in the middle of her back and pushed gently. "We've got a lot to see and only six hours to do it in."

"Can you imagine what it would be like if you were just swimming along minding your own business and happened to run into one of these things? One bite and you'd be history."

"Whales don't eat people."

"Tell that to Ahab." Before he could answer,

she was on to something else. She pointed to a two-story tank with so many people on both levels that it was impossible to see inside. "What's in there?"

"Otters."

"Real otters?"

He laughed. "As opposed to . . . ?"

"You know what I mean."

"Yes, they're real otters."

"Oh, I want to see."

It took almost a half hour to work their way to the front on the top level, where they could see the otters in and out of the water. A woman appeared behind the Plexiglas, dipped into the bucket she carried, and began throwing pieces of fish into the water. Janice bobbed up and down like a piston as she followed the otters' movements as they dove and either swept the prize into their mouths with their hands as they swam or brought it to the surface, where they rolled to their backs and used their stomachs as a dining room table.

Noticing a couple of five-year-olds trying to get a better look, she let them crowd in front of her but stood her ground when their parents tried to follow. Finally the only way Chris could get her to leave to see the rest of the exhibits was by telling her about the touch pools where she could "pet" bat rays and sea cucumbers and whatever else happened to be on exhibit that day.

She asked a hundred questions. Those Chris couldn't answer, she asked the volunteers who worked at the pools.

At the kelp forest Janice challenged Chris to a contest to see which of them could find the most sea life. It looked as if Chris would win right up until the last minute, when three fish appeared simultaneously in front of Janice and she instantly identified them from the information plates in front of her.

"I win," she announced gleefully.

"Didn't anyone ever tell you it's not nice to gloat?"

"Who cares—it's fun."

He almost smiled at the mischievous look she gave him. "That sounds like something Tracy would say."

She grabbed the front of his shirt. "Take that back."

"And if I don't?"

"You walk home."

"You seem to forget, it's my car."

She thought a minute. "Oh, yeah."

He took her hand and led her back through the main floor to the jellyfish exhibit. Three hours later they made their last stop—the gift shop. Janice headed straight for the books. It took forever for her to decide which one she would buy. Chris thought she was being incredibly picky until she opened her wallet to pay. Without meaning to pry, Chris couldn't help but notice the book took half the money she had left.

"Guess what I'm going to be doing the next three weeks," she said as they walked outside.

"I'll go in half if you'll share," he said.

She smiled. "You can borrow it as much as you like while I'm here. But this puppy goes home with me."

He liked that she'd had a good time and wasn't afraid to let him know. A lot of the girls in his crowd would have acted bored because they thought it was sophisticated. Not Janice.

She was interested in everything and fascinated by almost as much. Halfway through the aquarium she'd announced, "The next time I come to California, I'm going to know how to dive. I want to see what it's like out there myself." She'd turned to him, her eyes filled with excitement. "Can you imagine actually swimming with otters? Could there be anything cooler?"

After the ten days she'd put in with Tracy, Chris was surprised Janice would ever want to come back.

They were on their way to the car when Chris asked, "Hungry?"

"Starved."

"Hamburger okay?"

"My dad said he'd shoot me if I didn't eat fish at least once while I'm out here. Would you mind if we make it today?"

"Sure. I don't know any special restaurant around here, but I guess we could ask."

They went into a T-shirt shop and talked to the clerk. He told them about a place not to be missed that made the best fish tacos north of Mexico City.

"Fish *tacos*?" Janice said when they were

outside again. "I don't think that was what my father had in mind. How about we find someone else to ask?"

"Thank God—I was afraid you were going for it."

She looked up at him through the longest lashes Chris had ever seen on anyone. "I don't know," she said. "Maybe we should give it a try."

"I will if you will," he said, convinced she would back down.

"Okay."

"You're kidding."

"What have we got to lose?"

"Our lunch, for one thing."

She laughed. "Come on, where's your sense of adventure?"

On their way home, Janice insisted she'd loved the tacos and would have them again. Chris told her she was crazy, that his grandmother's rhubarb-and-strawberry pie and the bellyache it had given him afterward had been a better experience.

Later that night the dessert Eric had promised turned out to be rhubarb-and-strawberry pie with vanilla bean ice cream on the side. Janice had to turn away to keep from laughing when she saw the look on Chris's face.

When they arrived back at the house and found it deserted, Chris decided to ask Janice to go with him to meet Charlie Stephens. He liked that he didn't have to talk her into it and that she acted properly impressed when they were introduced. But what Chris liked best was that her enthusiasm wasn't put on. She asked a lot of questions that Chris would have never thought to ask, even wanting to know why his 1984 Los Angeles gold medal seemed tarnished. When he told her the gold had rubbed off from the number of children who had handled it, Janice smiled and told him that he was her kind of hero.

Then she did something that left Chris in awe. Not only did she eat all of her own pie, she insisted on sharing his, digging out the inside and leaving him the crust. All in all, it was the second best day of his life.

Or so he thought until they thanked Eric and said good night to Charlie and started home.

"What a great guy," Janice said as they crossed the public pathway to the beach that separated the two houses. "Eric, too."

"Thanks for coming with me."

"You're welcome." She stopped in the middle of the path and held her arms wide, as if gathering the day's memories. Looking up at the sky, she turned in a circle. "And thanks for threatening to break my leg if I didn't."

He laughed. "It was your arm."

Pretending to lose her balance, she purposely bumped into him. "Arm—leg, same difference."

On impulse he bent, picked her up, and threw her over his shoulder in a fireman's carry. "If anyone sees us, they're going to think you're drunk."

"And if they see me like this, they'll think I passed out and you had to carry me home."

She hardly weighed anything; he'd carried heavier grocery bags. He could have held her forever, but he hadn't thought how short her dress was when he'd picked her up or considered the possibility that lace-trimmed panties would end up inches from his face.

Sensing the change in Chris, Janice put her hands on his shoulders, propped herself up, and slid down the front of him. Neither of them moved as they looked into each other's eyes.

Heavy ocean air, still warm from the heat of the day, wrapped them in an intimate cocoon.

Slowly, confident only of his own feelings, Chris moved to kiss her. His heartbeat thundered in his ears, blocking all other sounds, even the rolling roar of the ocean. She tilted her head to meet him, her lips open in anticipation, the tip of her tongue reaching for his. With a low groan Chris wrapped his arms around her and deepened the kiss. When it was over, with his chin gently touching the top of her head, he said, "I don't know where that came from."

"Boy—me either."

"Did you mind?" He felt like an idiot for asking, but he needed to know.

She didn't answer right away. Finally, looking up at him, she said, "I'm not sure. Maybe if you did it again, it would help me decide."

A feeling came over Chris he recognized but had never experienced in this way before. He didn't just want to kiss her, he wanted to make love to her.

Her mouth was unbelievably sweet, the touch of her tongue intoxicating. The way she put her arms around his neck and stood on her toes to bring herself closer sent his mind rushing ahead days and weeks and months with pictures of them together, laughing, loving, intimate.

What he'd felt for Tracy was in his imagination. This was real.

And it was so much better.

"No," she whispered.

"No?" he repeated.

She smiled as she dropped from her toes to stand flat-footed again and looked up at him. "I didn't mind."

He touched her cheek. "Want to go for a walk?"

"Yes."

She didn't have to say anything else. It was enough to let him know they shared the same thoughts, the same feelings.

They headed for the stairs. As they stepped on the beach, Chris took Janice's hand. She looked at him and smiled. His legs were moving, but his feet weren't hitting the sand. Was this what it was like to walk on air?

"I'm going to be gone when you get up in the morning," he said. "And I'm not sure when I'll be back."

"Where—"

Finally he told her about the movie. She

was wide-eyed with excitement. "When you get home tomorrow I want to hear everything, even the smallest detail."

He hesitated. "I don't want Tracy to know. . . ."

She nodded, not asking or needing an explanation.

Chris sat on a salt- and sun-bleached log washed up by some long-ago storm and pulled Janice down to sit next to him. They talked about school, their friends, their hopes, their dreams. They talked fast and free and nonstop, as if trying to make up for all the time they'd wasted.

Everything about Janice fascinated Chris, from her allergy to olives to her love of Irish folk songs. They found a hundred things they had in common, from politics to philosophy, and a dozen they didn't, from *Star Trek* to which was the best fast-food restaurant.

They continued to talk as the moon moved across the night sky, as the high tide moved in and claimed more and more of the beach, as the still night air became a breeze, and as the temperature dropped steadily.

A lifetime was hard to share in one meeting, but they tried. It was as if each held desperately important information that had to divulged before they could be sure what was happening to them was real and lasting.

In the end, it was the cold that drove them from the beach. Despite having Chris's arms around her, Janice could hardly talk, she was trembling so hard. Still, she told Chris she didn't want to leave, but he, reluctantly, insisted they should go in.

Though it was less than six feet from his own, Chris walked Janice to her bedroom door. He kissed her good night, and then she kissed him back. He marveled how perfectly they fit together, as if they'd been custom fitted. She felt it, too. He could tell by the way she put her arms around him, the way her hips nestled into his.

"Will you wait up for me tomorrow night?" he whispered.

"Yes," she breathed against his ear.

He started to say something more but heard a sound coming from inside Janice's room. The last thing he wanted was to have Tracy find them together. He gave Janice one last kiss and crossed the hall to his own room. "I'll get home as soon as I can."

"I'll be here," she said softly.

Chris dreamed when he went to sleep that night, but for the first time in years, it wasn't about Tracy.

CHAPTER

9

Chris rolled from his side to his back, tucking his hands under his head and staring, unseeing, at the ceiling in his bedroom. He couldn't sleep. His mind simply wouldn't shut down.

His two-day crowd scene in the movie had turned into a small speaking role that lasted four days and kept him on the set from early morning to late at night. During that time he'd seen Janice for an hour or so when he came home at night and a half hour every morning when they ran together on the beach, but that was all. She insisted she didn't mind. He hoped she was saying it only to be polite, because he sure as hell minded being away from her.

Just when Chris thought his role was over, Robert showed up on the set and asked him to hang around a few more days. He'd almost forgotten the conversation at Tony's party when Tony and Robert had said he looked like some David guy they both knew, but that night Chris had been reminded in a way he wasn't likely ever to forget.

It turned out David wasn't a person but a character in a book that Robert was making into a movie. They'd been looking for an actor to fill the role for over six months. But no one they'd come up with so far could win the author's approval. The deal had been about to fall apart when Tony spotted Chris.

Then tonight, the unimaginable had happened.

Robert offered him the role.

Now all Chris had to do was figure out what he was going to do about it.

When Chris told them there was no way the author would want someone who didn't have enough acting talent to talk his way out of a traffic ticket, Robert informed him that there had been half a dozen people from the project on the set that week, including the author. They'd come specifically to look him over, and all concurred—he was the perfect David.

Chris had been flattered at first, but close on its heels had come dry-mouthed fear. Robert was dumbfounded when Chris told him that he wanted some time to think about the offer first.

Before he'd left the set that night, the people Robert had brought with him began anticipating Chris's doubts and potential problems and supplying answers. School wouldn't be a problem; he'd have the best tutors available. It didn't matter that he'd never acted; he was a natural. Whatever he didn't know, they could teach him. The studio would arrange and pay for a place for him and his mother to live; they would even provide a car and driver. If he didn't like acting, it was only one movie, not a lifetime commitment. Chris couldn't help but notice that the last was said with about as much conviction as a kid left alone in a candy store promising not to eat anything.

The kicker, the argument Chris couldn't ignore, was the money. They wouldn't give a solid offer, telling him it was up to the agent he hired to work out the final figure, but the hinted amount could pay his way through Yale *and* Stanford and still leave enough for a down payment on his house at the beach.

How could he say no?

God, how could he say yes? Being in movies wasn't something ordinary people like him did. You had to be special, you had to want it so badly that you waited tables and lived in dumps and sacrificed.

Robert's staff had insisted he could pull it off, but what if they were wrong? What happened if they started filming and he was terrible? Everyone would know. It was the kind of thing you read about in newspapers and saw on those entertainment shows on television.

What if he made it through okay and the critics turned thumbs down?

It wasn't even an action flick that they wanted him for, something where it didn't matter whether he could act or not because all any-

one cared about was how many cars and buildings were blown up. This story was about a kid
in a small town in the Midwest whose father is
wrongly accused of child molestation. The book
had been on the best-seller list forever. Millions
of people who had read the book and who
would see the movie had their own ideas of
what David should be like. There was no way
he could please them all. He was Chris Sadler,
not this David character.

The problem was Chris loved everything
about making movies, or at least everything he'd
seen so far. He'd even started daydreaming
about being an actor someday, but it was a long
way from dreaming to doing. He felt as if he'd
been told he'd qualified for the Olympics, but as
a platform diver.

He rolled back on his side, doubling the
feather pillow and propping it under his head as
he gazed out the window at the passing clouds.

Janice had waited up for him that night, as
she had every night that past week. He'd spilled
his news like a glass of milk, fast and all over
the place. She hadn't said anything for a long
time afterward. It was almost as if he'd dumped
a load of compost in her lap and she couldn't
figure out if it was for flowers or garbage.
When the surprise had worn off and they'd
finally talked about it, she'd said aloud all the
things that were bothering him. She understood
why he was more terrified than excited about
the chance he'd been given and why, in spite of
everything, he'd be an idiot to refuse.

What if five or ten years from then he decided acting was his thing? He wasn't so naive to think opportunities like this came along every day.

As Chris left the set that night, Robert let it casually drop that he'd set up a screen test for Chris in Los Angeles in two days. He assured him that it was just a formality, that no one who'd seen him had any doubt he could handle the part.

Chris had a feeling a lot of the stuff they were feeding him was crap, but he had no way to know for sure.

Bottom line—did he want to trade his last year in high school and a chance to repeat as state wrestling champion for what could either be the best or the worst thing that had ever happened to him? He had to make up his mind before he said anything to his mother. It was important the decision and its consequences be his, not hers.

He'd started to roll onto his back again when he heard the door open and someone come inside. Thinking—hoping—it was Janice, he propped himself up on his elbow and asked softly, "What's up?"

"I knew you'd be awake," Tracy whispered. "I have something to show you."

As confused as he was surprised, Chris sat up and peered at the dark figure at the foot of his bed. "Now?"

"You didn't leave me much choice. You're never here anymore," she said in a pouting voice. She ran her fingers through her long hair to fluff it before sweeping it forward to lay on her shoulders.

He was dreaming.

He had to be.

But why this dream? And why now? He was over Tracy, at least that was what he'd told himself.

It was dark in his room, but Chris had no trouble seeing Tracy when she moved into the light coming from his window. She had on a short, silky bathrobe untied and open far enough to reveal a skimpy matching gown. His heart did a somersault before it slammed against his ribs.

She came around the side of the bed and sat next to him, drawing her leg up until it touched his. "It's boring around here without you."

Jesus, it wasn't a dream. Not only could he feel her heat, he could smell her perfume, a heavy, musky odor that permeated his lungs and left him sucking for cleaner air. "What do you want, Tracy?"

She smiled. "First you have to promise you won't tell."

It took a while to sink in that she was flirting with him. He would have been less surprised if a giant wave engulfed them and washed them out to sea. "Look, I'm tired and—"

She put her hand on his leg, high up near his groin. "Come on, Chris, all I'm asking is one little promise."

Angry that she thought he was so gone on her that all she had to do was touch him and he would do whatever she asked, Chris took her hand off his thigh and moved to the middle of the double bed. "You're after something, Tracy. Why don't you just tell me what it is so we can skip all this other shit."

She took some time before she answered. "It's really hard for me to admit this." She did the thing with her hair again. "But Janice made me see how wrong I've been about you. We only have two more weeks." She shrugged, bringing her shoulders forward and exposing the tops of her breasts. "I want to make the best of them."

She was lying. He could see it in her eyes. "Sorry," he said, feeling an intoxicating sense of power. "I'm not interested."

"Janice told me that you were still mad about the other night," she said, providing her own explanation for his refusal. She smiled seductively. "She tried to convince me it was serious, but I told her you've been mad at me before and that it never lasts very long."

"Look, Tracy, I don't know what game you're playing or why, but I've got to get up early. If you've got something to tell me, either get it over with or save it until I get home."

"Where are you going?"

She'd asked in such a way that it was obvious she already knew the answer. Like looking at the back of the crossword puzzle book, he suddenly understood, and everything fell into place. Somehow Tracy had found out about his being in the movie. "No place special," he answered her.

"Can I go?"

"Why?"

"If I don't get away from here, I'm going to go crazy. You know what a pain in the ass my mother can be when she gets on one of her kicks." This time her smile was coy. "Besides, she'd have an absolute shit fit if she found out what I did."

She'd thrown the line, knowing there was no way he could resist taking the bait. "What did you do?"

"First you have to promise you won't tell."

She didn't care about any promise; it was getting him to do what she wanted that mattered. For the first time in all the years they'd known each other, he had the upper hand in something. "Forget it," he said. "I don't want to know."

"Why are you being such a—" She caught herself. "Why are you being so stubborn? All I'm asking for is— The hell with it. I guess I'll just have to trust you." She turned on the lamp beside the bed, sat back, spread her legs, and waited for Chris's reaction.

A shaft of heat hit his testicles. He felt himself grow hard—which was precisely what she'd been after. Instead of being turned on, he was pissed. Big time. She'd made a fool of him again.

"Well, what do you think?"

"About what?" he asked coolly.

"The tattoo."

Even knowing it was a mistake, he couldn't

stop himself from looking. There, high up on the inside of her thigh, an inch below the elastic on her blue bikini panties, was a rose encircled in barbed wire. All Chris could think about was how long she'd sat with her legs spread while some stranger got his rocks off branding her.

"Isn't it great?" she said.

"Yeah, I guess. Whatever makes you happy."

"You want to touch it?"

He stared at her. All this because he'd had a couple of lines in a movie? "No thanks."

She moved closer. "I don't mind. It's kind of—"

A light tapping drew their attention. The door eased open before Chris could answer. Janice came inside and closed the door behind her. She was wearing shorts and a sweatshirt with LIFE'S A BEACH printed across the front.

Tracy smiled triumphantly. Chris didn't move.

"I thought I'd find you in here," Janice said, returning the smile.

Tracy turned and settled in next to Chris, leaning her back against the antique carved oak headboard and her shoulder into his. "You might want to wait for an answer before you come barging in next time." With deliberate movements, she closed the front of her robe. "What do you want, anyway?"

"You need to work on your timing," Janice said. "This is when Chris and I go running every morning."

If Janice had been a little closer, Chris would have kissed her. "Give me a minute. I'll meet you outside."

Janice nodded and left.

"I thought you said you wanted me to leave so you could get some sleep," Tracy said accusingly.

Chris reached for the shorts he'd left on the chair beside the bed. "I figured you'd be uncomfortable if Janice found us together."

"Why should that bother me?"

He looked at her over his shoulder. "I don't know, maybe I thought it might screw things up for you if she told your boyfriend about me when you got home."

She flung herself out of his bed. "You're a loser, Chris Sadler. You always were and you always will be. You and Janice deserve each other."

He pulled his T-shirt over his head. "Thanks. And just think, it's all your doing. We never would have met if you hadn't insisted she come along."

Tracy flung the door open and almost ran into Margaret, who had just come from the bathroom. They stared at each other for several seconds before Tracy said through clenched teeth, "Would you please get out of my way?" Margaret stepped to the side, and Tracy went into her own room, slamming the door behind her.

"Want to tell me what just happened here?" Margaret said to Chris as he came around the bed.

"Later." He put his hands on her shoulders and gave her a quick kiss on the cheek. "Janice is waiting for me outside. We're going for a run." Almost as an afterthought, he added, "Don't go anywhere. We need to talk."

"Yes," she said to his retreating back. "We do indeed."

CHAPTER

10

Chris and Janice were almost to the rocky promontory that held the house Tony rented before either said anything. Finally Chris turned and faced her while he ran backward. "Thank you for rescuing me." She'd come to get him an hour and a half early. "How did you know?"

"I didn't for sure. I just woke up, saw that Tracy was gone, and made a wild guess." She spoke without lifting her eyes to look at him.

Chris dipped his head to put himself in her line of vision. "Are you mad at me?"

"Disappointed."

"I didn't ask Tracy to come to my room."

"Maybe not, but you obviously didn't ask her to leave, either."

"I did. She wouldn't."

Janice stopped and stared at him, her hands planted on her hips. "Oh? And just how hard did you try?"

He smiled. He loved that she was mad and that she'd cared enough to risk everything, including her pride, to rescue him from Tracy. "You are unbelievably beautiful."

"Don't even try that crap on me. I know how you feel about Tracy."

"How I felt," he corrected her.

"You can't just turn something like that off. It takes—" She caught her bottom lip between her teeth and turned away from him.

Chris came up behind her and wrapped his arms around her shoulders. "You scare me," he said.

"Yeah, right. I'm one tough babe."

"I'm falling for you, Janice, and I don't know what to do about it."

She was very still. "What do you want to do?"

"Keep you here with me—move to St. Louis, practical things like that. But there's not a damn thing I can do. At least not now. That's what makes it so hard."

The fight left her like an outgoing wave. She leaned her back into his chest. "How did we go from hating each other to this?"

He tightened his arms around her, snuggling his chin into her neck. "I don't know and I don't care. You're the best thing that's ever happened to me. Somehow we're going to find a way to make it work."

"Promise?"

This one he could give easily. "I promise."

She turned to face him, tilting her head back

and reaching for a kiss. "We've got now. We'll worry about tomorrow later."

He'd never tasted anything as sweet as her tongue as she explored his mouth. He grew hard with wanting her, but this time the reaction was as mental as physical. With desire came a wondrous need to love and be loved. He wanted to fight battles for Janice, to give her flowers and oceans and sunrises. He wanted to hold her hand when they went places together, and he wanted to lie down naked with her in front of a roaring fireplace. He'd never made love. Yesterday his virginity had been an embarrassment. Today, knowing the first time would be with Janice, he was glad that he'd waited.

He held her close, letting the feel of her body imprint itself onto his. "I'm going to see if I can postpone the trip to L.A. until the end of the month."

"So you've made up your mind you want to do the movie after all?"

The statement had just come out. It was as if an enormous weight had been lifted from his shoulders. No more angst, no more putting it off, no more indecision. "I guess I have."

"Have you told your mom?"

"Not yet." He saw that the sky had started to clear, going from a gray black to dark purple. This was his last day on the set with Tony. He really couldn't miss it. "I have to get back. Tony's picking me up early today."

"Let's go someplace tonight," she said, taking

his hand as they retraced their steps to the house. "Just us."

He bent to kiss her. Where they went didn't matter. Knowing they would be alone was enough to send liquid fire coursing through his veins. "I'll get home as soon as I can."

Chris didn't get back that night until almost midnight. Tony was leaving for Los Angeles in the morning to prepare for some upcoming interior shots, and the crew had planned a surprise party for him. Chris had felt obligated to attend. After six attempts to reach Janice and receiving a busy signal four times and letting it ring ten times twice with no answer, he finally gave up. He'd told her before he left that morning that it might not be possible to get away early. She'd said it was okay, that they could postpone their plans for another day. At the time it had been easy to say and hear because neither believed it would happen.

Tony gave Chris his address and phone number when they got in the Jeep, insisting he would be put out if Chris didn't use them. On the way home they'd talked about what Chris should expect when he went in for the screen test, about joining the Screen Actors Guild, and about what to look for in an agent.

By the time they pulled off the highway, Chris had been indoctrinated with Tony's philosophy on "being in the business." He conceded it was an exciting way to make a living, but that Chris was never to forget that first and foremost *it was a business*. Along with that piece of reality, Tony had delivered a short, stern lecture about Chris living below his means and investing every dime he could get his hands on against the day it would all come to an end— and he wasn't ever to try to fool himself about that: his career as an actor would come to an end one day.

Most of all, he was to keep his head out of his ass when it came to Hollywood parties and the hangers-on who were always around trying to buy friendships with free drugs.

It was the speech Chris had expected from his mother that morning. Instead, after about fifty questions, he'd gotten a remarkably calm acceptance and not one thing about talking to his dad first or the possibility he would some-day regret giving up his last year of high school.

"I'm going to be watching you," Tony said when they reached the house. "Screw up and I'll be on your case so fast, you'll think I was hiding in the closet the whole time. You get in trouble, you've got my number."

Chris couldn't decide whether he brought out some big brother instinct in Tony or if Tony had stuck his neck out to get Chris his chance. The reason didn't matter. The friend-ship did. He wouldn't let Tony down.

"I'll let you know how it goes." Chris got out of the car. "The test, I mean."

"We'll do something to celebrate when I finish this shoot."

Chris closed the door and stepped away from the Jeep, waiting until Tony drove away before going in the house.

The lights were on, but no one was around. "Mom?" He waited a second. "Janice?" Still no answer. He headed for the kitchen to see if they'd left a note and almost fell over a suitcase left sitting beside the sofa. He bent to pick it up and saw that it was packed.

His mother came in from the deck through the sliding glass door. "I thought I heard you in here."

He looked down at the suitcase and then at her. "What's going on around here?"

She put her finger to her lips and motioned for him to follow her into the kitchen. Even though they were out of earshot for anyone at the back of the house, she still spoke softly. "Beverly is taking the girls home tonight. They're leaving on a red-eye out of San Jose."

She might as well have told him she'd staked a claim in Alaska and they were heading there in the morning. Janice leaving? Beverly flying out of San Jose? None of it made sense. "I'm not following you."

"Tracy and Beverly have been going at it all day, or at least since Tracy got back from town this afternoon. You won't believe what she did."

"Yes, I would," Chris said, understanding dawning. "How did Beverly find out about the tattoo?" He couldn't believe Tracy was dumb enough to tell her mother what she'd done, but then he was beyond questioning anything Tracy might do.

"What tattoo?" Margaret asked.

"The one on her—" Chris caught himself. "If Beverly doesn't know about the tattoo, what got her going?"

Margaret hesitated.

"What?" Chris prodded.

"Nipple rings."

"Jesus." Tracy was really over the edge. "How did Beverly find out?"

"They started bleeding. The doctor said—"

Janice came into the room. Her eyes were red and swollen. "Would it be all right if Chris and I went outside to talk?" she asked softly. "I need to tell him something."

"Of course," Margaret said. She looked at the clock over the stove. "I wouldn't go too far, though. You only have a few minutes."

"Why does Janice have to go?" Chris demanded as Margaret moved to leave. "Why can't she stay here with us?"

It was obviously not something she'd considered. "I guess she could . . . at least it's all right with me." She looked at Janice. "How do you think your parents would feel about you staying?"

"I don't know. I'd have to call my father and ask." A glimmer of hope lit her eyes. To Chris she said, "Were you able to talk them into waiting for the screen test?"

He'd forgotten that he was leaving himself

in two days. "They said it was already set up, and that there were too many people involved to put it off." He couldn't just let her go. "But I'll be back in—"

"I don't want you to miss your chance because you're worried about getting back to me." She blinked to clear fresh tears.

"But you can't just leave," Chris said, reaching out and taking her in his arms. He held her as if the contact were what would keep her there. "When will we see each other again?"

She burrowed into his shoulder, no longer fighting the tears. "I don't know. Maybe I could come out the week after Christmas."

"But that's forever," Chris said.

"I'll write you every day."

"I'll call you as soon as I get to L.A."

"I'm going to leave you alone," Margaret said, tenderly touching Chris's arm as she left.

"It's not fair," was the last thing Margaret heard Janice say before she closed the door to stand guard outside. She looked at her watch and calculated the minimum time it would take Beverly to get to the airport, seeking another minute or two for Janice and Chris to be together.

Any way she figured it, they had less than fifteen minutes. No matter what happened to their relationship in the months to come, their love would never be as intense or as painful as it was for them at this moment. Nor would it ever be as sweet.

Margaret's heart broke a little for them . . .

while a part of her envied them, too. Seeing them together had made her remember how it felt to love and be loved. Until then she'd managed to convince herself the feelings were ones she could live without. She knew now that she was wrong.

Margaret propped a note of welcome against the seashells she'd gathered and left on the table in lieu of flowers for Joe and Maggie. She was leaving five days early to meet Chris in Los Angeles and didn't want them greeted with a wilted bouquet. She'd already made one pass through the house, checking to see that everything was dusted and polished for their arrival, and was about to make another when an overwhelming sense of melancholy came over her.

She went out on the deck. An early morning fog cloaked the ocean, muting the sounds of waves and shore birds. Drops of water fell silently from the eucalyptus leaves overhead, as if even they mourned her leaving.

The past three and a half weeks had seen another circle completed in her life. The beach house was where Chris had taken his first tentative step as a baby and where, seventeen years later, he'd taken the step that would leave his childhood behind. She and Beverly had watched their children grow close and then apart, their paths to adulthood as disparate as life above the ocean surface from that below. This was where she and Kevin had come to make an attempt at reconciliation, and where she'd finally told him she wanted a divorce.

The days she'd been at the house alone had given her something she rarely had at home—time to think and reflect about where she'd been and where she was going. Margaret had vicariously experienced Chris's pain at being separated from Janice and his nervous excitement about a film career. On the sideline she experienced his emotional roller coaster while he was the one taking the ride. It had been that way for years. Mentally she'd known Chris would leave one day, but it seemed she'd never accepted it in her heart.

Her emotional dependence on him couldn't go on. No, it *shouldn't* go on. She needed a life of her own. And thanks to her son and Janice, she now knew she didn't want to live the rest of her life alone. They'd made her remember how much sweeter life was when it was shared. From now on she would give the men she met a chance. They couldn't all be like Kevin. Somewhere there had to be a man who believed in the miracle of second chances, who watched PBS but couldn't understand opera, who ate scampi and fast food without complaining about either, and who didn't think stretch marks and wrinkles automatically precluded an interest in sex.

Even with the fog, people were already beginning to fill the beach, determined that not even the weather would steal a day of their vacation. For Margaret, it was time to leave. She had an appointment to meet Chris that afternoon at the William Morris Agency office in Beverly Hills and had a long drive ahead of her.

She got into her trusty old Volvo and took one last look in the rearview mirror as she drove away, sad at what she was leaving, excited at what lay ahead.

PART THREE

J U L Y

CHAPTER

1

Sixty-five years they'd been married and Joe still thought that in the eighty-eight years he'd been alive, Maggie remained the most beautiful woman he'd ever seen. At times, like this morning, it was as if he were looking at her from a place outside himself, seeing her the way she had been on their wedding day—golden haired, a lone dimple high on her creamy left cheek, her dark brown eyes alive with love for him.

Back then she'd believed him the most handsome, intelligent, caring man on earth. The wonder of it was that she still did.

Now Maggie's hair was a soft white and her dimple a reward that came with a smile. Only her eyes were the same—challenging, beckoning, playful, and mysterious in turn. And, lately, edged with pain.

"Do we have everything?" she asked, calling to him from the back door of the bungalow they'd bought five years after they were married.

Joe closed the trunk lid. "We have everything that was on the list."

"The plastic tarp?"

"In the box with the food."

"The letter?"

"In your suitcase."

"Josi's toys?"

"In my suitcase."

"Well, I guess that's it." She put her hand against the door frame and stood very still.

"Another dizzy spell?" Joe asked.

"Just a small one."

It took every ounce of willpower to stay where he was. He'd learned that nothing would hurry her recovery from the dizziness, but that creating a fuss could, and often did, make things worse. She wanted him to go on as if the moment were but a slight inconvenience. "Did you check the front door?"

She nodded.

"Turn off the air-conditioning?"

Again she nodded.

"Then I guess we're ready."

She brought her hand down tentatively, waited several seconds to check her balance, and stepped onto the landing. "My purse is on the table. Would you mind getting it for me?"

Joe came around the car and held out his hand. He was both pleased and disheartened that she took his help without protest and that she let him help her into the car.

"This getting old stuff is for the birds," she said. "I don't like it one bit."

It was a familiar refrain, first uttered the day Maggie turned sixty-five and a teenager had innocently asked her what someone like her was doing at a Grateful Dead concert. Until then Maggie had somehow managed to remain blissfully unaware of the barrier her age created in young people's minds.

Joe bent and gave her a quick kiss, as much for the physical contact as to assure her that she would always be young in his eyes. "I'll be right back."

When he returned, he had Josi tucked under one arm and Maggie's purse under the other. He closed her door, checked to make sure the lock had caught, and got in his side of the car. Josi dug her claws into the back of the cloth seat to have one last good stretch before settling down between them, her head resting on Maggie's leg.

Automatically Maggie's hand went to the cat's head to scratch her ears as Joe slipped the key into the ignition. The purr of big Chrysler and the twenty-one-pound Maine coon cat began at the same moment and continued the hour and a half it took them to drive from San José to the beach house.

"Will you look at that," Maggie said as they turned the final corner and at last spotted the house. "With all Julia's been through she still found the time to plant flowers. That's a really good sign. Wouldn't you agree, Joe?"

The garden provided a palette of color, a vivid contrast to the gray, overcast day. A love of flowers was the first thing Maggie and Julia had discovered they had in common. That initial bond led to dozens of later discoveries and eventually to a friendship that belied the fifty-five-year age disparity. Maggie had mourned Ken's loss, but her grief had been boundless for the lost young woman who'd grown blind to a future without her beloved husband.

"I thought she was beginning to sound more like herself when I talked to her last month," Joe said. "Coming here without Ken must have been hard on her, though."

Maggie reached past the cat to put her hand on Joe's leg. "But she did it." She gave him an encouraging smile. "Now the next time will be easier. This place is too special to lose because of memories. I told Julia she had to mix some new times in with the old, that if she stayed away now, she'd never be able to come back. That's the last thing Ken would have wanted."

Joe patted her hand. "From the looks of it, I'd say she listened to you."

"I know what I'm talking about, Joe."

He pulled into the driveway, stopped the car, brought her hand up to his lips, and pressed a kiss to knuckles swollen from arthritis. "In all our time together, have I ever doubted you?"

She smiled. "I think if I put my mind to it, I might be able to come up with one or two times."

"If it was more than two years ago, it doesn't count."

Now she laughed. *"In all our time together?"*

Impatient to move around now that the car had stopped, Josi stood and arched her back before stepping gingerly onto Maggie's lap to look outside. Maggie flinched. Joe reacted instantly, reaching for the cat and lifting her.

"She's all right," Maggie said.

"I meant to trim her nails before we left." It was easier for Joe to blame the pain on Josi's nails than Maggie's cancer. "They're like daggers."

"Did you bring the clippers?"

Their conversation settled into the ordinary as they moved from the car into the house. Once inside, Joe insisted Maggie relax on the deck while he unloaded the trunk and put things away. Uncharacteristically, she didn't argue but let him seat her in one of the redwood chairs. Before going back inside, he propped her feet up on the chair's matching stool and tucked a blanket around her legs to protect her from the cool afternoon breeze. When she was settled to his satisfaction, he handed her the note he'd found on the kitchen table.

"I assume it's from Margaret or Beverly," he said.

Maggie unfolded the parchment-colored paper and read the short missive. "Margaret says both families had to leave early for various reasons and that she has left us a refrigerator and cupboard full of food." Maggie read on in silence. "The postscript is certainly intriguing."

"Oh?" Joe prompted.

"She says she may have some exciting news for us in our Christmas card, that she and Chris have experienced some intriguing changes in their lives."

"I wonder what it could be."

"Whatever it is, I hope it works out for them. I can almost feel her enthusiasm coming through the paper."

"Would you like me to bring you something to read while you're sitting out here?"

She shook her head. "I think I'll just watch the ocean for a while and listen to the waves."

"I'll be right inside if you need me."

She smiled. "I always need you."

He pressed a kiss to her forehead before he left.

From where Maggie sat she couldn't see the beach, only the trees that surrounded the house and the ocean itself. She would have preferred sitting farther out on the deck where she could feel the breeze on her face and see the waves, but she could give Joe so little these days that yielding to his nurturing without complaint had become her habit.

Unlike Joe, who'd always preferred quiet over crowds, she loved the noise and energy of summer and liked to be a part of the activity. Smiles came easier to people who'd come on vacation determined to leave their troubles behind, if only for a week or two. Here, where everyone was a stranger, it was okay to greet each other, it was even okay to stop and talk to someone you didn't know. Best of all for

Maggie, it was even okay to say hi to the children.

She understood the reasoning that drove this generation of parents to instill fear in their children, why they trained even their toddlers to run away from an unknown, smiling face, but she had never stopped feeling the loss. Without children of her own, Maggie had been an aunt and then eventually a grandmother to the children in their neighborhood. Joe had been their uncle, and then grandfather. The back door to their house was always open. Cookies were baked to be shared, and Sunday comics were meant to be read aloud. Joe's tools and nuts and bolts container had been gathered by him with broken bikes and wagons in mind.

The decorating of the Chapman Christmas tree had been a special occasion every year. Always as tall as the ceiling, the Douglas fir held more handmade ornaments than store bought. None of the neighborhood children were satisfied until they found their own creation proudly displayed.

Two generations of children had grown up in the neighborhood before things began to change. Eventually the small houses surrounding them became home to families whose lives were too busy or incomes too small to maintain yards or keep up routine maintenance. The children disappeared into day care and then school. Those who were home alone in the afternoons stayed inside to watch television, hiding from strangers, even those right next door, who might do them harm.

Almost as if Maggie's thoughts had conjured a genie who'd granted her a wish, a little girl appeared on the old abandoned path to the beach that ran in front of the deck. She looked to be five or six years old, had golden hair caught up in twin ponytails, a round face, and enormous questioning brown eyes.

She put both hands on the railing that ran around the deck and swung down to peer through the slats at Maggie. "Hi."

"Hi," Maggie said back.

"I'm Susie. Who are you?"

"Maggie."

"Do you live here?"

"Sometimes."

"Do you have any kids I could play with?"

"I'm afraid not."

Susie shrugged, as if it really hadn't mattered. "My mom and dad don't live together anymore. They're divorced."

It was said with an ease that tugged at Maggie's heart. "Are you here with your mom?"

"My dad." She pulled herself back up and propped her chin on the railing. "He used to be a doctor, but now he's making a book."

Julia had mentioned there was a doctor staying in Andrew's house, but she hadn't said anything about his daughter being with him. "Where is your dad now?"

"With Jason."

"Jason?"

"My brother."

"And where is Jason?"

She pointed behind her. "They're making a sand car."

"*Susie*—," a man's voice called, the panic not yet full-blown.

She turned toward the sound. "I'm over here."

Seconds later a tall man with wind-tousled gray hair and the beginnings of a mustache rounded the house. He was carrying a mesh beach bag filled with plastic shovels, molds, and buckets. "How many times have I told you not to wander off by yourself, young lady? Jason and I have been looking all over for you." His relieved expression didn't match his stern voice.

"I told you I had to go to the bathroom."

"But you didn't say you were leaving."

He dropped the bag, scooped her up, and flung her over his shoulder. As he bent to pick up the bag again, he glanced toward the house and noticed Maggie. "I'm sorry—I didn't see you sitting there."

Susie began to squirm, and he put her back down again. "You must be Maggie. I'm Eric Lawson—" He waited a second to see if his name would register before adding, "The guy staying in Andrew's house. Julia said she'd tell you I was handy if you needed anything." A boy appeared. He was half a head taller than Susie and had light brown hair cut short on the sides and long on top. When he saw Maggie, he moved to stand close to Eric.

Maggie tugged on the blanket Joe had wrapped around her legs, but he'd done his usual thorough job and she couldn't readily free herself.

"Don't get up," Eric said. "We can't stay."

Susie tilted her head back to look up at him. "How come?"

"Because I have to start dinner," he said.

"What are you making?" she asked.

"Spaghetti."

"Not again," she moaned. "We had that last night."

Maggie chuckled. "Warmed-up spaghetti isn't my favorite, either. Joe and I were thinking about having a pizza delivered," she said to Eric. "Would you and the children like to join us?" They'd been thinking no such thing, but the chance for company was too tempting not to offer a small bribe.

"I don't know," Eric said.

"*Please,*" Susie wailed.

Eric looked down at the boy beside him. "What do you think, Jason?"

His only answer was to lift his narrow shoulders in a noncommittal shrug.

"Your place or ours?" Eric asked.

"Here would be fine." Whether it was a mile or right next door, the actual distance didn't matter; one seemed as daunting as the other. The trip down had taken its toll on her energy reserve.

Eric placed his hand on the back of his son's neck. Jason leaned into the embrace, resting his head against Eric's hip. "When would you like us to come over?"

"Six?"

He glanced at his watch. "Perfect. That will give us time to clean up."

"Oh, please don't bother," Maggie said. "Come as you are."

Jason glanced up at his father and said softly, "But I have sand in my shoes."

"Then by all means you must do something about that," Maggie said. "We wouldn't want you to track sand into your father's house." She always marveled how different children from the same family could be. Jason was obviously a literal, serious child, while Susie was spontaneous and free. Did one's actions allow, or perhaps even dictate, the other's?

"It's not my daddy's house," Susie said. "It belongs to his friend. We live in Daddy's old house now, and he lives here all by himself."

Maggie looked to see how Susie's blunt assessment of her father's situation affected him. He took it in stride, but she did notice what seemed to be a small flicker of regret. "What kind of pizza should I order?" she asked, purposely changing the subject.

"No garlic," Susie said. "I don't like it. And no mushrooms. Jason doesn't like them."

"Yes, I do," Jason said.

"No, you don't," Susie insisted.

"Do too," he countered.

Maggie smiled. "How does sausage and pepperoni sound?"

"Wonderful," Eric said.

"With olives," Susie added. "Lots of olives."

Maggie looked to Eric for confirmation. "I'm afraid she's serious," he said. "Maybe you could get them to put a few on a couple of slices?"

"I'll see what I can do."

Eric shifted the beach bag to his shoulder and held out his hand to Susie. "Come on, short stuff. Let's go home and make a salad to go with the pizza."

She grabbed his hand and brought her legs off the ground for him to swing her. "We'll be back," she called to Maggie.

"I'll be waiting for you," Maggie called after her.

Seconds later Joe came to the sliding door, opened the screen, and came outside. "I thought I heard you talking to someone."

"You did," she said. "We're having company for dinner."

"Then I'd better get to the store."

She loved that he didn't ask who or how many or why she'd extended the invitation, considering the circumstances. But then it was only one of a thousand things she loved about the man she'd married all those years ago. "That won't be necessary. We're having pizza." Again she struggled to free herself from the blanket, and again she had to give up. "All we have to do now is find some place that will deliver."

"You hate pizza," Joe reminded her.

"You'll understand when you see who's coming."

"I'm not even going to ask how this came about. I'm just going to let you surprise me." He untucked the blanket. "When will our guests be arriving?"

"Six."

"Good. That gives you time for a short nap."

"You promised you wouldn't do that," she reminded him gently.

"And you promised that if I brought you here, you wouldn't wear yourself out trying to do everything at once."

Taking care of her had always been as much a part of Joe as his blue eyes and deep, rumbling laugh. How could she have expected him to be any different now? "All right, but no more than half an hour."

"A half hour it is."

CHAPTER

2

Jason said little during dinner, eating his pizza without looking up, as if being there for a meal were punishment instead of a treat. Susie chattered with the ease of a practiced hostess, keeping the conversation flowing with questions and comments and tidbits of family gossip that frequently left Eric at a loss for words.

When they had finished eating, Susie excused herself and went to the bathroom and Joe and Eric got up to clear the dishes, leaving Maggie and Jason alone together. Taking advantage of the moment, Maggie held out her hand to him and asked if he would mind helping her into the living room. She'd sensed that he'd assumed the role of caretaker after his parents' divorce and that it was a way she could breach the invisible barrier that stood between them. He looked at her wrinkled, knobby fingers and hesitated a moment before slipping his small, perfectly formed hand into hers.

She let him lead her into the adjoining room,

moving even more slowly than usual. "Should we sit with Josi, or over there next to the table?" she asked, shamelessly using the cat as bait to tempt Jason into sitting next to her rather than in the single chairs by the table.

Jason stared at the cat stretched out along the back of the sofa, its length making it seem even larger than its twenty-one pounds. "Does she like kids?" Jason asked.

"Almost as much as I do," Maggie answered.

He moved toward the cat tentatively, as if stalking prey. Josi noted his approach through one partially opened eye. With his knees pressed into a cushion, Jason put out his hand. Before making contact, he looked back at Maggie. "Are you sure it's okay?"

"I'm sure."

He touched Josi's foot. Her other eye opened. He moved to the thick thatch that covered her belly. Her head came up. Slowly he ran his hand along her side. She yawned and stretched, then put her head back down and turned on her purring motor.

Jason grew wide-eyed at the loud, rumbling sound. He pulled his hand away and held it against his chest. "What's that?"

"It means she likes you."

"It does?"

Maggie sank into the cushion next to Jason. Josi dropped her tail possessively over Maggie's shoulder. As if drawn by an irresistible force, Jason reached out to run his hand along the length of the cat's thick fur. His fingers brushed

Maggie's cheek, and she felt as if he were petting her also.

Susie came into the room. "Can I pet him?"

"It's not a him," Jason said. "It's a her."

"Can I?" She looked to Maggie for her answer.

"Of course you can. She likes it best when you're very gentle."

Susie crowded in beside Jason. With her hand open flat, she touched Josi's head. "What's that noise?"

"It means she likes me," Jason said.

Again Susie looked to Maggie. "Does it really?"

Maggie nodded. "It means she likes you, too."

Impulsively Susie leaned forward and gave Josi a kiss on the end of her nose. "He smells funny," she announced.

"It's because she eats a lot of fish."

"Yuck," Susie exclaimed, and backed away, losing interest. "Do you have any toys?"

"I have books," Maggie said, only then remembering there were several children's books tucked in the game cupboard. "Would you like to read one with me?"

"Okay."

Joe did a quick check of the goings-on in the living room as he finished drying a glass. For all that had been fair and wonderful in Maggie's life, the cruelty was that she'd never been able to have a child of her own. They'd tried to adopt but had been turned down when the agency found out about Maggie's epilepsy. By the time a medicine came along to effectively control the seizures, they were old enough to be grandparents.

"She's really good with them," Eric said when Joe came back to put the glass away.

"I sometimes wonder if God didn't keep her from having her own children because there were so many others who needed her."

Eric didn't say anything for a long time. Finally, gently, he asked, "Is it cancer?"

Joe looked at him. "How did you know?"

"After a while you can see the battle signs even when someone is trying as hard as Maggie is to hide them."

"She never complains." Because he didn't know what else to do, Joe dipped a sponge in the soapy water and began wiping down the counters.

"How far along is it?"

"They don't give her much time." The words scraped his throat on the way out. He should have been used to the pain by now, but it came on fresh each morning when he foolishly allowed himself a moment to believe he was waking up from a nightmare. "One doctor said a month or two, another one told us she could still be here Christmas."

"No one, I don't care how good he or she is, can predict that kind of thing with any certainty," Eric said. "I've had patients who should have lived a year or more who died within weeks after being diagnosed. And others who confounded every medical tenet and lived weeks or months or even years beyond what anyone believed possible."

"But most people die when you expect them to, I suppose."

"Yes, most people do."

Joe nodded.

"If there's anything I can do to help while you're here, please let me know," Eric told him.

"Julia was sure you'd feel that way."

"You talked to Julia about me?"

"Maggie or I give her a call every couple of weeks. She's had a pretty hard time of it since Ken died, and sometimes she just needs someone to talk to. She said you and Ken were a lot alike in some ways, kinda like you were cut from the same fabric, only one of you was plaid and the other stripes."

Eric fished the last of the silverware out of the dishwater. "Ken must have been pretty special."

"The best. I've known a lot of people in my life, and not one of them was his match." Joe had taken Ken's heart attack almost as personally as Maggie's cancer. "He and Julia were one of those once-in-a-lifetime kind of things. She's gonna be a long time finding someone to replace him—if ever." He picked up the dish towel again and then the silverware Eric had dropped in the drainer, fanning them out to dry each one separately.

"She's a young woman," he went on. "It's hard to think of her living all that time without anyone." His voice softened when he said, "I can't imagine living all that time without Maggie."

"How long have you been married?"

"Sixty-five years this past March. Maggie was twenty and I was twenty-three when we tied the knot." He shook his head. "I think of all that's happened since—how the world has changed and how we've changed right along with it—and it still seems like it was just yesterday that we were standing in front of the preacher in that little chapel in Reno."

"You were married in Reno?"

"You probably thought that was something your parents' generation started," he said, grinning. "But it goes all the way back to me and Maggie." He folded the dish towel and hung it over the sink. "Before I forget, if you happen to be talking to Julia any time soon, I'd appreciate it if you didn't say anything about Maggie. With all she's been through since Ken died, we decided not to tell her until . . . well, you know what I'm saying."

"I understand."

"How about a cup of coffee? Wouldn't be any trouble to make a pot."

"We should probably be going," Eric said. "I don't want the kids wearing out their welcome."

"Couldn't happen," Joe told him. "They're better medicine for Maggie than anything she's been given so far." He stopped before entering the living room to give Eric a chance to see for himself. Susie sat at Maggie's feet, playing with the seashells Margaret had left on the dining room table. Jason had curled himself into Maggie's side and was listening to her read *Lassie Come Home* while Josi rumbled away, her head taking up most of Jason's lap.

"They don't get to visit their grandparents very much," Eric said. "I can see now I'm going to have to do something to change that."

"Maggie and I would be more than happy to pinch-hit while they're here with you." The offer was more self-serving than benevolent. He would do anything, strike any bargain, to give Maggie something to look forward to when she got up in the morning.

"I'd like that." Eric stared at his children, the depth of his love and caring reflected in his eyes. "Jason needs a lot of attention and under-standing right now. He really took it hard when I moved out two years ago. His mother has just remarried, and he's had to accept that the four of us are never going to be a family again."

Eric stuffed his hands in his pockets and went on. "She's on her honeymoon. Which is why the kids are with me now instead of August."

"If I'm not prying," Joe asked with hesita-tion, "how do you feel about the marriage?"

"It was inevitable. Shelly's a beautiful, car-ing woman."

"Daddy," Susie called to him. "Come see what I made."

Joe hung back to watch Eric with his daughter. Eric crouched down on the floor next to her while his hand slipped around Jason's swinging foot. He was a man who communicated through touch. Joe liked that. And he liked that Eric wore his heart on his sleeve when it came to his children.

Maggie looked up and caught Joe's eye. She gave him a contented smile and then went back to her story.

When they'd first found out about her cancer, Joe had tried to talk her into staying home that summer, terrified of anything that might tire her and possibly steal a minute of the time they had left together. But she'd insisted they come to the beach house, and he could see now that she'd been right. She had one last gift to give and had found the perfect little boy to give it to.

Jason probably wouldn't remember the lady with the cat who had read him stories and shared a pizza with him, but somewhere deep in his mind Maggie would make a difference by letting him know that he was special and worthy of the gift of her time.

CHAPTER

3

It's a beautiful morning," Maggie said as she stared out the living room window. The feeder had drawn a flock of house finches. They swooped and landed, darted and chased, as they vied for prime positions while down below, crested sparrows calmly and peacefully went about cleaning up the spilled booty.

Joe came over to stand beside Maggie, moving slowly as he worked out the kinks that came from a hard night's sleep. He put a finger under her chin to tilt her head back for a kiss. "What are you doing up so early?"

She put her arms around his waist and laid her head on his shoulder, the touch and smell and feel of him as familiar and welcome as the air she breathed. "I couldn't sleep."

"Are you okay?"

"I'm fine. I was thinking about Jason. He's special, Joe. I know it's a lot to say after only just meeting, but I don't believe I've ever known another little boy like him."

"How so?"

"He has a gentle soul. All that time he and Josi were together, he never once teased her by tweaking her ear or tugging on her tail. And he didn't panic or try to get away when she grabbed hold of his hand to stop him from rubbing her tummy. Something like that isn't calculated, Joe, it's a part of who Jason is."

"Susie's pretty special, too."

Maggie smiled. "If I could have custom-ordered a little girl for us, she would have been just like Susie."

He pressed the second kiss of the day to her temple. "What can I fix you for breakfast?"

"An English muffin—and tea." She didn't feel like eating; she rarely did anymore. It was one of the ironic things about dying. For what had to be the first time in fifty years she wasn't worried about putting on weight. Her clothes hung on her, making it difficult to pretend, even on the good days, that she wasn't in the midst of her last journey.

She didn't regret dying; in a way she was grateful it had come the way it had and that she would be allowed to handle it on her own terms. Her heartache came from leaving Joe. Given the choice, she would have had him go first. Bearing the sorrow and loneliness would have been her final act of love.

Even in heartache, Joe would survive. After his last physical the doctor had told him that as long as he stayed out of the path of a speeding truck, he easily could live to be a hundred.

That day Maggie had been the only one to see the forlorn look in Joe's eyes at what should have been good news. It was then she'd made up her mind that when she left him, it would be with memories of their long life together, not of a death prolonged by ever-incapacitating cancer.

Beneath that decision rode one more compelling and urgent. From the day she'd been diagnosed, what she'd feared the most was something she could never share with Joe. She knew this man who'd been her best friend and lover for sixty-five years. He was incapable of simply letting her go. In his mind he could deal with a "do not resuscitate" order, but never in his heart. For whatever years were left him, he would wonder if he'd let her go too soon; he would imagine the day or week or month she might have lived to be the most important they had ever shared.

If she lingered, Joe would sell his very soul to make her last days as easy as possible, and he would allow her no say in the matter. She could not bear the thought that the cold reality of the cost of dying could leave Joe to live the rest of his life in poverty.

It had taken weeks of impassioned persuasion to convince him that her final moments ought to be of her own choosing. She wanted to be lucid when she told him good-bye, not in a vegetative state with machines and clinicians controlling her final moments. After the life they had shared, how could she leave him any other way? When, at last, he understood it was not cowardice or fear that drove her, but a rational and reasonable wish, he relented.

Maggie had chosen her birthday because its symbolism had irresistible appeal. She thought of the day as a circle, marking her life's beginning and its end. Joe had held her in his arms for a long time after she told him, saying nothing. Finally he'd said he would go along with all that she'd asked—save one thing. He would not leave her to die alone. She'd argued and then pleaded, but he wouldn't budge, telling her that she should have known he was too stubborn to let her have everything her way.

"You've left me again," Joe said. "Are you thinking about Jason, or is it something else this time?"

She looked up at him. "I was thinking about us. I must have done something really special in my last life to be rewarded with you in this one."

"If that's true, you're going to have one heck of a life next time around."

She shook her head. "This is it for me. It simply doesn't get any better."

"You're right," he said softly.

"What are we doing today?" Unlike the past, where their August at the beach house had been unstructured, this time they'd made plans. Some were purely sentimental—watching the hummingbirds at Carmel Mission and looking for otters off Point Lobos. Others were things they'd always meant to do but had put off because of finances or circumstance—a round of golf at Pebble Beach for Joe while she drove the cart and a picnic on Fremont Peak.

"Today is lunch at the Steinbeck house."

It was a treat they hadn't missed giving themselves in years, even when they'd been so broke that they had to cash in the change Joe kept in an old whiskey bottle at the back of his closet in order to go. "Did you make reservations?"

"Yes," he replied indulgently. "Last week."

She smiled. "And you chose today because . . . "

"Your favorite quiche is on the menu."

"Ah, it's truly wonderful how you spoil me."

He gave her a surprised look. "But you told me that you wouldn't marry me unless I did."

"Did I really? How clever of me." It was her turn to give him a kiss. "Remind me what else I made you promise."

"That I would wash the dishes and do my own laundry."

"Hmmm, we seem to have let that one slide a little."

"Maybe it was vacuum and clean the bathroom?"

She gave him a playful poke in the ribs. "I think it was probably more along the lines of convincing me I was the most beautiful woman in the world and doing it with a straight face."

"No, you would never let me off that easy."

The wonder of it was that in sixty-five years, the desire had never faded from his eyes. "What time are our reservations?"

"One."

"And how long does it take to get there?"

He eyed her for several seconds. "Are you saying what I think you're saying?"

"I must be losing my touch if I have to spell it out for you."

"Are you sure?"

"The spirit is willing. I don't see why we couldn't give the flesh a chance."

He grinned. "You won't believe what you just did to me."

She took his hand and started toward the bedroom. "I will if you show me."

When Joe removed Maggie's nightgown it wasn't skin ravaged by time and gravity that he saw, but the body of the young woman who had lain beneath him on their wedding night, her breasts full and firm, her stomach flat, her thighs as smooth as a calm sea and as soft and beckoning as a lover's whisper.

He knew her body as well as his own, where and when to touch her, how to move once he was inside, when that alone would bring her to climax and when she wanted or needed more. There were sighs that told him when she was ready and a quick, barely audible intake of breath that let him know to move faster.

In his care not to hurt her, he awoke a poignancy buried months earlier by fear. Unlike Maggie, Joe had been slow to master the ability to live each day as it came without thinking about what was ahead. With the diagnosis, the once easily put aside knowledge that life was finite no longer provided a shelter. At eighty-eight, with all but a handful of their contemporaries gone, he should have been better prepared for the inevitable. But he could not bear to acknowledge that the rules of life applied to them, too.

In the end he'd drawn his strength from being allowed to give her this one last gift. She would not be the one left behind to mourn his loss.

After they had made love, Maggie curled into Joe's side and smiled contentedly. "There is no better way to start the morning."

"Are you okay? I didn't hurt you, did I?"

She ran her hand over his chest. "Did I act as if you were hurting me?"

"Well, I did hear you moan once."

"Only once?" she said teasingly.

He drew her closer. "It's been a good life, Maggie. I couldn't have asked for more."

"We've been truly blessed, my love. Even being given this time together to say good-bye." She moved to free her arm to try to ease the ache in her shoulder. For days now she'd been putting off increasing her pain medication, preferring the discomfort to lightheadedness. But she couldn't hide what she was going through from Joe much longer. As long as he believed she wasn't suffering, he could handle what was happening to her. At times, the lack of outward manifestations of the disease even made it possible for them to forget for a while.

"I've been thinking a lot about Julia and

Ken since we got here," she said. "They were so happy together. Do you remember that time we all went to dinner at Winslow's and Ken made that toast where he said all he wished out of life was to live as long and happily with Julia as we had with each other?" She put her hand over Joe's where it lay on her stomach. "I never doubted for a moment that his wish would come true."

"Now Julia either lives the rest of her life alone or settles for second best," Joe said.

"Not necessarily second best. No one could take Ken's place, but someone could create a new one of their own." She turned her head to look at him. "I don't want you to close yourself off to the possibility you could find someone else, too."

"Why would you say something like that? You know it's not going to happen." He leaned back against the pillow and stared at the ceiling. "I love you, Maggie. I always will. There could never be anyone else for me."

"I wouldn't mind, you know."

He sat up with his back to her. "I don't want to talk about this."

"Please, Joe. It's important to me. Let me go knowing you'd at least consider the possibility."

"Why are you doing this?"

"Because it breaks my heart to think of you alone."

He swung around to look at her. "Leaving me alone, at least doing it now, is your choice."

She flinched at the attack. "I thought you understood."

The stiffness left his spine. He closed his eyes against a sudden welling of tears. "I'm sorry. I shouldn't have said that."

She put her hand in his. At that moment she would have given anything to take away the pain, but she clamped her jaw tight to keep from saying the words he so desperately wanted to hear. She couldn't give in. Nothing had changed.

"Do you want to take a shower before we leave?" he asked, putting them on safe ground again.

"If we have the time."

He glanced at the clock on the nightstand. "We can make it"—he summoned a mischievous smile—"but only if we take one together."

"I love you, Mr. Chapman."

He brought her hand to his lips for a kiss. "And I love you, Mrs. Chapman."

CHAPTER

4

The next morning Maggie stepped outside to pick up the newspaper just as Jason came running across the pathway that separated their houses. "I've been waiting for you," he called to her. "Dad said I couldn't come over until you were up for sure."

She smiled. "Well, I'm up for sure now. What can I do for you?"

"Want to go see the fireworks with us?"

The question caught her by surprise. She'd forgotten it was the Fourth of July. "I'd love to. Is it okay if Joe comes, too?"

He nodded enthusiastically. "I'll tell my dad to make some more sandwiches."

"What time are we leaving?"

He gave her a blank look.

"Can I bring something?"

"You mean like toys and stuff?"

"Well, I was thinking more along the lines of food and stuff, but I suppose I could pick something up at the store for you and Susie to play with."

"Do you have any chocolate chip cookies?"

"No, but I could make some."

His eyes grew big and round. "You could?"

"Are they your favorite?"

He nodded.

"What about Susie? Does she like them, too?"

"Yeah, but not as much as me."

Eric came out on his front porch and waved. "I see he found you."

"Yes—and has graciously invited us to join in your Fourth of July celebration."

"I hope you can come," Eric said.

"She can," Jason answered for her.

Susie joined Eric. "Can I come over?" she called to Maggie.

"Of course. If it's all right with your father."

Eric put a hand out to stop her from launching herself off the porch. "I don't think the two of you need to be—"

"It really is all right," Maggie said. "Joe and I were going for a walk on the beach. We'd love to have them join us."

Eric lowered himself to his haunches in front of Susie, said something to her, and waited until she'd replied with a sincere bobbing of her head before standing back up and holding out his hand to her. They walked across the pathway that separated the houses.

"I'm glad you're coming with us tonight,"

Eric said. "I wish I could take credit for thinking to ask, but it was Jason's idea."

"What time, and what can I bring?" She saw a stab of disappointment cross Jason's face and quickly added, "Besides chocolate chip cookies."

Eric frowned at Jason. "I suppose the cookies were your idea?"

"I just told her I liked 'em."

"They're Joe's favorite, too," Maggie said. "And I love picnics."

Susie wrapped her arms around Maggie's legs. "Daddy said it's gonna be just like making flowers in the sky."

"What a lovely way to put it," Maggie told him.

He laughed and jokingly put his hand over his heart. "I am a writer, you know. Or at least that's what I keep telling myself."

"I don't imagine you've been able to get much done this past week." She moved to give Jason room to stand beside her.

"I work for a couple of hours after they go to bed and then before they get up. I'm a little amazed at how much I've been able to get done in just those few hours."

Joe came to the door. "I thought I heard someone out here."

"We've been invited to a Fourth of July picnic," Maggie said.

It took a second for the information to register. "My goodness, I'd forgotten it was the Fourth." He looked at Jason and Susie. "Are you coming, too?" He came out to join them.

Jason nodded and Susie grinned broadly.

"And will there be fireworks?" he asked.

"Big ones," Susie said. "Like flowers in the sky."

"If there's no fog," Eric reminded her.

"A picnic and fireworks and my best new friends," Joe said as he put his hand on Jason's narrow shoulder. "I can't think of a better way to spend the day." He looked at Maggie and smiled. "The only thing missing is peach ice cream."

The words triggered a memory so intense, her tastebuds responded in anticipation. The strict diet Joe had gone on after his stroke had spelled the end of a tradition they'd started their first Fourth of July together—cold fried chicken, potato salad, and homemade peach ice cream.

"Where do you suppose we'd have to go to find an ice cream maker?" she asked Joe on impulse.

"There's got to be a dozen places around here we could try," he said.

"Can I go?" Susie asked.

"I don't think that's such a good idea," Eric said before Joe or Maggie could answer.

"We don't mind," Joe said. "That is, if you don't."

Eric hesitated, as if trying to give Joe a chance to change his mind. Finally, a trace of doubt in his voice, he said, "I guess it would be all right."

Jason looked up at Maggie longingly, his huge brown eyes asking his question for him.

"Would you like to come, too?" she said.

He looked to his father. "Could I?"

Eric glanced from Joe to Maggie and back again. "The two of them can be a real handful at times."

"We'd love to have them," Maggie added.

"What about Josi?" Jason asked, his enthusiasm building by the second.

Maggie laughed. "I think Josi would much rather stay here. But I'm sure she'd love to see you when we get back."

Jason looked up at Eric. "Dad?"

"All right, but I'm drawing the line at your moving in with them. So don't bother asking."

Eric tried to work while they were gone but found it hard to concentrate. He'd never seen Jason and Susie take to anyone the way they had Joe and Maggie, but then he had to remind himself that he didn't know his children as well as he liked to think he did. For all he knew, they were as open and loving with everyone they just met.

Still, Eric was troubled about allowing the friendship to deepen any more than it already had. There was something special going on among the four of them, especially between Jason and Maggie. How many times could Jason survive his world being turned upside-down because he'd lost someone important to him?

But that was crazy. Maggie was a summer

friend, someone likely to become a distant memory halfway into the new school year. To deny something now because of what might someday be bordered on paranoia.

He leaned back in his chair and stared at the fog bank sitting offshore. The woman he'd talked to about the fireworks in Monterey had warned him they'd had fog three out of the four past years and that the display was likely to be limited to puffs of colored light in the gray; but he'd never been put off by long odds. If he had, he'd never have gone to medical school. No one had given him much of a chance of making it, not coming from a high school in a backwoods logging community with twenty-three in its graduating class. But he'd proved them wrong—and then up and quit.

He wished he had some sense that it was more than need that drove him to write, that he actually had something to say that someone would want to hear. Not that he was writing for posterity; he wanted to entertain, to provide an escape, if only for a couple of hours, to people like the uptight patients he used to see in his office. Television had been a luxury when Eric was growing up, reading a necessity. Already he could see the same signs in Jason and looked forward to the day when they would discuss favorite authors.

Any link was important and to be nurtured when he didn't live in the same house anymore.

The phone rang. Eric's first thought was

that something had happened to the kids. "Hello," he said anxiously.

"Eric? Is that you?"

He'd never heard her voice on the phone but knew instantly who it was. He responded in a way that surprised him, as if Julia had been gone only a couple of days and he'd been expecting the call. "Yes, it's me. You caught me at the computer."

"Oh, of course. I should have known you'd be working now. Why don't I call you back later?"

It was the last thing he wanted. He would do anything, say anything, to keep her on the phone. Not a day had passed since she left that he hadn't thought about her. "I was just about to take a break. What can I do for you?"

"I've been trying to reach the Chapmans— they're the couple I told you about, the ones staying in the house this month. Have you seen them, by any chance?"

He leaned back in his chair and propped his feet up on the desk, remembering how she'd looked that last morning as they'd followed the otter from one end of the cove to the other. "Just about an hour ago, as a matter of fact. They took Jason and Susie shopping with them."

"Jason and Susie?"

"My kids."

"Oh, of course." She sounded embarrassed that she hadn't remembered.

Her voice washed over him like a warm

summer rain, the kind you tilted your head back to let the drops hit your face, where you licked the moisture from your lips and closed your eyes to concentrate on the utter sensuality of the moment. "I have them for three weeks. Their mother is on her honeymoon."

For a heartbeat, she said nothing. Then, in a voice soft with understanding, "Are you okay?"

Was her compassion born of pain, or had she always been as sensitive to others? "I'm better than okay. I'm happy for Shelly . . . and for the kids."

"I believe you."

He hadn't realized until then that it was the kind of thing someone might say to try to impress the listener. "Did you need to get in touch with Joe and Maggie right away? I might be able to find them for you."

"I was just checking to see if they needed anything. I've tried calling for a couple of days now and haven't been able to reach them. Then I tried them at home and they weren't there, either, so I started to get a little— Never mind. You told me what I needed to know."

His heart did a quick turn at the depth of concern he heard under the forced nonchalance. He understood now why Maggie wanted to keep the news about her cancer from Julia. "How are things with you?"

"Better."

"As in 'better than they were' or 'better than you'd hoped they would be by now'?"

She hesitated. "Surprisingly, a little of both.

I still get blindsided by things every once in a while, but I'm actually having days where I don't have to remind myself that the rest of the world expects to see me wearing a happy face by now."

"Maggie and Joe talk about Ken a lot." He was taking a calculated risk in talking about Ken to Julia. Bringing him into their fledgling friendship could as easily put a barrier between them as break one down. "I think they had mentally adopted him."

"I know. He felt the same way about them."

"Well, now they're the ones who've been adopted—by my kids. If I let them, Jason and Susie would be over there all day every day." Innately, he knew they would feel the same way about Julia. She and Maggie were a lot alike.

"I think that's wonderful. And it's probably just what Maggie and Joe need."

"We're going on a picnic this evening and then over to Monterey to watch the fireworks."

"I'm going to a party." It was said with a distinct lack of enthusiasm.

He wanted to ask if she was going to the party alone but couldn't come up with a way to slip it into the conversation. "I always grumble about going to parties and then have a good time when I get there." Trite, but true. His grousing about their extended social life was just one of the wedges he'd created between himself and Shelly.

"I'd much rather be going on that picnic with the five of you."

How could what had obviously been an off-hand statement make him feel as if he'd won the lottery? Was he lonely or simply jealous over how happy Shelly had sounded when she'd last called to talk to the kids, wanting some of that happiness for himself?

"I could drive up to get you." Damn, it hadn't come out the way he'd intended. Instead of a breezy reply to a casual statement, he'd come across as serious and needy as a televangelist asking for money. He dug his fingers into his mustache and scratched. One more week and that was it. If the itching didn't let up, the damn thing was going.

"I just might take you up on your offer if this wasn't one of those command performance kind of things."

He couldn't tell whether she meant it, or if she was so good at sidestepping invitations, she could let people down without them feeling the impact. "I assume you're still taking an active position in the company."

"I tried staying home a couple of days last week, but almost went crazy knowing there wasn't anything or anyone who needed me."

"Which is why you go to work every day—to satisfy that need?"

She waited a long time before answering, and when she did, it was as if she were making a confession. "I have to do something to keep busy, but the business was Ken's love, not mine."

"I understand."

"Somehow I knew you would."

There it was again, that inexplicable connection. "So what are you going to do?" he asked.

"Keep trying. It's the only thing I can do."

A half dozen clichés came to mind, but he refrained from using them. She was as smart as she was beautiful and sure as hell didn't need recycled advice from him. "Do you want me to have Joe or Maggie call you when they get home?"

"Just tell them I checked in and that I'll try again in a couple of days."

"And if they want to reach you?" He sensed she was getting ready to hang up and didn't want the conversation to end.

"They have my number. But I don't think I gave it to you—just in case something happens and you need to reach me," she added quickly.

"I have a pen right here, go ahead."

She read off the ten numbers and then had him repeat them to her. "Before I go . . . how is the book coming?"

"The agent asked to see the first half, so I sent it to him a couple of days ago."

"Is that good?"

He laughed. "I don't know."

"What happens now?"

"I don't know that, either. I guess he reads it and either tells me to keep going or to round-file it and start on something else."

"Did he say how long it would be before he got back to you?"

"No, and I didn't ask."

"Which means your heart is in your throat every time the phone rings."

How could she know him so little and yet know him so well? "I had no idea the waiting would be so hard."

"Will you call me when you hear?"

It was difficult, but he resisted making more of the request than she'd intended. "Sure. If you're not home, I'll leave a message on the machine."

"Take care," she said.

"You too."

He hung up and glanced out the window at the beach. It was even more crowded than usual with the influx of people for the holiday. The ocean was active and foamy, agitated into white peaks and green valleys by a far off Pacific storm. The sky was a Dallas Cowboy blue, with brightly colored kites sprinkled across the horizon. If he'd spent the morning listing his requirements for a perfect day, he couldn't have come up with one better than the one he'd just been given.

Julia tossed the pen she'd been holding onto her desk and leaned back in her chair. She had five minutes before her meeting with John Sidney and his staff to discuss the quality control problems they were having with their shipping boxes. Her initial reaction had been to let John handle the supplier himself, but that wasn't the way things were done at HCF.

Although Ken's first love had been prod-
uct development, he'd been a hands-on boss,
involved in every aspect of his business
through daily minimeetings with the managers
of the different departments. When Julia took
over she felt overwhelmed trying to cope with
Ken's loss and learn the business at the same
time and had cut the meetings to twice a
week. The drop in morale had been immediate
and startling.

The men and women who worked at HCF
were in her corner, willing to go the distance
and do whatever necessary to facilitate her
takeover. Their loyalty was unquestioning, their
enthusiasm intimidating. If she'd run into resis-
tance—and it wouldn't have taken a great
deal—she could have convinced herself it would
be better for everyone if she sold the company
and let someone who knew what they were
doing take over. Instead she faced a kindness
and sympathy and patience that made it impossible to walk away.

A light knock sounded on the door. "Come
in," Julia said.

Pat Faith, her secretary, popped her head
in. "I just heard that John Sidney's wife miscar-
ried last night. I knew you'd want to know."

Julia was certain they'd met at one or
another of the company parties, but she couldn't
summon a mental picture. "I can't remember
who she is."

Pat stepped inside and closed the door
behind her. "She's really quiet, but very

pretty—long blond hair with a mole under her right eye."

"Always wears a dress, even to the picnics?"

"That's her." Pat started to leave, then remembered something else she wanted to ask. "Did you find Joe and Maggie?"

Over the sixteen years Pat had been Ken's secretary and then Julia's, she'd become as much friend as employee to both of them. "Yes—no. I didn't actually find them, but at least I know where they are and that they're all right. It seems they've been adopted by their new neighbor at the beach house."

"The writer?"

Julia had forgotten she'd told Pat about Eric. She nodded. "His kids are staying with him, and you know how Joe and Maggie feel about kids."

"Oh, he's married, then?"

It seemed an odd question. "Divorced."

Pat smiled. "Glad to hear it."

"Now why—"

"I like the way you look when you talk about him and just don't want to see you getting yourself into something sticky."

Julia's mouth opened in surprise. "You're imagining things. I don't look any different when I talk about Eric than I do when I talk about any other friend."

"I'm not saying there's anything wrong with finding someone you're interested in," she protested. "It's bound to happen sooner or later. It's just that you've got to be a lot more careful than someone like me."

She'd heard the warning in one form or another from every one of her and Ken's friends. Not only were they convinced she was a stationary target for every fortune-hunting man on the planet, they couldn't imagine why she would ever allow another man in her life again, no matter how wonderful he was.

After having the best, why—*how*—could she ever settle for less?

Another knock sounded on the door. "It's probably John," Julia said. "I'll see if there's anything he and his wife need. In the meantime why don't you call McLellan's and have them deliver whatever orchid they have in bloom now. Be sure they know we want something especially nice, and make it in white or pink or yellow, nothing dark. Keep the note simple and sign it from all of us."

Pat nodded. "I'll take care of it."

Julia got up to meet John at the door. If losing Ken had done nothing else for her, it had taught her how much it meant to have someone show they cared. She couldn't give John what he wanted most, but she could give him that.

CHAPTER

5

The five of them arrived at the pier early, armed with blankets, books, and games for Jason and Susie, a folding chaise longue for Maggie, and chairs for Joe and Eric. Sea lions barked in the background as if setting up their protest early to be sure their feelings about the intrusion were heard while Eric kept an eye on the fog bank sitting offshore.

Stuffed from fresh peach ice cream and a variety of picnic excesses, they were content to sit the two hours and wait for the show to begin. After several minutes of polite but pointed encouragement, Joe sprawled out on the blanket, Susie on one side, Jason on the other, and began reading aloud the books Susie had brought with her.

As others drifted in to fill the spaces around them, Eric and Maggie watched the sun lazily make its way to the fog-pillowed horizon.

"How are you doing?" Eric asked, his voice low so that only she could hear.

Maggie studied him for several seconds before answering. "You know, don't you?"

"Joe confirmed what I'd already figured out the night we had pizza."

She nodded. "I'm a little tired," she admitted. "But I wouldn't trade one minute of being here for a truckload of energy."

"You know, you really should try to pace yourself."

Her only answer was to look at him.

"I'm sorry. That was a pretty stupid thing to say."

"Did you say things like that to your patients when they knew they were dying?"

"I may have. I honestly don't know. One of the reasons I quit was that I saw myself turning into the kind of doctor I swore I'd never be."

"My aunt once told me that even death has a beginning, that it's simply another of life's journeys. I think about that whenever I begin to feel weighed down by everything that's happening."

"I like that. Would you mind if I use it?"

"In what way?"

"There's a scene I'm working on in the book that could use a philosophical touch."

"My aunt would be most pleased." Maggie smiled. "And so am I."

Eric reached his arms up over his head to stretch, stuck his legs out in front of him, and crossed them at the ankles. "Julia said you and Joe have been coming to this area for a long time and that you used to own her house."

"We spent our honeymoon in Santa Cruz and have been back every year since. Sixty-five of them, all told."

"I understand you used to own Julia's house."

"Bought it over fifty years ago, right after the doctor told us we wouldn't be needing to add any more bedrooms to our house in San Jose. Then Joe had his stroke just after he retired and we sold the place to Ken. He made the deal contingent on our staying here during the summer—said he was afraid to let the house stand empty all those months." She smiled at the memory. "Of course, the way he made it sound, we were the ones doing him the favor. We didn't take the whole three months. Joe found renters for June and August, good solid people he was sure would take care of the place. We thought we were doing Ken a favor helping him out with the payments that way." She chuckled. "Can you imagine?"

"I think I've been infected with whatever bug bit all of you," Eric said. "Now that I've been here a while, I don't want to leave. It's going to be hard to turn Andrew's house back over to him when he comes home."

"I wish you could have seen what it was like around here when we first came. It's not that I don't like what the cities and towns have become, it's more that I sometimes miss what they were."

"I'd love to hear what it was like back then."

"Goodness, I wouldn't know where to begin." Rarely did she let herself slip into stories of the past, believing that doing so was more barrier than connection to others, but as they sat and waited for dusk Eric began to ply her with questions about the area, how it had changed and how it had stayed the same.

She told him of the stink and noise that had made up Cannery Row when the money had come from sardines and not tourists, how boats had unloaded and processed the larger fish at the end of piers now filled with restaurants and shops. She described the unspoiled charm of Carmel when ordinary working people had lived in the cottages that now sold for more than any of these people could have hoped to make in a lifetime.

Over their years of exploring the Monterey Peninsula she and Joe had made friends with artists and fishermen and farmers. And then slowly the makeup of the area had begun to change. Tourists arrived with hefty wallets, liked what they saw, and began to buy pieces of paradise for themselves. The cypress- and pine- and oak-covered hillsides soon sprouted No Trespassing signs on solidly gated driveways.

To accommodate the visitors who came on a budget, T-shirt shops now dotted Carmel's Ocean Avenue. They were located between, across the street from, and around the corner from galleries that sold paintings that left all but the most affluent slack jawed. Once meticulously clean, the still quaint village now suffered from tourist overload. Candy wrappers and beverage cups spilled from trash containers, while, at times, sidewalks barely accommodated the shoulder-to-shoulder pedestrians. Visitors arrived by the busload, laden with cameras and fanny packs and secretly hoping to catch a glimpse of Clint Eastwood so they would have something to tell their friends when they got back home.

Eric was still asking questions about Carmel and Monterey when nightfall settled and enveloped them. He'd barely gotten to Santa Cruz and the effects of the 1989 Loma Prieta earthquake when the first of the fireworks, a set of three rings in red, white, and blue, lit up the sky. Maggie promised they'd finish another time as she moved deeper into her chaise longue to make room for Jason. Susie crawled onto Joe's lap and put her hand on her father's arm.

Appreciative ooohs and aaahs filled in the spaces between reverberating booms.

"Daddy, they really are just like flowers," Susie said in awe. "I wish Mommy could see, too."

Maggie's heart went out to her. People you loved were supposed to love each other. The absence of that love was a hard lesson for someone so young to have to learn. "You could draw her a picture tomorrow. I'll bet she would like that."

"I'll draw her one, too," Jason said, his gaze never leaving the sky.

"And one for Roger?" Eric suggested gently.

"Okay," Susie said.

"I suppose," Jason added.

Maggie could see how much the peace offering had cost Eric. It was obvious that given the choice, he wouldn't have wanted to share his children with another man, but no matter the possible consequences, he would always put their needs above his own.

Without warning a breath-stealing stabbing pain shot through Maggie's midsection. She gripped the armrests as she waited for it to pass. Could she have forgotten to take her medication? No, it wasn't possible. Joe delivered the assortment of pills with unerring regularity.

Eric started to say something, turned, and saw what was happening to Maggie. Without drawing attention to them, he circled her wrist with his hand, his fingers probing the pulse point. After several seconds he quietly reached for her purse and pulled out a plastic bag filled with dark orange prescription bottles. After scanning the labels, he chose one container, opened it, and removed two tablets. With deft, subtle movements, he slipped them into her mouth. "Do you need water?" he asked softly, slipping her hand into his.

She shook her head, leaned back, and closed her eyes as she waited for the narcotic to take effect. Joe had been adamant that she be put under the care of an oncologist as concerned with quality of life as cancer. The doctor had warned them that the time might come when pills weren't enough, but they were supposed to have several more months before that happened.

The narcotic lapped at her pain like waves hitting the shore, gradually washing it away until she was left with nothing but its memory and the fear of its return.

Maggie opened her eyes and saw Eric watching her. "I'm fine now," she mouthed. The incident had occurred so fast and with so little fuss, not even Joe had picked up on what was happening. "Thank you."

Eric gave her hand an affectionate squeeze. "If you ever need me, just call. Anytime."

Jason looked at his dad. "What for?"

"Anything," Eric told him, ruffling his hair.

"How come Maggie would need you?" he pressed, refusing to be put off.

Maggie believed the surest way to lose a child's trust was to lie to him, but now was not the time or the place to tell Jason that she was sick. "To help make more ice cream."

The explanation seemed to satisfy him. "Can we?"

"Of course we can," she said.

Jason's attention was drawn back to the fireworks as a series of explosions marked the spectacular finale, lighting up the sky with an entire garden of the ephemeral flowers.

As if on cue, the fog rolled forward. Maggie watched the last flaming blue trailer fall into the ocean through the encroaching mist and felt a strange peace come over her. In part, the beauty of the display had come from its transitory nature. As much as she didn't want to leave Joe, neither had she a desire to live forever. She regretted that she hadn't worked harder to be a better caretaker of her small corner of the world.

She should have done more to let people know how many birds died because of balloons released at celebrations, or entered the battle to institute mass transit systems throughout the bay area.

She was proud of the awards she'd received for convincing people to neuter their pets and lowering the number of kittens and puppies that died at local shelters and the work she'd done to help the homeless—but she should have done more.

"Ready?" Joe asked.

It took a second to register what he was asking. She smiled an acknowledgment as she moved to extract herself from the chaise longue. "My, that was wonderful. I'm so glad we came." She looked at Jason and Susie. "Thank you for asking us."

"You're welcome," Susie said.

Jason gave her an impromptu hug. "You can come with us next time, too."

She put her arms around him and pressed a kiss to the top of his head. "Thank you," she said simply.

The ride home was quiet as first the kids, and then Joe, fell asleep in the backseat of Eric's car. As they neared the power plant at Moss Landing, Eric glanced over to see if Maggie had fallen asleep also. Seeing that she was still awake, he said, "I know how annoying it can be to have people constantly ask how you're doing, but I'm going to risk it anyway. How *are* you doing?"

"Right now, or overall?"

"Both."

"As well as can be expected." She caught his look of surprise and grinned. "I'm sorry, I've always wanted to say that to a doctor. Frustrating, isn't it?"

He laughed. "Extremely. It's also a very good way to tell me to mind my own business."

"I'm winding down, Eric. I'm sure you know the process, and I really don't have anything new to add." She put her hand on his arm. "But please don't think your caring isn't appreciated, or that I won't take you up on your generous offer and call if I need you."

"I wish there was something I could do to help."

"You're a nice man. I hope you find someone to share all the wonderful things that are ahead for you."

"Which wonderful things are you referring to? If you've had some revelation about the book, I wouldn't mind hearing it. I had no idea waiting could be so hard."

"I was talking about life. The book will take care of itself."

"Remind me of that every so often, will you?"

She might not be his friend for long, but she would be the best she could be while she was there. "It would be my pleasure."

CHAPTER

6

Joe pushed open the bedroom door with his hip and backed in, a tray of tea and toast balanced in his hands, Josi at his feet. "The fog has set in with a vengeance."

Maggie propped her pillow against the headboard and sat up. Josi joined her, butting her head against Maggie's hand to have her ears and chin scratched, rewarding the effort with a loud, body-rumbling purr. "It's making up for last night," she said, running her hand along Josi's back.

Joe waited for Josi to settle before putting the tray on the bed and pouring a cup of tea for himself and Maggie. The pot was one they'd picked up in London thirty years ago on their one foray over the Atlantic Ocean. He opened the blinds before joining her on the bed. "How did you sleep?"

She hadn't, but he would only worry if she told him. "It was a perfect night. I had the most wonderful dreams."

"What would you like to do today?"

She took a tentative sip of her tea to test it. She didn't know whether it was the cancer or the medicine, but she was losing her sensitivity to heat and cold and had burned herself several times lately. The tea was perfect. She curled her hands around the bright yellow mug and took another sip.

"I've been thinking about something."

He cocked an eyebrow as one corner of his mouth lifted in an anticipatory smile. "Yes . . . ?"

Instead of answering, she looked at him as if it were for the first time. "You are without a doubt the most handsome man I've ever seen."

He chuckled. "That said, you can be assured you now have my complete attention."

"You really are, you know. No one who didn't know you would ever believe you're almost ninety." She shook her head. "*Ninety*, Joe. Did you ever think we'd be around this long?"

"If it weren't for you, I wouldn't be here at all."

"Sure you would. You were the one who taught yourself to walk and talk again. All I did was stand back and watch and offer a little encouragement every so often."

"Oh, is that what you're calling it now?"

She hid her smile by dipping her head to take another drink of tea. Time and distance had mellowed the memories of what had been a horrendous two years in their lives. Worry and frustration over Joe's stroke had driven them to the very edge of their coping abilities. But they'd come through even stronger and with a profound appreciation for the lengths they would travel for each other.

"So tell me what you've been thinking about," Joe said.

"I know we made a lot of plans before we got here, that there were a lot of places we were going to go and things we were going to see . . ." She wished she knew for sure whether the itinerary they'd made up was for her benefit or for his. "But I've been thinking—now this is just a suggestion, it doesn't mean we have to do it if you don't want to. Anyway, I was wondering—now I want you to tell me the truth about how you feel, this is just an idea I came up with . . ."

"Why don't you just spit it out, Maggie?"

Josi rolled to her back and stretched, her length taking up half the bed. "What do you think about having Susie and Jason stay with us in the mornings while Eric works on his book?" she said in a rush. "It wouldn't be that long. They're only going to be here another week. With the ice cream and everything else we did yesterday, I never got around to making Jason's chocolate chip cookies. If he and Susie were here, they could help me. Then when we were through, you could help them with the fireworks pictures they were going to make for their mother and their new stepfather."

"Are you sure you want to do this? What about all the plans you made?"

"They don't seem so important anymore."

"Whatever makes you happy makes me happy, Maggie. That's all I've ever wanted."

"It's more than being happy. I don't think about *me* so much when I'm with them." And she knew Joe didn't, either. While making a pilgrimage to familiar and well-loved places of their past together had seemed like a good idea at the time, she'd come to realize how maudlin the whole thing could become. She wanted Joe to remember her smiling and living each day in the present, not the past.

She looked into his eyes to see if he understood, but all she could see was the now familiar mixture of love and sorrow and pain. "Are you sure it's okay? This was your time, too. I don't want to take anything away from you."

"As long as we're together," he said, "none of the rest matters."

"We still have to convince Eric—and the kids have to want to come."

"We might have our work cut out for us with Eric, but I know exactly what the kids will say."

"There's something else." She put her mug back on the tray. "It's important that you answer me truthfully."

"I always do, Maggie."

"But this is different. I think you would do anything to please me now."

"I can't give you an answer until you tell me what it is."

She ran her hand through her hair, experiencing a small mental blink at the unfamiliar feel. Once so thick she purposely had it thinned with each haircut, it now barely covered her scalp. "Am I being selfish? Is it unfair to Jason and Susie to let them become my friends?"

He put the tray on the floor and settled her into his arms. "Fair or not, my love, it's too late. They're already attached."

"Our time here was supposed to be so simple. How did it get so complicated?"

He kissed her and touched his finger to the end of her nose. "I guess life had one last lesson to teach you." He laid his cheek against the top of her head as she nestled deeper against his shoulder. "How about if I talk to Eric and we let him decide?" he suggested.

"Listen," Maggie said softly.

"What are you hearing that I'm not?" he asked after several seconds.

"The ocean and Josi's purring have the same rhythm." Joe's heartbeat was part of the mix, steady and strong in her ear where her head rested on his chest. They were the sounds of life, each with its own cadence, its own meaning, and its own duration.

Eric stood at the screen door and watched as Jason and Susie walked off hand in hand with Joe and Maggie. Bundled up in jackets and sweats against a fog that had hung on tenaciously for two days, the four of them had decided to brave the cold and head for the beach to build sand castles. Eric would come down later to judge their efforts, the winners to be excused from helping to clean up after lunch.

Joe hadn't tried to hide his surprise when Eric agreed to his and Maggie's proposal to watch the kids so that he could work. What Joe didn't know and Eric didn't tell him was that he'd already given a lot of thought to their concerns about Jason and Susie becoming too attached. While the eventual loss of someone they loved wasn't a lesson he would have purposely chosen for them that summer, when balanced against the joy of knowing someone as special as Maggie, there was no question which Eric would choose for his children.

If he had a regret, it was that they hadn't met sooner. Shelly's parents had had a difficult time accepting a grandparent role. Jason and Susie dated them in a society where youth and its trappings were coin of the realm. Visits were limited to occasional holidays, preferably at Shelly and Eric's house, far removed from the possibility of running into one of their friends. This was accomplished with a subtlety and skill of a queen controlling worker bees.

His own parents were gone, killed in a hotel fire when he was a junior in college. By the time the litigation cleared, he was a startlingly wealthy, twenty-five-year-old orphan.

Joe and Maggie were the closest Jason and Susie would ever get to the ideal for grandparents. He wasn't about to deny his own kids something he wished he'd had for himself.

Absently scratching his mustache, Eric closed the door against the fog and went back to work.

Maggie packed wet sand into a tomato sauce can that had both ends removed. She then carefully released the sand, creating a corner post for her and Susie's horse corral. Lying on her belly, her gaze intently focused, Susie shoved a stick into the post to act as railing.

"Good job," Maggie said.

Susie looked up and smiled, swiping a hand across her forehead where her bangs had escaped her jacket hood. Sand caught in her eyebrows.

"Come here a second," Maggie said, reaching for her. She instructed Susie to close her eyes while she removed the sand. Instead of going back to work, Susie climbed up on Maggie's lap.

"How come we couldn't bring Josi?" Susie asked.

"I'm afraid she's not much of a beach cat."

"'Cause she doesn't belong here?"

"Something like that."

"The way me and Jason didn't belong with Mommy and Roger on their honeymoon?"

"Not exactly. We don't let Josi play in the sand because she'd get it in her tummy when she licked herself." The second part was a lot harder. "Your mommy and Roger went on their trip by themselves so they could become even better friends. Best of all, you and Jason get to be with your daddy."

"And you." She put her arms around Maggie and gave her a hug.

"And me," Maggie said.

"Will you come and see me and Jason when we go home?"

"I would if I could, Susie, but I'm going to be a long way away."

"That's okay, you could drive your car."

"Even farther than that."

"But how will I see you?"

Maggie touched her hand to Susie's chest, covering her heart. "You'll see me in here."

Susie thought a minute and then frowned, obviously confused. "In my tummy?"

Maggie laughed. She ran her fingers over Susie's stomach, tickling her. "Yes, right in your tummy. Every time you eat homemade ice cream or chocolate chip cookies, I'll be there giving you a great big hug."

Laughing, Susie squirmed out of Maggie's grasp and landed in the middle of their carefully constructed farmhouse. When she saw what she'd done, instead of being upset, she laughed harder. Falling backward, she rolled from the house to the corral.

As Maggie joined in Susie's merriment, the ache in her side that she'd been trying to ignore for the past half hour began to gain control. In spite of the warning, Maggie lay down beside Susie and rolled along behind her. When she sat up again, it wasn't pain that stole her breath, it was an overwhelming sorrow. It seemed she wasn't as ready to abandon the life still left to her as she'd believed.

She looked up and saw Joe and Jason heading toward them, their hands full of shells and rocks and various other intriguing items they'd picked up on their walk.

"We're going to build a spaceship," Jason said. "Wait till you see the stuff we got for it."

Joe came over to check on Maggie. "What happened here?"

Susie giggled, bending over and hiding her face with her hands.

"You don't want to know," Maggie said.

He studied her before saying, "Pill time?"

She nodded.

After adding his stash to Jason's, Joe reached in his pocket and surreptitiously handed Maggie her medicine. Brushing sand from her back and shoulders, he said, "I assume this is something I don't want to know about, either?"

"We were smashing the house," Susie said.

"I see." Joe said. He looked at Maggie. "And you were doing this because . . ."

"It was fun?" she suggested.

"You do realize, of course, that this creates a serious handicap for you in the contest."

He would stay there until he saw that she was all right. Just as he would stay at her side for as long as it took her to die, at home or at the hospital. He would be there when she was put on machines that would prevent her from ever uttering another word.

Even if she wasn't afraid of the expense, how could she allow her and Joe's time together to end like that?

Her moment of indecision washed away, clearing her mind the way each outgoing wave cleared the sand. She was glad that the questioning had come this one last time. When she left Joe there could be no doubt that she was doing the right thing.

CHAPTER
7

Maggie was with Eric when he got the call that sent her on a wild journey between joy and despair. She was still on that journey two days later.

Shelly had wanted to know if Jason and Susie could stay with Eric another week while she and Roger settled into their new home.

Of course, Eric had told her, he would love having them, as, he was. sure, would their new friends, Joe and Maggie.

Which meant they would be there for her birthday.

Which meant her life could not become the tidy little circle she'd so carefully planned.

She delayed telling Joe until that night when they were alone. No additional words were necessary as they sat on the sofa in the living room and held each other, Josi draped across their laps as if she, too, were a part of the decision-making process.

"I'm sorry," Joe said. He understood her turmoil as readily as he understood her reasoning.

"Thank you for not trying to convince me that their staying an extra week is part of some big master plan."

"A master plan would mean someone had found a cure, or a way to stop the pain. I've accepted that isn't going to happen, Maggie. At least not in time for us."

She hated that he believed her a coward, but she could not burden him with the truth. He would give his life to save her. She knew this without question. And he would sacrifice everything for her. This, too, she knew without question. To Joe, relinquishing his financial future was simply to whisper "I love you" as he told her good-bye.

Josi tucked her nose under Maggie's hand, instantly responding with a purr when Maggie scratched her ears. "Now I have to pick another day."

"Not tonight you don't."

"If I put it off, I'll only think about it more." She was afraid that without a set time, she would wake up each morning and find a reason to stay the day. She loved fog as much as sunshine, tea and toast as much as a cozy dinner. Her heart soared whenever she spotted a hummingbird at one of the flowers, and Josi never failed to make her smile. But as important as every breath she drew was Joe. If she could have loved him only a little less, she could have stayed.

She wasn't sure what happened when someone died. As a young girl sitting in catechism classes, her belief in heaven and hell had been as unquestioning as her belief in neighboring towns. As she grew older and ventured into the world, her faith suffered damaging blows from unanswered questions. How could the God she'd been led to believe loved children let so many die such cruel deaths? Was He, as so many sincerely believed with prayer and behavior and avowed appreciation, so busy determining the outcome of basketball and football and baseball games that He had no time to help those beset by famine, flood, and pestilence?

In the end she'd decided it wasn't God she questioned so much as His organized believers. Not until she'd completed her religious journey did she discover Joe had traveled the same road, only years ahead of her.

Their church was small, just her and Joe and God. They tithed by working to preserve the earth He'd created and the animals that called it home. Only one word was in their gospel, and they relayed it by action, not preaching. That word was love.

"Are you awake?" Joe asked softly.

She tilted her head up to look at him. "I was just thinking."

"About?"

She hesitated telling him, afraid he might interpret her questioning as doubt. But an insistent inner voice demanded she take the chance. "What happens when we die."

"And?"

"I know what I'd like to happen."

He gave her a heartbreakingly tender kiss. "So do I. What do you suppose the chances are that it will?"

"We'll be together, Joe. That's the one thing I know for sure. If there's no heaven where I can wait for you, I'll always be in your heart."

"Oh, Maggie, we were so blessed to have found each other. We really have no right to ask for more." A sob caught in his throat. He swallowed. "But I want it all. I want to spend eternity with you."

"If there's a way, my darling, I'll find it. Even if it's on a cloud in another universe, I'll go there and make a place for us."

Three days later, after they had lunch with Jason and Susie and Eric, Maggie told Joe she was tired and that she was going to take a nap. When Joe went in an hour later to see how she was doing, he found her curled up in a fetal position, her skin damp, her heart racing.

"The medicine . . . isn't working," she said, looking at him through pain-filled eyes. "Get Eric. He'll know what to do."

Joe said a silent prayer that Eric was still home. During lunch he'd said something about taking the kids to a movie that afternoon. He glanced out the window as he picked up the phone and saw with relief that Eric's car was still there.

Eric took one look at Maggie, bundled her up, and put her in his car. The five of them were at the hospital ten minutes later. Joe stayed with Jason and Susie while Eric saw Maggie through the maze of admission and diagnosis.

Caught up in his own spiral of fear and grief, Joe didn't notice the effect their rush to the hospital had had on Jason until he became aware that he was no longer sitting with Susie. He was pressed against the wall, watching the now empty hallway where his father and Maggie had disappeared.

Joe went up to Jason and laid his hand on his shoulder. "I saw a soda machine in the lobby. Would you like one?"

Eyes wide with concern, Jason looked up at him. "What happened to her?"

"Maggie's sick, and the medicine that's been helping her stopped working. Your dad is helping her get some new medicine."

"Is she going to die?"

It was a question that needed a parent's answer. Joe didn't know what to say.

"She is, isn't she?"

Joe nodded.

"Can I tell her good-bye first?"

Closing his eyes against the familiar feel of tears burning the back of his throat, Joe nodded again. With an innocent love and caring Jason had summed up something Joe had struggled with for months. It was a gift to be able to say good-bye, to share the last moments, to say one last time "I love you."

"She would like that," he told Jason.

He leaned against Joe, drawing support, giving comfort. "I don't think we should tell Susie."

Joe glanced over his shoulder. Susie was watching cartoons on the television that had been mounted to the wall. She was oblivious of the drama being played out around her, protected by her years and innocence. "You're a very special big brother, Jason."

After they got home from the hospital, Maggie slept the rest of the day and through the night. The next morning she was groggy from the new medication but eager to see Eric and the kids. Susie arrived first, bounding up on the bed without hesitation or thought that the trip to the hospital had been anything but routine. She settled in beside Maggie, reaching for Josi and digging her fingers into the cat's thick mane.

"Daddy said we couldn't stay," she said, plainly believing Maggie would get him to change his mind.

Eric stood at the doorway, Jason at his side. "How are you feeling?" he asked.

"Very well, thanks to you."

He smiled. "I'd be happy to take the credit, but I think it really belongs to those yellow-and-blue capsules the hospital sent home with you."

Maggie saw fear in Jason's eyes, and it broke her heart. Had she known he would be exposed to her illness this way, she never would have let their friendship grow. "I'm sorry if what happened yesterday scared you," she told him. "But you can see how much better I am today."

Still he didn't say anything.

"I told them they could only stay long enough to see you and say hi," Eric said. "If it's all right, we'll come back for a little while this afternoon."

Susie looked up at Maggie, a plea to be allowed to remain in her eyes.

"Of course it's all right," Maggie said. She put her hand over Susie's. "I have a job for you when you come back."

"You do?"

"I've tried and tried and can't find Josi's red ball. I thought maybe you could help me look behind the sofa."

"I could do it now," Susie said. "I could look under the TV, too."

"We'll check on the way out," Eric said, holding his hand out to her.

Jason stayed behind as Eric led Susie into the living room. "I'm sorry you're sick."

"Me too. But most of all, I'm sorry about what happened yesterday."

"It wasn't your fault. You didn't want to be sick."

"You're a special young man, Jason," she said. "I'm so glad you came to stay with your father so you could become my friend."

He stood very still, as if torn between being there and running away. Finally, he came into the room and crawled across the bed, flinging himself into her arms. "Joe said I could say good-bye, but I don't want to yet."

She glanced up and saw Joe standing in the doorway. The look in his eyes told her all she needed to know. She ran her hand over Jason's shiny, sweet-smelling hair and pressed a kiss to the top of his head. "We have lots of time," she said softly.

"Promise?"

"I promise. How many more days before you go home?"

"Five."

"I'll be right here for every one of them."

Eric came back. "Jason, it's time to go."

"I'm going to draw you a picture of me and Susie and Dad," he told Maggie.

"That's a wonderful idea. Will you bring it with you when you come this afternoon?"

"Is that okay, Dad?" He inched toward the foot of the bed.

"Maybe if you're feeling up to it, we could come for dinner and order another pizza."

"I'd like that," she said. "What do you think, Jason?"

"I found it," Susie squealed before Jason had a chance to answer. "Here it is." She poked her head between her father and Joe, her hand held aloft. She tossed the ball onto the bed in Josi's general direction. Josi waited for it to come near, slapped it with one paw, watched it roll away, and laid her head back down on the comforter.

"It's nap time," Maggie said in an attempt to explain Josi's lack of interest. "I'm sure she'll feel more like playing this evening when you come back."

"It wouldn't hurt you to take a nap with her," Eric said to Maggie. He gathered Jason and Susie and started them down the hall. "Call if you need anything," he told Joe. "Anything at all."

When they were gone, Joe came in and moved Josi so that he could sit next to Maggie. The cat gave a low rumble of protest, stuck its paws out for a stretch, and flopped over on its side. "She's getting a little thick around the middle," Joe said.

"It's all the treats the kids have been feeding her. They love to see her sit up and beg."

He took her hand in his. "How are you feeling?"

"I'm going to let you get away with asking that because of the new medicine."

"If I get to ask, then I'm entitled to an answer."

"I'm a little lightheaded and a little tired, but there's no pain."

"None at all?"

Because he was asking about the cancer, she could give him an honest answer. She wouldn't tell him about the ache in her heart or how her throat hurt from holding back tears.

"None at all," she told him truthfully.

CHAPTER

8

An ocean breeze swept through the leaves of the eucalyptus as Joe and Maggie stood in the middle of the road and waved good-bye to Eric and Jason and Susie. Their week was up and they were going home. Jason's face was still pressed to the glass when their car rounded the corner and disappeared.

"He's going to miss you," Joe said as he brought his arm down.

Maggie ran her hand across Joe's back in an affectionate, familiar gesture. "Eric talked to Shelly. She knows that Jason might need some extra attention when he gets home."

"What would you like to do this evening?"

She looked at him. "It's time, Joe."

He felt gut punched. "But we—"

"It has to be now," she stated flatly, leaving him no room to maneuver.

God, how he wanted to challenge her, to demand she give them another week, at the very least another day; but all he had left to give her was the right to decide for herself. "Are you in pain?"

"It doesn't matter."

"Would you like to go for a walk on the beach first?"

She shook her head and touched her hand to the side of his face. "I have to do this now, Joe."

He took her into his arms. "There are a hundred things I still want to say to you."

"Pick one."

In the end, the choice was obvious. "I love you," he said simply.

They walked toward the house hand in hand. Before they went inside, Joe stopped to pick a perfectly formed, miniature red rose. When Julia and Ken were married and Julia took over the care of the garden, she'd selected the roses she planted around the house on the basis of fragrance over beauty. This one had both. Joe wove the stem into Maggie's hair and kissed her lightly on the lips.

Maggie took her stash of carefully hoarded pills with her into the bathroom, insisting Joe not be with her when she actually took them. She'd told him he would carry enough mental images of this day without adding one more. When she came out, he helped her to the bed, sat down beside her, and took her hand.

Touching his cheek, she said, "I want you to leave now."

He smiled sadly and shook his head. "I'm overruling you on this one, Maggie, my love."

She looked into his eyes, telling him silently of her love, letting him see how sorry she was to go, but that she wasn't afraid. "I love you, Joe Chapman," were her last words as her gaze lost its focus, her eyes closed, and she gently drifted off to sleep.

He stayed until she drew her last shallow breath and her heart fluttered to a stop, then stood and brushed a kiss to her forehead. The rose in her hair filled his lungs with sweet memories of summers past.

"Wait for me, Maggie," he whispered. "I won't be long."

A half hour later the afternoon sun stole through the window and filled the bedroom with a soft orange light. Joe came in to retrieve the container of pills he'd hidden in the back of the closet. They were contraband, acquired during a fishing trip to Mexico that he'd gone on the month after Maggie told him about her plans. He'd known from the moment she was diagnosed that he had no desire to live in a world without her. She had been a part of him for sixty-five years. To go on alone would be simply a matter of consuming space. What they'd had, what they'd been, demanded a better ending.

When he returned from the kitchen, Joe settled into the bed next to Maggie. Gently he drew her into his arms. "Did you really think I could let you go without me?"

He closed his eyes and waited. Slowly the pills narrowed his consciousness to a small point of light. As he felt himself drifting free, he called to Maggie, telling her that he was coming. At his last breath the light flashed and surrounded him with prisms of color.

And then he was at peace.

And he was not alone.

CHAPTER

9

Eric arrived home late that night. He'd planned to stay in Sacramento and visit the friend who'd taken over his practice, but he was hit with such an empty feeling when he dropped the kids off that he knew he would be lousy company. He begged off, telling his friend that he was concerned about his summer neighbors and thought he should get back to check on them.

The lights were off at Joe and Maggie's, and the last thing he wanted to do was disturb their sleep. For the first time in days, the moon was visible, its light casting a silver sword across the water. Or was it a path for the dreamers who had stayed up late enough to catch the magic?

Instead of going inside immediately, Eric went for a walk.

All the way back he'd fought an unreasoning jealousy at Shelly's obvious happiness. Given the option, it was what he would have wished for her. Still, it was hard to see the contrast between how it had been for them in the end and how it was for her now.

How had he let himself become so self-centered that he'd failed to see what he was doing to her?

He wanted what she now had. The only thing saving him from complete depression was knowing that he no longer wanted it with Shelly. He'd let her go, physically before mentally, but the break had been complete for over a year now.

As hard as he tried, he couldn't keep Jason and Susie out of the mix. It had been a fist to his gut to see them standing on the porch waving good-bye, the four of them a complete family unit.

He walked to the far end of the cove and started back. Ahead of him, he spotted something white and round left behind by a retreating wave. He stopped to pick it up. It was a perfectly formed, unbroken sand dollar, the first he'd seen in over three weeks of searching with Jason. He checked to see that the resident creature was no longer alive before slipping the shell into his pocket.

He would call Jason in the morning to tell him about the find. Somehow the small connection made him feel better, and his footsteps were lighter as he headed back to the house. He actually smiled when he saw Susie had left her play shoes by the back door. She had staked her claim and left a gentle reminder that she would be back.

* * *

The next morning Eric got up from the computer every half hour to look outside, watching to see if Joe had picked up his newspaper. At nine-thirty he became concerned, at ten he decided he'd waited long enough.

He spotted the note on the front door from the walkway and pulled it up in midstride. For long seconds he stood and stared at the piece of paper that had his name printed in neat block letters. Instinctively he knew what was inside.

How could he have missed the clues? They were so goddamned obvious—in hindsight.

An overwhelming sadness filled his chest, squeezing out the air. Death was a part of living. It was one of the first things he'd learned in medical school. If you were going to feel sorrow, you saved it for the child who went without ever tasting the sweetness of life or the young mother who should have been saved to see her children grown. To want a career as a doctor and to let yourself feel more was a sure path to burnout down the line.

Joe and Maggie had lived a long and glorious life, blessed by a love that was as rare as the black bear that had once roamed freely throughout the Santa Cruz mountains. It was right that they should die as they'd lived—together.

His hand as heavy as his heart, he removed the note and looked inside. Unexpectedly, tears pooled in his eyes and he was unable to read the carefully scripted words.

Damn it, he didn't want them to be gone.

He wiped the tears from his eyes with the backs of his hands. What made him so sure the note was what he thought? An instant spark of hope ignited and flared like one of the sparklers of his childhood. Maggie could have experienced trouble with her medication again. Maybe they were still at the hospital, both of them traveling in the ambulance. Maybe they wanted him to go there and pick them up.

His hopes lasted as long as it took him to read the opening line in Joe's note.

Dear Eric,

> I'm sorry to involve you in this, but I couldn't figure what else to do. Maggie made the decision months ago to end her life on her own terms. I know I don't have to explain why I would choose to go with her or to tell you that she wasn't aware of my decision. I thought I had everything taken care of, that all I would have to ask you to do was call the coroner.

> But that was when I planned to take Josi with us. I honestly believed she'd be happier that way, but Jason and Susie made me see how wrong I was. The old gal still has a lot of good years ahead of her. I just couldn't bring myself to take them

away. Besides, I know Maggie would never forgive me.

Which brings me to the favor. Could you find a new home for Josi? It's hard as hell not to give you a long list of things to look for in her new owner. At the very least she'll need someone willing to put up with her belief that she's the best thing that could have happened to them. I guess as long as you can find someone who believes it, too, that's enough.

It's hard to say good-bye, even in a letter. Love is a word used so freely that it's lost a lot of its meaning, but it's the only one I know to tell you how Maggie and I came to feel about you and Jason and Susie.

I'm sorry we'll miss the party when your book sells to the movies. Raise a glass to us, would you? Somewhere we'll be doing the same.

Joe

Eric slowly folded the paper and put it in his breast pocket. He would trade everything he had—hell, he would trade everything he could ever hope to have—to experience the kind of love that Joe and Maggie had known.

Pausing to run his hand through his hair and take a deep breath, he went inside.

Josi came running out to meet him, a soft

meowing sound marking her steps. She circled once, wrapping herself tightly around his legs, and then headed back to the bedroom, stopping to look over her shoulder several times, checking to see that he was following. She jumped up on the bed at Joe's and Maggie's feet, looked at Eric, and let out a long, plaintive cry.

"Me too, Josi," he whispered as he took in the sight. "Me too."

Eric spent the rest of the morning answering a police officer's questions. When all the spaces on the forms were completed, the woman officer handed Eric the picture they'd found clasped in Joe's hand and asked what he knew about it. Eric stared at the drawing Jason had made the day after they'd come back from the hospital. It was a picture of him and Jason and Susie standing in front of their house. He was in the middle, Jason and Susie on either side. He and Susie were smiling, Jason had marks on his face that Eric first mistook for freckles and then saw were tears. Jason's hand was raised as if he were waving good-bye.

"Can I have this?" Eric asked.

She thought a minute. "Sure, I don't see why not."

Jason's private expression of grief tipped the emotional balance for Eric. He had to get away. "Do you need me here or is it all right if I go home for a while?" When she hesitated, he added, "I just live across the pathway. The green-and-white house."

"As long as you don't go anywhere else. At least not while we're still here. Just in case I have more questions."

"I'm not planning on going anywhere."

Josi was at the door to greet Eric when he arrived home. She circled his legs so tightly, he couldn't walk. Finally, frustrated, he bent and picked her up, surprised at how readily she settled into his arms.

Taking her with him, he went into the kitchen to make coffee. When he tried to put her down, she planted her paws on his shoulder and held on. Rubbing the side of her head against his chin, she pushed hard enough to move his head sideways. It was obvious she wanted something, but he had no idea what. The food and water he'd put down earlier appeared untouched.

Finally, as if realizing she wasn't getting through to him, she changed her approach, jumped down, ran to the front door, and howled.

Understanding at last, he said in a choked voice, "They're gone, Josi. I know how you feel, but I don't know what to do about it any more than you do."

Later, when the coroner arrived to take Joe and Maggie, Eric went back to the house. He didn't need to be there, but he couldn't stay away. Several neighbors had stopped by, but they stayed only long enough to learn there was nothing to be done and then returned to their own homes. A collective sorrow seemed to fill the air, silencing all but a few oblivious beach visitors.

When everyone was finally gone, a profound silence settled over the house. Eric purposely listened, but not even the sounds of waves or gulls or birds at the feeders broke through the dark curtain that had descended. It was almost as if the house itself had gone into mourning.

As the policewoman left she'd shown Eric the list of people Joe had left to be contacted, asking him if he wanted to take care of it or whether he'd prefer they did. Needing something to do, he told her he would do the calling.

The list included a lawyer for the will, an accountant who would act as executor, a doctor in San Jose who had been as much friend as physician, and a neighbor who would simply want to know. Last was the number for the Neptune Society with a note explaining that arrangements had been made for their cremation, for their ashes to be mixed, and for them to be scattered at sea.

As Eric wandered through the house, he realized Joe had thought of everything. The house had been cleaned, their belongings packed and placed by the front door, the cupboards cleared of food with a note asking that everything be donated to a homeless shelter.

Joe and Maggie had died as they had lived—giving whatever they could to others.

CHAPTER

10

Eric decided to wait until he'd had a week or so to deal with Joe's and Maggie's deaths and to take care of calling the people on Joe's list before he would drive up to Sacramento to tell Jason and Susie. Although he would have liked to wait to tell Julia, too, it just wasn't possible.

The next morning, while Josi sat on his manuscript and stared at him, he tried to reach Julia, first at her house and then at work. Her housekeeper told him she'd left an hour before he called, her assistant told him she wouldn't be in for a couple of days.

He tried working but couldn't concentrate and gave up to go into the kitchen for his fifth cup of coffee that morning. He wound up back at the computer, staring at a blank screen. Josi moved from his desk to the front door, where she stood on her back legs and tapped the handle with her paw.

"You're supposed to be an inside cat," Eric said.

She looked at him and meowed.

He still hadn't decided what to do with her. He'd never owned a cat, not even as a kid, and had no idea what they required beyond food and water and a litter box. The ideal solution would be to give her to the kids, but Shelly had asthma and was allergic to damn near everything on four legs.

Again Josi meowed, this time putting both paws around the handle.

Eric got up and opened the door a crack to see what she would do. She stuck her nose into the opening, and before he knew what was happening, she'd forced her head and then the rest of her body through.

"Josi—come back," he shouted as she took off. He threw open the door to go after her. It didn't seem possible a cat so big could run so fast, but she was out of sight before he made it out onto the porch.

He found her pressed against the corner of Joe and Maggie's front door as if she could gain entry by squeezing through the crack. When he tried to pick her up, she hissed and then let out a low, plaintive howl.

Eric took the key out of his pocket and let her inside.

She raced to the back of the house, going from room to room, her calls becoming increasingly more frantic.

"They're not here," Eric said after she'd come back into the living room, an accusing look in her eyes. "I know I'm not much, but from now on, I'm all you've got." Not until that moment was he aware that he'd made up his mind what he was going to do with her. Despite a truckload of doubts, he would keep her himself.

He heard a car pull into the driveway and looked at his watch. The shelter he'd called about taking the boxes of clothes and food said they wouldn't be able to pick them up until sometime after noon. He went to the window. His stomach did a slow roll when he saw Julia getting out of her car.

He met her at the door. "What are you doing here?" he asked.

She took a step backward, surprised at finding him there. "The police called me."

"God, I'm so sorry you had to find out that way. I was going to come up and tell you in person, but there were some things I had to take care of first."

"Then it's true . . . ?" She looked past him into the house. "They're dead?" Her voice dropped to a whisper. "Both of them?"

She seemed to fold into herself, the shoulders of her Armani suit growing larger as she slowly disappeared inside. "I hoped it was a mistake. I prayed it was."

Thinking she was about to collapse, he brought her into his arms. She held on to him as if she were in free fall and he had the only parachute. Eerily silent sobs shook her thin body.

Eric took her inside. They sat together on

the sofa while he continued to cradle her. As the sobs lessened, she started to move away, but he held on, gently letting her know it was all right to stay. As if his action had granted her whatever mental permission she needed, she relaxed in his arms.

He handed her tissues from the box on the end table. She wiped her eyes and blew her nose and finally asked, "Do you know why they did it?"

"My guess is that Joe couldn't imagine a life without Maggie."

"I don't understand. What made him think—"

"She had cancer. Pretty far advanced, from what I could tell. It was only a matter of time, and I think she wanted the time to be one she chose herself."

"She never even hinted there was something wrong when I saw her in March."

"I'm convinced she didn't know that Joe planned to go with her." Absently he ran his hand along her arm. The soft wool yielded to his touch like fine silk. "What I can't figure out is why she chose here." Eric had struggled with the question since finding them. It was obvious Joe and Maggie cared deeply about Julia. How could they have added to her grief over Ken's death by dying in her house?

She spread a tissue in her lap and methodically began to fold it over and over again until all that was left was a small square. "She probably didn't have anywhere else to go. And I'm sure she knew I would understand." Her hand closed around the tissue. "She thought Joe would be living in their house after she was gone, and she didn't want him to have to remember her dying there."

Eric had witnessed this type of thing between women all his life, and still it never failed to amaze him. He didn't doubt for a moment that Julia was right. What she said made perfect sense. So much sense that it was as if Maggie herself had told Julia, as if she'd left behind an invisible capsule with her thoughts and feelings for her friend to discover.

"I know they thought the world of you," Eric said. He'd meant his words as comfort; instead they triggered fresh tears.

"Oh, God, I don't want them to be gone."

He looked at the suitcases and boxes lined up by the front door, at Josi sitting in the front window, waiting for Joe and Maggie to return, and at the gurney tracks on the carpet. If he felt the room closing in on him, what must it be like for her? He stood and held out his hand. "Let's get out of here."

"Where?"

"My place. I'll fix you lunch."

"I'm not hungry."

"Coffee, then."

She glanced around the living room. "I should—"

"The hell with that," he said. "Whatever 'shoulds' there are that need doing, I'll take care of later. Right now it's you I'm worried about."

She wiped her cheeks with long, tapering fingers, the nails sensibly short and buffed to a shine. "I'm fine."

"Sure you are." He helped her up and guided her toward the door.

"What about Josi?" she asked.

"I'll come back for her later." It was obvious the cat was in the midst of her own mourning process and could not leave until it was convinced Joe and Maggie were really gone.

Julia waited with her arms folded across her chest as Eric locked the door. "Someone has been working in the garden," she said. "The flowers look beautiful."

To protect herself, she had focused on something inconsequential, the way people waiting for life-and-death surgery counted ceiling tiles. "Joe was teaching Jason how to garden."

"Jason?

"My son."

She pressed the flat of her hand to her forehead as if trying to contain a headache. "Oh, of course. Are Jason and his sister still here?"

"They went home two days ago."

"Oh . . ." Julia frowned as if struggling to remember something. "But Maggie and Joe were still alive when they left?"

Eric nodded.

A look of understanding came over her. "Maggie must have planned to die last week on her birthday," she said with conviction. "But she couldn't because the kids were here. How like her. Even at the end she put others ahead of herself."

He dipped his head and reached up to rub a stiff muscle in his neck. He noticed Julia was wearing three-inch-high heels and sheer, glossy nylons. "I was going to suggest we go for a walk on the beach, but you can't go like that." He needed to get away, if only for a little while. "I don't suppose you brought any other clothes."

"The police called just as I was leaving for work." She glanced up at the sound of a passing car. "I came right down. I don't know why. They said it wasn't necessary." In a voice so soft Eric had to strain to hear, she added, "But I couldn't stay away." She stopped and put her hand to her mouth to hold back a sob. "I thought about coming last week for Maggie's birthday, but I had all those damn meetings. . . . Maybe seeing me would have made a difference."

"It wouldn't have," he told her.

"How can you be so sure?" The look she sent begged him to give her an answer she could believe.

"Maggie had cancer, Julia. She was dying. Nothing you could have done or said was going to change that."

"At least I could have seen her one more time," she said, almost choking on her regret.

"And made her leaving twice as hard."

"But what they did was so wrong. They should never have died that way. Life is too precious not to hold on to every minute."

Plainly she'd never seen anyone in the last stages of bone cancer. The pain Maggie had been in was only the beginning. Eventually the narcotics she would have required just to make it through the day would have stolen the Maggie that Joe had known and loved. Her final breath would have been nothing but a formality.

When they reached his house, Eric opened the door and led Julia inside. She stood in the middle of the room, looking lost and unsure what to do with herself.

"Would you prefer tea?" he asked.

She gave him a blank stare.

"Rather than coffee. Or there's soda."

"I don't think I want anything now. Maybe later." She wandered over to the window and stared out at the ocean. "Sometimes it's hard to remember how much I used to look forward to being here."

"You'll feel that way again."

She shook her head. "On the way down I decided that when I leave this time, I'm never coming back. The real estate agent I talked to when I was here in May said I didn't have to come down when the house sold, that everything could be accomplished through the mail."

The thought of never seeing her again hit Eric like an unexpected wave, knocking the wind out of him while it sent him scrambling for his footing. "Is that how you handle all your problems—by running away?"

She turned on him, her face radiating anger. "How dare you say that? You know nothing about me or my problems or how I handle them."

He'd expected a reaction, but nothing like this.

"You have no idea what my life is like," she went on. "Every day I'm trying to do a job people under me are ten times more qualified to do. I'm hanging on by my fingernails because I know if I sell the company, half the people who helped Ken build the business into what it is today will more than likely lose their jobs. I can't do that to them . . . no matter what staying does to me."

Julia turned so that her back was to him, closed her eyes, and bit her lip. But it was too late; the angry words were out, and there was nothing she could do to take them back. What was wrong with her? Why had she attacked Eric when he'd tried so hard to help?

She jumped when she felt him touch her arm. He turned her to face him again. She didn't see the expected anger in his eyes. In its place was something else, something she didn't understand. "I'm sorry," she said. "I guess I needed a target, and you were the only one handy. I know it's not a great excuse, but it's the only one I have."

In a move that seemed to surprise him as much as it did her, he kissed her. When his mouth closed over hers, it wasn't friendship or understanding or tenderness he relayed, but a raw, needful passion. She hesitated at the force of the demand, then responded on a primitive level, realizing instinctively how desperately she wanted what he offered.

For almost a year death and its aftermath had been a constant companion. No matter where she went or what she did, it was there in the memories, the demands, the expectations, the loneliness. Every holiday, every birthday, every dinner invitation with an uneven number of guests, the unending stream of mail that still arrived with Ken's name on it, the board meetings where he was more a presence than she was—they were like chips constantly being removed from the block of marble that was her sanity.

That morning the phone call telling her Joe and Maggie were dead had been the blow that threatened to topple her. And now Eric offered her a chance to taste life again. It simply didn't matter why. Sanity and reason were bit players in this drama.

She put her arms around his neck and pressed her body into his. Deepening the kiss, she opened her mouth and met his tongue with her own, thrusting with a deliberation that left no cloud to hide her intentions. She felt as well as heard the rumble of response that started in his chest and became a moan of primitive desire.

Julia pulled the shirt from Eric's jeans as if it were a barrier between her and freedom. She ran her hands up his tightly muscled back, digging her nails in as she moved down to his waist again. This was not the way she made love, it was not the way she asked to be made love to; it was a cry for help.

Eric reared back, captured her hands, and looked deeply into her eyes. "Is this really what you want?"

"Isn't it what you want?"

"Answer me."

"Yes—it's exactly what I want."

"I don't have any protection."

"I'm willing to take the chance." When he hesitated it felt as if she were lost at sea and that the ship sent to rescue her had sailed by. "But you're not."

Not until that moment did he realize how much he wanted her. "The hell I'm not," he said in a throaty rasp. With a determination of purpose that matched her own, he ran his hands up the front of her silk shell, grabbed the lapels of her jacket, and stripped it from her shoulders. Somewhere in the back of his mind a voice insisted he stop and think about what he was doing, that he consider the possible consequences and behave like the responsible, rational man he'd always been. For the first time in his life, he ignored the voice and gave himself over to instincts he barely recognized.

His breath hot, his mouth demanding, he kissed Julia until she began to move against him in heated insistence. He removed her top and cupped her breasts. As he caressed the lace-covered nipples with his thumbs, she arched her back to return the pressure.

"Take this off," he demanded.

She reached behind her and unhooked the bra while he pulled the straps from her shoulders. Now he held her breast and drew the nipple into his mouth with his tongue. Julia felt the tug all the way to her toes. She put her head back and bit her lip to keep from crying out.

Peripherally she heard the zipper on her skirt open, felt the skirt slide over her hips and thighs and drop to the floor. His fingers slipped into the waistband of her hose and lowered the nylon over her buttocks and then her legs. She looked down where his head lay against her belly as he lifted one foot and then the other out of her heels. It was everything she could do not to press his face closer, to assuage the need that had grown to a mind-numbing intensity.

"Please . . ." The plea rode on an escaped sigh. She was horrified when she realized the word had come from her. She'd never begged for anything and hated that she had so little control over what was happening to her now. Her only hope was that he hadn't heard.

Just as she reached to touch his head, she felt his hand on her inner thigh—and then his breath, hot and full of promise. Something—his tongue, his finger, she couldn't tell—touched the spot warmed by his breath and sent a shock wave throughout her body. Trembling with its impact, she put her hands on his shoulders to keep from falling.

She was hit by another wave and then another, as if she were standing in a storm-driven surf. Her legs began to shake. She leaned into Eric and held on as if he were the only thing keeping her upright. Seconds later the spasms began. They lifted her and spun her around, stealing her last semblance of balance. She cried out at the strength of the feeling.

Just as she was sure she was about to take flight, Eric stood, lifted her into his arms, and took her into the bedroom. She was unprepared for the hunger that resurfaced when he took off his clothes, pinned her beneath him, and entered her. The fury of his movements demanded she respond in kind. And she did, lifting her hips to meet each thrust. Their skin touched, their flesh bruised, and still Julia wanted more. She wrapped her arms and legs around him and moaned his name as if it were the magic word to open the door to the kingdom.

Again waves lapped at her consciousness, each one stealing more of her control until, finally, it was gone. She bit into his shoulder to keep from crying out at the same time he arched his back and buried himself deeper into her still.

Afterward Eric rolled to his side, taking Julia with him, cradling her in the protective circle of his arms. He brushed back her hair where it had come loose from the tightly pinned twist and kissed the dampness from her forehead.

Julia lay still, accepting his tenderness, wondering about the depth of his caring, and fighting to stay afloat in a whirlpool of recrimination.

When several minutes had passed and she still hadn't moved, Eric propped himself up on his elbow and looked at her. "Are you all right?"

CHAPTER

11

"M y God," Julia said in a choked whisper. "What have we done?" She crossed her arms over her breasts and sat up, turning her back to him as if she could erase his presence.

Eric sat up next to her. He'd expected questions—hell, he had a couple of dozen of his own—but not this extreme reaction. "We made love," he said, answering her obviously rhetorical question.

"We had sex," she corrected him.

"Whatever you want to call it, I'm not sorry it happened."

"Well, I am." She reached for his shirt and held it in front on her.

"I take it this kind of thing has never happened to you before?"

She nodded. "You take it right."

He wanted to bring her into his arms to comfort her but knew it wouldn't be welcomed. "How do you feel?"

"Are you crazy?" She tried to comb her hopelessly tangled hair with her fingers. "How do you think I feel?" Burying her face in her hands, she answered her own question. "Cheap—and stupid."

He pulled her hands away and forced her to look at him. After several tense moments of eye contact, he said, "You forgot to add sated."

A flush went from her chest to her neck to her face. "That, too," she admitted softly.

He leaned over, kissed her, and smiled. "You didn't ask me how I feel."

"I can't make light of this."

"I'm not asking you to. I just don't want you to make it into something it wasn't."

"Meaning?"

"I wanted—" He stopped. Why was he holding back? "I *needed* this just as much as you did."

"I know this is hard to believe, but Ken was the only man I ever made love to. . . ." She put her head back and stared up at the ceiling. "Before you."

"What makes you think that would be hard for me to believe?"

"The way I acted."

"If it's confession time, I suppose I should tell you that you're the first woman since Shelly."

She swung around to look at him, forgetting the shirt covering her breasts. "You're kidding."

"Why would I lie about something like that?"

"Because men don't—" She didn't finish.

"Don't what, Julia?"

She shrugged. "They're more free with their— It's easier for them—"

"I can't speak for the other men you know, but I've never thought of sex as a casual contact sport. I may have been as carried away as you were," he said. "But I knew exactly what I was doing. I've wanted to make love to you almost from the first moment I saw you."

"Why?"

"I don't know if I can put it into words."

"You're a writer, Eric."

"There are days I doubt even that."

She listened for something disingenuous in his voice but heard only her own thoughts and feelings being expressed with an honesty that had been beyond her since Ken's death. Her friends, the men and women who had become her advisers at the office, even her own family, refused to listen when she tried to express the fears and doubts that had plagued her this past year.

She took his hand. "I think I'd like that tea now."

He brushed his lips against hers, grabbed his jeans and shirt, and slipped into them before going to the closet to get his robe for her to put on. Pointing to a door, he said, "The bathroom is in there. Use anything you want."

She wound her arms into the plaid flannel, folded the excess material onto itself, and doubled the tie around her waist. "Including the toothbrush?"

"Including the toothbrush," he repeated without hesitation.

Of course she had no intention of using his toothbrush. She'd been baiting him, curious to see what he would say. For some idiotic reason, his answer pleased her. "Oh, by the way . . ."

"Yes?"

"I like your mustache."

Automatically his hand went to his lip. "I was thinking about shaving it off."

"Don't."

He smiled. "All right."

Not until she was alone in the bathroom did she realize the implication behind her request. What possible reason could she have for asking him to keep his mustache? When she left this time, she doubted they would ever see each other again.

Eric put a pot of water on the stove, then fixed a dish of food and water for Josi and took it to her at the other house.

She came running to the door expectantly when he opened it, her disappointment almost palpable when she saw who it was. He lowered himself to his haunches to pet her. She tolerated his touch for a few seconds, then went back to her perch on the windowsill.

The water was boiling when he returned. He took out two mugs, dropped in bags of Earl Grey, and brought them into the living room to steep. He was staring out the window at a red-and-yellow box kite floating across the gray sky when he sensed Julia come into the room.

She didn't say anything as she moved to stand beside him, her silence more comfortable than anxious. He could smell her perfume and knew that the spicy scent would forever remind him of her. He would flash back to this moment and the kaleidoscope of emotions that had changed shape and intensity and color as they tumbled through his mind.

She stood next to him, and Eric was filled with a physical ache spawned by a deep-seated need to be touched, not sexually, but with affection. It seemed an eternity since he'd known the kind of intimacy that came from caring, the reassuring hand, the comforting hug, the kiss that said "I'm here." He longed to have all of that in his life again.

And he wanted more—the inconsequential conversation in front of the fireplace, the cheese and crackers and bottle of wine shared on a hillside, the joke with the missed punch line that was funny because the clumsy telling was so familiar. He wanted to go to a party and look across the room and know there would be someone looking back.

"Can you do that?" Julia asked. "Fly a kite, I mean."

Finally he looked at her. Rather than put her hair up again, she'd left it loose. Her attempts at finger combing had failed, leaving her appearance bed tousled and incredibly sexy, something he knew would appall her had she known.

"Blindfolded and with my hands tied behind my back."

Cocking an eyebrow at him, she said, "I'd like to see that."

He laughed. "So would I."

"I should get dressed."

"Why?"

She plainly hadn't expected the question. "I don't know—I guess I feel a little peculiar standing around in your bathrobe." Actually, surprisingly, she didn't. She was simply giving voice to something her conscience told her she should feel. In reality she felt perfectly comfortable—good, even. The robe was old and had been washed so many times that the flannel was as soft as down against her bare skin. "Besides, you're dressed."

He held out his arms. "It's this or nothing."

"So you're a one robe kind of guy. I like that."

Turning serious, he said, "I'm a one woman kind of guy, too." Seeing how uncomfortable the statement had made her, Eric let it go. He reached for the blue mug and handed it to her.

Julia pinched the excess water out of the teabag and dropped it onto an empty saucer beside Eric's computer before she took a sip. "Perfect." She wrapped her hands around the mug, warming them. "I can't believe how cold it is for July. Has it been like this long?"

"A couple of days." He added his teabag to

hers, then set down his mug. "I'll be right back." When he returned from the bedroom, he handed her a rolled-up pair of socks. "Put these on."

She sat on the sofa, slipped the socks over her feet, and tucked her legs up under her. "What are you going to do with Josi?"

He shook his head. "I'm still working on that. I've considered keeping her myself, but I've never owned a cat. I don't know the first thing about them."

"Me either. I had a goldfish once. The guy I was going with at the time won it for me at a traveling carnival." She curled deeper into the corner of the sofa, as if settling in for a long stay. "The poor thing only lasted a week." Looking up at him over the rim of her mug, she added, "Which, as I recall, was about three days longer than the boyfriend."

Eric sat in the chair opposite her, propping up his bare feet on the weathered wood coffee table. He tried not to stare at Julia or let himself believe she was more than she was—someone who'd come into his life who had no intention of staying. "How did you and Ken meet?"

"At a computer trade show. I was taking care of a booth for a friend. Ken came by and started asking questions, and I stupidly tried to make him think I knew what I was talking about. We were married three months later."

"Maggie said she'd never seen two people more in love."

"She told me that, too." A tear appeared at

the corner of her eye, and she blinked several times before going on. "I know why Joe did what he did," she said softly. "If I weren't such a coward, I would have done the same thing."

The statement horrified Eric. "You can't be serious. Joe was eighty-eight, you're barely past thirty."

"Age has nothing to do with it."

"The hell it doesn't. Do you honestly think Joe would have done the same thing at your age?"

"You have no idea what it's like to face the rest of your life alone."

"Look around you, Julia."

She stared into the dark liquid in her mug. "You have your kids."

"For two days every other week, for as long as it doesn't interfere with one of their friends' birthday parties or a game of soccer or a hot date when they get older."

"But you and Shelly—"

"What? Didn't love each other as much as you and Ken? What if I screwed up the greatest love story of the century with my self-indulgence? Does that mean I can never hope for a second chance?"

"Ken was special."

"And I'm not?" It was as close to revealing how he felt as he could get.

"I didn't mean it that way. What I'm trying to tell you is that we were special together."

Her words knocked the fight out of him. "I

know—Maggie told me." A knock on the door saved him from having to say anything more.

The tow truck had come for Joe and Maggie's car. It was to be taken back to San Jose and sold along with the house.

When Eric returned, Julia was dressed and waiting for him. She'd even fixed her hair in the same tight twist at the back of her head. Their mugs and the spent teabags were gone, and he had a feeling that if he went into the bedroom, he would find the bedspread had been smoothed over and his robe hung up in the closet. Fleetingly he wondered what she'd done with the socks. He used the washing machine for a hamper and was willing to bet she hadn't looked for it there.

"I have to get back, Eric. There's a board meeting tomorrow that I really can't miss."

"I don't need an explanation, Julia. If you feel you have to go, then go."

She adjusted the front of her jacket, smoothing a nonexistent wrinkle. "There's a house-cleaning service in Santa Cruz that I've used several times over the years. I'll call them to come and take care of things. They have a key, so they won't have to bother you for yours."

"That's not necessary. You won't find a speck of dirt anywhere in that house. Joe took care of everything before he died. "

The news left her visibly upset. Stumbling over the words, she asked, "What about the bed?"

"They didn't use your bedroom, Julia." She

hadn't asked, but it was clear she was haunted by the thought. "They died in the back bedroom, the one with the double bed, and they used a plastic sheet."

She flinched and turned away.

He'd intended sparing her the details, but it was obvious she needed to hear them. "After the coroner left I took care of everything that Joe couldn't."

When she looked at him again, her eyes were glistening with unshed tears. "I have to go now."

"I'll walk you out to your car."

She was inside her Mercedes and about to drive away when she stopped and lowered the window. "I'm not sorry I came, Eric. And I'm not sorry about what happened between us."

It was more than he'd expected, less than he'd hoped.

But then he was a patient man—patient and determined. He would give Julia the time she needed, weeks, months, even a year. Three hundred and sixty-five days was nothing put up against a lifetime together.

CHAPTER

12

The next day Eric had just walked in from his third attempt to coax Josi into coming back with him when the telephone rang. It was Julia, and she sounded as if she'd been crying.

"I got a letter from Joe in today's mail," she said.

"I wondered why he didn't leave anything at the house for you."

"I understand now."

"Does it help?"

"I didn't think anything could, but it does. He asked me to forgive them. Can you imagine? He was so afraid I would stop going to the beach house because of the sad memories, and he didn't want that to happen." She paused. "I'm glad now that I didn't tell them I was going to sell the house."

"Maybe you should rethink your plans."

"I have."

"And?"

"I still feel the same. There's nothing for me down there anymore. Everything, everyone I loved, is gone."

Eric should have felt the sting of her words. Instead he thought of a picture he'd once seen of an Alaskan grizzly standing on a rock in the middle of a river, a salmon inches away from its open mouth. In that frozen instant, the salmon would forever shimmer with life. His feelings for Julia were like that.

"Then I guess it's simply a matter of deciding when you'll put it on the market." It was pointless to try to get her to change her mind, so he didn't even try. If he had to pursue her long distance, so be it.

"It may not come to that. Peter said he was interested and that I was to let him know when I'd made up my mind about selling."

"Isn't he supposed to be back soon?" He didn't care when Ken's old best friend, Peter Wylie, was due back; the question was simply a way to keep up his end of the conversation.

"Next week."

"And what about the family that has the house in August?" He needed to know how long he had to work things out with Josi.

"They usually wait until the first weekend to come down and then stay over Labor Day."

"You caught me as I was leaving," he said. He wanted her to feel a sense of loss, too, if only in their conversation.

"I'm sorry, I should have asked if you were busy."

"So, I guess this is it." Damn it. Why the lump in his throat now? "Have a good life, Julia."

She didn't answer him right away. "You've been a terrific friend. I owe you a lot."

Gratitude was not what he wanted from her, but plainly she wasn't ready to give anything else. "You don't owe me anything."

"Will you let me know about the book?"

"Yeah—sure," he said.

"Please? I really do care."

"Give me your address. If it sells, I'll send you a copy." He grabbed a pencil and wrote it down on the back of a manuscript page.

After that there was nothing left for either of them to say except good-bye. Eric hung up knowing he'd taken a risk by creating even more emotional distance between them, but she had to miss him before she asked herself why.

Two days later, Josi met him at the door when he brought her the first of the day's fresh food. Instead of eating, she sat at his feet and looked up at him expectantly.

"What's going on here?" he asked.

She circled his legs, wrapping her tail around his ankle as if it were a fifth appendage, meowed once, sat back down, and stared up at him. "You're going to have to be a little clearer than that," he said. "Remember, I'm not a cat person."

She stayed where she was, never taking her

eyes off him. Finally, figuring it was worth a try, he picked her up. She settled into his arms and let go of a purr that sounded like a drag racer warming up at the line.

Early the next morning, before he'd even had breakfast, Eric was back at the computer with Josi asleep on top of his manuscript when the phone rang.

"When can you come to New York?" It was his agent, Mel. "There are some people I want you to meet."

"What's up?"

"I went ahead and sent the first half of the book out to test the water."

"And?"

"You said it was important that you feel comfortable with your editor—it's time to decide which one it will be. You've got a half dozen to choose from."

"Someone wants to buy the book?" Eric said, incredulous. "But it's not even finished."

"There are a lot of someones, and they obviously had enough to make up their minds that they wanted it."

"They're offering me a contract—and money?" He was having a hard time accepting the concept. "And they're doing this before I've even finished? What if it falls apart at the end? What if it doesn't, but it's not what they expected?" Old doubts mixed with new, and he had trouble telling them apart. "I thought you told me I had to finish the book before anyone would look at it."

"That was before you sent me the first half. Stop worrying, Eric. It really is that good."

"I'm going to have to take your word for it." For the last couple of weeks he was convinced everything he'd written was crap.

"So, when can you get here?"

He looked at the wall where he'd hung the picture that Jason had drawn for Joe and Maggie. "I'll let you know in a couple of days. There's something I have to do here first."

He moved Josi's tail out of the cord's way as he hung up. Staring at her, he said, "And what do I do with you?"

With dry food and plenty of water she'd be all right while he was gone on an overnight trip to Sacramento, but there was no way he could leave her alone while he was in New York. Maybe he could have one of the neighbors come in. But what if they forgot, or what if she thought he wasn't coming back and took off?

Eric laid his arms along the length of his desk, propped his chin on his hands, and did an eye-to-eye with Josi. "I guess I could look for that good, loving home that Joe asked me to find for you."

She yawned and closed her eyes.

"You could at least have the decency to look worried."

That brought a sound Eric could only describe as a feline chuckle. He remembered something he'd read about cats a long time ago—you don't own a cat, they own you. Not until Josi had he understood what that meant.

Before he had time to reconsider, he picked up the phone again and called Julia at home.

She answered on the second ring. "Hello."

"It's Eric."

"Hi. . . ." How was it possible for her to feel excited and wary at the same time? Only days ago they'd said what she'd believed to be their final good-bye. Why the peculiar reaction now?

"I have a favor to ask."

"After all the favors you've done for me this summer I can hardly say no. Ask away." She carried the phone outside to the back deck and curled up in her favorite chair. A hawk circled overhead. She had an insane urge to tell Eric about it, to describe her surroundings, to share with him how the sweeping hills and dense forest brought her the only peace she could find anymore in her increasingly hectic life.

"I have to leave town for a couple of days and I need someone to watch Josi."

He could have given her a hundred guesses what his favor might be and she wouldn't have come close. She felt guilty about hesitating but knew that having Josi there would be a daily reminder that she'd lost Joe and Maggie, too.

God, she was becoming such a coward. "Of course I'll watch her," she said.

"I'll drop her off at your house on the way to the airport if that's all right."

"I'll fax you the directions. That was a fax machine I saw on your desk, wasn't it?"

"That's what they called it at the store. I'm

not even sure the damn thing works." He gave her the number. "You'll be the first one to use it."

"I'm glad you thought to ask me to take care of Josi. I was afraid the way we left things—" The words scraped her throat like emotional sandpaper, leaving it raw and tight. "I guess what I'm trying to say is that I finally figured out that I don't want to lose you as a friend."

"I don't want that to happen, either," he said.

Having Eric as a friend was a milestone of sorts. He was the first she'd made that past year and the only person she knew who hadn't known Ken. It was as if she'd finally taken a step into what was to be her life from then on. The realization left her a little sad. In her mind she'd known she couldn't live in the past, but her heart just hadn't been able to let it go. Now time and circumstance had made the decision for her.

"When should I expect you?" she asked.

"I'm not sure. I haven't booked the flight yet. There's something I have to do before I leave." A long silence followed. "I have to go to Sacramento to see the kids. They still don't know about Joe and Maggie."

Her heart went out to him. It was obvious in everything he said and did how much he loved his children. And now he had to tell them something that was sure to hurt them. "How do you think they'll take it?"

"Susie will do okay. She's still too young to realize what dying is all about. It's Jason who worries me. He figured out what was happening to Maggie when we had to take her to the hospital. I just don't know how I'm going to explain that Joe's gone, too."

"The picture," Julia said, remembering something she hadn't understood at the time. "*That's* what it was about."

"I don't know what you mean."

"The one Jason drew that you have hanging by your computer. I saw it when I was there, but couldn't figure out what it meant. Jason was telling them good-bye."

"Joe had it with him when he died."

"Don't worry about Jason, Eric. He settled up with Joe and Maggie before he left. It's all there in the picture."

"I hope you're right."

"I know I am. You can trust me on this one."

"I'll call when I know what day I'll be coming."

It was one of those lines meant to steer the conversation to a close. "I know it's none of my business, but where are you going? Never mind," she added quickly. "It really is none of my business."

For a second she thought he was going to tell her anyway, and then he said, "I'll see you in a couple of days."

"I'll look forward to it." What was wrong with her? She ended business calls with more warmth.

"Me too."

There was nothing more to say. "Good-bye, Eric."

"Good-bye, Julia."

Eric hung up, sat back in his chair, and stared at the blinking cursor on the computer screen. It was strange how some life-altering moments arrived with a clap of thunder and how some came so softly, it would be easy to miss them if you weren't paying attention.

He looked at Josi. Without the cat to prompt him, he might never have called Julia. And he might have missed hearing the whispered voice that insisted what he felt for her was real. He supposed there had been stranger romantic catalysts than a twenty-pound feline; he just didn't know any.

Eric put off calling Shelly until later that night. When he did reach her, he told her that he would be coming up in the morning to see the kids and why.

"I think Jason knows," she said. "He's been talking about them as if they were already gone. I've never seen him like this, Eric. It's as if he's a wise old man in a little kid's body."

"They were special people, Shelly."

"And it's the first time he's ever lost someone," she added.

He considered reminding her there were degrees of loss and that Jason had gone through far too many of them in his few years, but he knew he would only be taking out his frustration on her.

The trip went better than Eric had dared hope. Shelly had been right: Jason had already accepted his friends' deaths. He didn't even question that Joe was gone, too, as if instinctively understanding Joe and Maggie were a pair and that what happened to one happened to the other. He'd even guessed that Josi would come to him and Susie through their father.

Strung out from the emotional seesaw he'd been riding, Eric decided to drop off Josi when Julia was at work. He wasn't ready to see her yet. His defenses were down, and there was no way he could keep her from discovering how his feelings had changed. He wanted something she wasn't prepared to give. Maybe she never would be. Unlike him, she'd had the perfect relationship. Why would she want to take a chance on someone who'd screwed things up so badly his first time out?

The way he saw it, he had only one sure thing going for him—she loved him, too. She just didn't know it yet.

PART FOUR

AUGUST

CHAPTER

1

Peter Wylie spotted Eric getting off the long-term parking shuttle at the airport just as his rental car shuttle pulled away from the curb. Briefly he wondered if Eric was leaving because Andrew had returned from his around-the-world voyage, then decided it was more likely a vacation or business trip that had them both coming and going at the same time.

He liked Eric; at least he'd thought he did. But running into him again gave Peter a strange, uncomfortable feeling that took him the entire ride to the rental car office to figure out.

It was seeing Eric and Julia together that he hadn't liked. They no more belonged together than rain and baseball. And it wasn't that he expected Julia to spend the rest of her life alone; he just didn't think she should settle for less than she'd had. Which, Peter had to admit, was a damn tall order. There weren't many men like Ken. Truth be told, he couldn't remember ever having met a single one.

Perhaps it was that he resented Eric thinking Julia might be available to him, and there was no mistaking that was what Eric had in mind by bringing her lunch and helping her out around the house.

God, where had that come from?

Could it be he really did expect Julia to spend the rest of her life alone out of loyalty to Ken?

The shuttle pulled to an abrupt stop, bringing an end to Peter's thoughts about Eric and Julia. He took his suitcases from the shelf, went inside, and arranged his rental. A half hour later he was on 101 headed south.

His usual routine was to stop by to see Ken and Julia before going home, the detour being a longtime habit started the year after they moved into their new place in Atherton. The three of them would have dinner and catch up on the happenings during the two months they'd been apart. Peter would spend the night and be off again in the morning.

He'd considered calling Julia to tell her he was going to skip that year, that the three-hour delay at Heathrow and the long flight home had left him feeling like one of the walking wounded. But he was afraid he couldn't pull it off. No matter what excuse he gave she'd know the real reason. He simply didn't want to be there without Ken. Every time he'd tried he'd discovered the memories were too painful, Ken's absence too obvious.

Even when Ken had been there, Peter never

stayed more than a night. He'd tried once, but the thought that Katherine might have arrived at the beach house was like telling a punch-drunk fighter he could go into the ring one more time. After several years Ken and Julia finally stopped trying to talk him into staying longer, accepting his early morning departure as part of the routine. Sustaining the hope that Katherine would already be at the beach house when he arrived, despite the fact that it had never happened—not once—made about as much sense as falling in love with her in the first place.

Peter had never told anyone about Katherine. His feelings were too private, too lacking in hope, to share. He lived in fear she might find out how he felt someday, and that he would never see her again. Even knowing it would be a blessing to have it over and that telling her how he felt was the only way he could put his feelings behind him and get on with his life, he could do nothing to precipitate the confrontation.

In a perverted kind of reasoning, one of the things Peter admired most about Katherine was her dedication to her family. She loved her husband without reservation and was devoted to her two sons.

They were the perfect family.

Peter would have done battle with anyone who tried to break them up.

Why, then, couldn't he stop dreaming about her?

He pulled the car into Julia's long driveway, stopped beside the intercom outside the gate that Ken had had installed after a stalker decided he was the living Satan, and announced his arrival. The excitement in her voice let him know he'd been right to come. She'd lost so much already, he was glad he hadn't taken this small ritual from her, too.

The tree-lined road took him to the top of the mountain and a house generally acknowledged to be one of the most beautiful in an area known for beautiful homes. Nothing had escaped the architect's fanatic attention to detail or Ken's instructions that the house must blend with the land that surrounded it. There were breathtaking views from every window, none of which were obstructed by blinds or curtains.

For all its size, the home was as comfortable and welcoming as the beach house. There wasn't a chair that wasn't used, a cabinet that wasn't functional, or a locked display case.

Julia met him at the door, her arms open wide. "It's so good to see you. How have you been? You look fantastic." Wrapped in his embrace, she leaned back and studied him. "No, you don't. You look like hell. Come inside and let me fix you a drink."

He smiled. "It's good to see you, too."

She led him into the living room. "Scotch?"

"Club soda. I'm afraid if I have anything stronger, you'll have to prop me up for dinner."

She went to the bar and got his drink. "Where are you back from this time?"

"London. I was staying with some friends in Connecticut and they talked me into going over with them. We saw some plays and went to some parties."

She gave him a questioning look as she handed him the cut-crystal glass. "Doesn't sound like your usual idea of fun."

"Diplomatically speaking, the week was pure hell."

Julia sat in the corner of the plush white sofa, kicked off her shoes, and tucked her legs under her. She motioned for Peter to join her. "So tell me what went right this trip. I can't wait to hear how the movers and shakers of the art world are doing."

He stepped out of his shoes, too, sat down next to her, and put his feet up on the coffee table. When Ken and Julia first moved into the house, Peter had been slow to accept the lack of formality. He would sit on the sofa or a chair with his back as straight and rigid as the trunk on one of the pines outside. Finally Julia had told him to loosen up or she'd do it for him.

"They're still buying my pictures," he told her. "My agent told me she's getting a little worried about me becoming too popular."

"But I thought—"

"If you knew her, you'd understand. She couldn't function if she didn't have something to worry about."

Josi sauntered into the room, sat across from them, and gazed out the window at the birds visiting the feeder.

"What's that?" Peter asked, startled.

Julia smiled. "A temporary houseguest. She's only been here a couple of hours and has already settled in."

"When did you take up baby-sitting friends' pets?"

"This is a special case." She put her hand out and called to Josi but was ignored in favor of the birds.

"Josi? Isn't that what Joe and Maggie call their cat?"

"This is their cat," she said.

"What are you doing—" He had a feeling he wasn't going to like what he was about to hear. "Did something happen to them?"

She didn't answer right away. Then, in a voice filled with sorrow, she told him about their mutual, longtime friends.

For Peter, Joe and Maggie were inexorably tied to his friendship with Ken. Their history linked them to a time before his summer trips to avoid the fog and tourists, and Ken's mansion in the Atherton hills. Despite several years of seeing them only a few days each summer, Peter felt a very real and deep sense of loss. Still, he was too much a romantic not to see the poetry and rightness of Joe and Maggie writing for themselves the final chapter to what had been an incredible love story.

"You said Josi was your houseguest. I take it that means you're not keeping her?"

"I would have, but she and Eric seem to have worked things out already."

"Eric Lawson?" The question was automatic. "The guy who's staying in Andrew's house?" He knew exactly which Eric she was talking about. For someone who'd come to the beach to get away from everything and everyone in order to write, Eric Lawson had managed to insinuate himself into the lives of a hell of a lot of people living at the cove.

"He was wonderful to them. I'm not surprised they asked him to take Josi." Julia smiled when Josi looked up at the sound of her name and sauntered over to sit on the sofa next to her. Scratching the cat's upturned chin, she said, "I don't think I've ever known anyone who loved an animal more than Joe and Maggie did this one."

"I take it you went down to visit them while they were at the house."

"Why do you say that?"

"I just assumed it was Joe and Maggie who told you how wonderful he was to them."

She stopped petting Josi to study Peter. "What's going on here? Do you have a problem with Eric?"

"Don't you think it's a little strange the way he's always showing up in people's lives?"

"Like that day you were shot and needed someone to keep you from bleeding to death?"

Agitated, Peter got up and went over to the bar to freshen his club soda. He wished he knew what it was about Eric that bothered him. He seemed okay on the surface, but underneath there was something about him that just wasn't right. "What do you know about Eric that he hasn't told you himself?"

"If you're trying to make a point, Peter, just make it."

"There are a lot of con men out there who specialize in rich widows." At last his suspicions had found form.

She blinked in surprise. "Let me get this straight. What you're saying is that you think Eric befriended Andrew when they were in college because he knew that someday Andrew would live in a house next door to one that Ken bought and that Ken would die of a heart attack at thirty-nine and leave a rich widow who would be an easy con?"

"I know it sounds pretty farfetched when you look at it that way."

"Is there any other way to look at it?"

"Maybe Eric didn't plan what happened," he conceded. "But that doesn't mean he's not taking advantage of an opportunity."

"And you base this on . . . ?"

She had him. "It's a feeling. I can't explain it. It's just there."

"He must have done something to create this feeling," she insisted.

"I'm not imagining this, Julia." He stopped to think and take a drink. "Anyone who saw the way he looked at you would have picked up on what he was thinking."

"And that was. . . ?"

Peter shrugged before saying, "He was like a little kid whose best friend just won tickets to the World Series. There wasn't a dance he wouldn't have done to impress you."

"I seem to remember you saying something along the same lines about me to Ken when we first started dating. You didn't think I was good enough for him, either."

The accusation stung—because she was right. From the minute Ken laid eyes on Julia he was convinced he'd met the love of his life. "Maybe that's the problem," Peter finally, reluctantly admitted. "Maybe I don't think anyone else will ever have the right to look at you that way." He realized that in his mind, Julia would always be Ken's wife. For it to be any other way was tantamount to tearing down the pollution-damaged Taj Mahal to put a stainless-steel building in its place. Ken could not be, should not be, replaced.

The insight was as startling as it was abhorrent. What possible right did he have to expect Julia to spend the rest of her life alone?

"Forget I said anything," he told her. "It's obvious I don't know what I'm talking about."

"Give Eric a chance, Peter. Get to know him when he comes back. I think you'll like him."

He put his elbows on the bar and took a drink as he looked at her. "Is this your way of telling me—"

"Eric and I are friends—nothing more. I'm a long way from letting anyone in my life again."

"Why do you say that?"

Instead of the quick, easy answer he'd expected, Julia took a long time before answering. "You aren't the only one who thinks Ken is irreplaceable. Everyone I know believes it's a given that I'll become the business world's Jackie Kennedy—minus the Onassis mistake, of course. All of them expect I'll have a few discreet affairs eventually, and that would be all right. But to actually marry someone would be unthinkable. How could I settle for second best after I'd had Ken?"

How could he deny something he'd thought himself? "I had no idea . . ."

"No one does." She got up and went over to the window. "The worst part is that I'm as guilty as everyone else. I don't fight being put into their nice tidy little mold because it's the way I see myself." Turning to look at him, she added, "The problem is Eric doesn't play by the rules. Probably because he doesn't know them." She shoved her hands in the pockets of her off white silk pants and smiled disparagingly. "But he's a quick study. I doubt he'll try again."

"Do you want him to?" Peter couldn't believe he was asking the question, let alone fearful of the answer.

"Sometimes—when I'm alone at night and realize that's the way it's likely to be from now on. The rest of the time I make sure I'm too busy to think about anything but work."

"You can't keep that up forever."

"Who says?"

"That's no way to live, Julia."

"What are my choices?"

"Just because Eric isn't the right guy doesn't mean one won't come along." What in the hell was he saying? She knew as well as he did that any man she let take Ken's place would mean she was settling. Not even loneliness could drive her to that.

"Out of curiosity, what makes you think Eric isn't the right guy?" she asked.

"You're kidding, right?"

"Humor me."

"You need someone who could help you run the business. Eric hardly—"

"Why?"

"Why what?"

"Why do I need someone to help me run the business? Are you saying I'm not capable of doing it myself?"

"No, of course not." He couldn't tell if she was spoiling for a fight or really wanted to know how he felt. "But you need someone who'll fit into your world, at least. What does Eric know about the kind of life you live? More important, does he care?"

"I didn't know anything about corporate life when I married Ken."

"But you weren't purposely headed in the opposite direction, either. Eric dropped out, Julia. He walked away from a practice he'd spent ten years building. I think that says a hell of a lot about the kind of person he is."

Her shoulders slumped as if he'd dealt her a defeating blow. "I never wanted Ken's job."

"He'd be really proud to see how you stepped in and took over."

"Don't do that." Hit by a sudden, inexplicable anger, she rocked back on her heels, gritted her teeth, and stared at the ceiling.

Peter watched as a dozen emotions played themselves out on Julia's face. This was a woman he didn't know, tortured and confused by all that had happened to her, her fingertips raw from trying to hang on. Until now she'd presented herself as the regal, grieving widow, accepting her fate with a graciousness that allowed even those closest to her to go on with their own lives without a backward glance.

"I don't know what to say," he told her.

"Neither do I," she said, and smiled.

She'd given him an escape route by smiling. Much to his shame, he took it. "Why don't we go out to eat? How about that place where Ken ordered the curried shrimp that—" God, how could he be so stupid?

"It's all right, Peter," she said in resignation. "I'll call down for a reservation while you put your bags away."

She would forgive him anything. After all, he'd been Ken's best friend. The thought brought little comfort when she realized that he, above everyone else who knew her, should have understood what it was to live without someone to love.

CHAPTER

2

Katherine Williams stood in the driveway of the beach house and directed her youngest son, Paul, as he backed up the station wagon. She motioned for him to stop when the tailgate was in direct line with the front door.

"Why'd you bring all this stuff?" he asked, coming around to help her unload.

She could have reminded him that she'd come earlier than usual that year, or admitted she'd packed more out of habit than reality, but she knew it wasn't the "stuff" Paul was concerned about. He was afraid she might be harboring the hope that he or his brother, Michael, would change their minds and stay the month with her instead of just coming down for the promised Mondays and Tuesdays. "You never know, I might decide to open a homeless shelter while I'm here. Think of all the interesting people I'd meet."

"Homeless people don't live at the beach."

"Open your eyes, Paul. There are homeless

people everywhere." She picked up a bag filled
with groceries and started in the house. Living
in a small town his entire life had left Paul iso-
lated from some of the harsher realities of life,
especially in bigger cities. Although only twenty
miles from Sacramento and in the midst of a
building boom, Woodland would still be considered a small town by anyone's standards.

He grabbed a suitcase and followed. "Not
the kind you'd want to take care of. The homeless people around here are that way because
they want to be."

She heard the trace of concern in his voice
and knew better than to carry the conversation
any farther. Paul was her worrier. He could
never leave her alone at the beach house if he
thought she really needed him to be there with
her. His fledgling sense of freedom required not
only her approval, but her example. Which was
why she'd decided to spend her August precisely the way she had for the past twelve years.
Paul needed whatever routine she could still
provide.

"Don't worry," she said. "I promise I won't
do anything I wouldn't do if you and Michael
were here with me." She dropped her bag on the
kitchen table and automatically looked for a welcoming note from Joe and Maggie. At the same
instant she remembered Julia's phone call telling
her why there would be no note that year.

Katherine's sorrow and sense of loss were
tempered by the knowledge that Joe and Maggie
had died the way they had lived—together. Her

grandparents had expressed the same hope and wound up living in different long-term-care facilities miles apart, rarely even seeing each other the last two years of their lives. Who had the right to judge what Joe and Maggie had done? Certainly not her. Given the same circumstances . . . But then those circumstances no longer applied to her, so it was useless to speculate what she might do.

Paul gave her a mischievous grin. "Does that mean me and Michael can't do anything we wouldn't do if you were home?"

"Don't even start with me." She took a box of cereal out of the bag and put it in the cupboard beside the sink. "Besides, you're going to be so busy while I'm gone you won't have time to get in trouble."

"How much time does it take?"

She put her hands on her hips and looked at him through narrowed, threatening eyes. "You know, I can always change my mind about staying here."

Instead of acting properly intimidated, he laughed. "I love it when you do that, Mom. All my friends do, too."

Katherine tried, but she couldn't keep a smile from forming. She swatted him playfully. "Get out there and finish unloading the car."

"What time is Michael supposed to get here?" he called over his shoulder.

"He said not to look for him before ten. He wanted to stop by Allison's first."

Paul groaned. He came back, his still growing

sixteen-year-old body filling the door frame. "If he does, he's not going to get here until tomorrow. What do you want to bet he calls at midnight and says he's too tired to drive all the way down here tonight?"

"What difference does it make whether he gets here tonight or tomorrow morning?" Michael was nineteen and chafing at the self-imposed restraints that came from living at home two months out of the year and being on his own at college the other ten. That summer, while he'd been with her, she'd tried to give him as much freedom as she could.

The question clearly made Paul uncomfortable. "None, I guess." He headed back to the car before she could answer him.

He was anxious to leave, to get back to his friends and his new job. A sadness spurred by fear threatened to engulf her. She was bone weary of the process of letting go. Damn the psychologists and philosophers and anyone else who preached she should find fulfillment in watching her children proclaim their independence. She wasn't ready for the next step. She loved having her sons around, loved the laughter, the teasing, the introspective moments.

A year ago the four of them had been the happiest, most well-adjusted family in their wide circle of friends—in Brandon's entire congregation. Everyone had said so. They were held up as the standard for the community. The good minister and his wife not only represented the ideal marriage, they were the perfect parents, actually managing to be involved in their children's lives without suffocating them.

Could that really have been only a year ago?

Katherine pulled crackers and canned chili out of the bag and put them away. She'd had no idea what to bring or how many she'd be cooking for, so she'd wound up taking a little of everything out of the cupboards at home. As if afraid to come right out and say they wouldn't be coming down on the promised two days a week, Paul and Michael had acted as if she should automatically expect them. Later, she'd hear one and then the other making plans with friends that would keep them at home.

As much as she wanted her sons' company, she didn't want them there out of a sense of obligation. If she was lonely, it was her problem.

"Hey, what's this—daydreaming on the job?" Paul came in, a bag in each arm.

She forced a smile. "It's the salt air. Does it to me every time."

He dumped the bags on the counter. "You love this place so much, maybe you should think about moving here."

She reeled at how casually the suggestion had rolled off his tongue, as if he'd already accepted that she and Brandon would never get back together. Her experience working with families in their church who were going through divorce was that the children were willing to do whatever necessary to get their parents back together again.

"And where would you live?" she asked.

"I meant after I'm out of school," he answered quickly.

"High school or college?"

He grinned sheepishly. "I suppose it depends on where I get accepted to college."

He was infected with the same disease that had hit every teenager she'd ever known—self-centeredness. To expect anything different would be to expect bees to stop making honey. She folded the bag she'd finished unpacking and put it away. "Don't worry," she said. "I'm not planning to move until you and your brother are—"

"Where is everybody?" Michael called from the living room.

"We're in the kitchen," Katherine called back.

Paul lit up like a new convert at a prayer meeting. "When Mom said you were stopping by Allison's, I figured you wouldn't get here before tomorrow," he said as Michael appeared in the doorway.

"Naw—there's nothing to keep me there," Michael said, grinning.

"Since when?" Katherine asked.

Michael reached around him and pulled Allison into view. "Since I brought her with me."

"Hi, Mrs. Williams," Allison said. "I hope it's all right that I came. Michael wouldn't let me call first."

"Of course it's all right," Katherine said. She had to be careful not to let them see just how "all right" it was. Given the opportunity, she would have had both Michael and Paul invite all of their friends to stay with them—the entire month.

"How long are you staying?" Paul asked.

"Allison doesn't have to be back until Monday," Michael said.

It was impossible to miss the flash of disappointment that crossed Paul's face. "That's great," he said with forced enthusiasm.

"Allison's never been to the boardwalk," Michael said. "I thought we could all go tomorrow."

Katherine gave Michael a private smile. She knew what he was doing and loved him for it. "I think that's a wonderful idea. It's been years since I've been there."

The weekend was almost perfect. They tried, but not even the distraction of having Allison with them was enough to cover Brandon's absence. The most telling moment was Sunday morning when Michael suggested they skip services and go to Big Sur instead and everyone agreed, something unthinkable had Brandon been there with them.

On Monday the three of them lingered over breakfast before heading home. Katherine stood in the driveway and waved good-bye, waiting to turn away until the taillights of Michael's Honda disappeared in the fog. Realizing she would feel more alone than she already did, she was reluctant to go back into the empty house. Instead, with only a long-sleeved shirt to ward off the cold, she slipped out of her shoes and headed for the beach.

When Peter arrived home a half hour later, the first thing he did was drive by Julia's house to look for signs that Katherine and her family had moved in. Finding none, he went about his usual routine of opening up the house and unpacking from his two-month-long trip. As always, a sense of home settled over him like an old, familiar blanket that brought as much comfort as warmth. His homecoming was a reminder why he continued to live in a house too small for his needs, at times irritatingly close to his neighbors, and in constant need of small and large repairs. This was home. More than anywhere else on earth, in this house he was free to be himself; it was a place where he could escape the fawning expectation that came with being the current luminary of the art world, a place where he could work undisturbed.

And it was only a three-minute walk, a look out his kitchen window, an impossible dream away, from Katherine Williams the entire month of August.

Peter opened the blinds in his studio and absently noted the fog showed no sign of lifting that day. After two months of unrelenting sunshine in the six states and two continents he'd visited, the gray provided a nice contrast. He went to his easel and looked at the sketch of an otter and her pup he'd made before leaving. He'd promised to do a watercolor for a charity auction to be held that fall in San Francisco and still hadn't come up with something that satisfied him.

Otters in any form were a cliché in the Monterey Bay Area. Every gift shop, gallery, and drugstore had them printed on cards, etched in glass, cast in bronze, or painted on canvas. Still, for years Peter had wanted to make his own statement about the sleek, spirited creatures, something unsentimental and real that had never been said before.

Ignoring his still packed bags, Peter sat at the easel, put on a fresh sheet of paper, picked up a charcoal pencil, and started sketching. Sometime later he was working on the muted image of an otter swimming through a forest of kelp and was actually pleased with the way it was turning out.

Which was the reason he swore at the knock on his front door that broke his concentration. Normally he wouldn't have answered—he never did when he was working—but this time something compelled him to see who was there.

With a pencil stuck behind his ear, his face fixed in a frown, he yanked open the door.

Katherine took a step backward at the greeting. "I was on my way home . . . I saw your car and thought I'd stop by to say hi. But I can see that you're busy, so I'll come back later."

The practical side of Peter's brain refused to

let him believe she was really there. Wishes
didn't come true, at least not for him. If they
did, Katherine would have been standing on his
doorstep a long time ago. He must have been a
hell of a lot more tired than he thought—so
tired that he'd fallen asleep at his easel and
dreamed her there. It was the only reasonable,
sane explanation.

"Peter?" She moved closer to look at him.
"Are you all right?"

Dear God, she really was there. "I'm fine,"
he said. "You caught me in the middle of something." It wasn't much of an explanation, but it
was the only one that came to mind. Lamely he
added, "I wasn't expecting you until next
Monday."

"I decided to come early this year."

"How are the boys . . . and Brandon?"

She hesitated before answering and then, in
an oddly cheerful voice, said, "Great—they're
all just great. Busy, too. Really busy. I'm not
sure any of them will be spending much time
here this year."

How was it possible that she grew more
beautiful while everyone else simply aged? He
always thought he had every detail memorized,
the way her naturally curly auburn hair became
unwieldy in the fog, the way her eyes turned
soft and seductive when she smiled, the way she
tilted her head when she looked at him. Yet
every year he discovered something new, something that fed his soul during the months he
lived with nothing but her memory.

"I'm sorry, I should have asked you in," he said, embarrassed. He stepped out of the doorway and motioned for her to come inside. When she did, he automatically asked, "Would you like something? Coffee? I think there are some teabags left over from the last time you were here." He never drank it himself, but knew it was her beverage of choice.

"No thanks." She went into the living room and sat in the Morris chair by the fireplace. "The room looks different than it did the last time I was here."

"The chest and rug are new. I went to a charity auction a while back and got caught up in the bidding." Peter started to sit in the chair next to hers, then changed his mind and sat on the sofa several feet away. This was the first time she'd been there without Brandon or one of the kids for him to use as a shield, and the last thing he wanted was for her to pick up on an unguarded expression.

"Are you sure I can't get you something?" he asked.

"Actually, I came by to see if you'd like to have dinner with me tonight. I forgot I was on my own this week and made a chicken casserole big enough to feed the entire neighborhood."

"What happened to the boys?"

She smiled wryly. "They grew up. Michael's going to be heading back to school in a couple of weeks and can't bear the thought of being away from Allison, his girlfriend, for even a day. Paul started a job at the grocery store two weeks ago and promptly fell in love with the owner's daughter. I have a feeling I'll be lucky to see him again the whole time I'm here."

"And Brandon?" Peter asked because it was the thing to do.

"He has a new assistant pastor he's showing the ropes."

She shifted in her chair and looked down at her hands. Just as Peter was beginning to think there might be something wrong, she looked up and gave him a dazzling smile.

"You know Brandon," she said. "He likes to think that his congregation can't get along without him."

"So you'll be here alone . . . the whole month?"

"It looks that way."

Peter was hit with the sudden and sure knowledge that the next month would either be the best or the worst of his life.

CHAPTER

3

Katherine closed the door and leaned her back against it as she listened to Peter's footsteps fade into the night. The dinner had been a success, just what she'd needed to make her forget—if only for a couple of hours—that it was likely her last year at the beach house.

She felt guilty about lying to Peter, even if the lie was by omission. The decision not to tell him that she and Brandon were separated had been an impulse. For months she'd been bombarded with well-meaning advice and endless questions from both friends and acquaintances. She was sick to death of their sad faces and suspicious sidelong glances and didn't want to go through it with Peter, too.

She desperately needed some normalcy in her life—if only for the month she would be there.

Normalcy? What a joke. She hardly knew what it was anymore. Normal had been when they were a family, when Brandon thought her the second best thing that had happened to him, putting her right up there after his calling to be a minister. She'd never minded being second. How could she be jealous of God?

Coming from a family that had reserved Sundays for football, she'd had to work hard to become the perfect minister's wife. What she'd been too young to realize was that it was the process of turning her from "sinner to saint" that intrigued Brandon. Once there, she stopped being a challenge. He began to take her for granted and then found her incredibly boring and easy to dismiss.

Which was precisely the way Brandon had put it the night he asked her to move out of the home the congregation had provided for them. He said once he realized how dangerous his boredom had become, he'd been on his knees night after night for more than a year, praying for guidance. Still, he found himself thinking about women in the congregation the way he should only be thinking about his wife.

He'd told her that he'd fought laying blame, but honesty made him acknowledge that his straying thoughts were her fault. She'd allowed the spark to go out of their marriage. The sex had become perfunctory at best, the companionship no more stimulating than the sex.

The congregation had been wonderfully supportive—to Brandon, at least. While no one actually said anything to her, it was obvious they thought she was the one who'd pushed for the separation. Of course Brandon insisted the decision was mutual, had even said so at the Sunday services when he made the announcement, but no one believed him. It had to be her fault. Reverend Williams didn't have it in him to turn his back on anyone, let alone his own wife.

She'd stopped going to Brandon's church at his request when she moved out of their church-owned house and into a two-bedroom apartment across town. The place was painfully small, but it was all she could afford until she finished the units she needed for her teaching credential and got a job.

That summer, for the first time in their lives, Michael and Paul had shared a bedroom. Neither one liked it, and after a couple of weeks Michael had moved in with his dad. Which was where they were both staying while she was at the beach.

Katherine glanced at the clock on the mantel. It was almost midnight and she wasn't the least bit tired. If she went to bed now, she'd just lie there. If she didn't at least try to sleep, she'd be useless in the morning.

She went to the bookshelf and started reading titles. There was a lot of technothriller stuff. Julia had said Ken was a fan. Katherine wasn't. She'd already read the mysteries, contributing several herself. Margaret Sadler left romances. Katherine picked one up that looked interesting, read the outline, and put it back. Even if it was fiction, she didn't want to read about someone succeeding where she'd failed.

She finally settled on a biography of Doris Duke, a woman so far removed from Katherine's own life that it was like reading fiction. Before curling up on the end of the sofa, she opened the sliding glass door to let in the sounds of the ocean.

Hours later, cold despite the afghan she'd put over her legs, her neck stiff from falling asleep sitting up, Katherine finally went to bed.

Strangely, her last thoughts were of Peter.

She decided he was precisely what she needed while she was there, a friend who neither wanted nor needed anything from her, someone who would share a meal or walk or conversation without prying or giving advice. Someone who had no reason even to think about her eleven months out of the year.

Two days passed before Peter broke down and went to see Katherine. He'd done everything possible to facilitate an "accidental" meeting, watching the beach to see if she was there and walking by her house whenever he could come up with a plausible excuse. The closest he'd come to making contact was a quick wave as she drove past him on her way out.

She came to the door wearing a one-piece navy blue swimsuit, her hair in a single braid down her back, sunglasses propped on top of her head, a towel draped over her arm.

"You just caught me," she said. "I was on

my way down to do some good old-fashioned, decadent sunbathing." She gave him a smile that belonged on a poster in a dentist's office. "I was beginning to think the fog was never going to go away."

Peter wondered fleetingly if there was a special place in hell for men who lusted after preachers' wives. "I have to go into town later and thought you might like to come along—if you're not doing anything, that is."

She smoothed back a strand of hair that had come loose from her braid. "What time?"

The motion exposed the soft curve of the side of her breast and almost stole Peter's composure. "Around noon?" When she didn't answer right away, he added, "It doesn't have to be then, I just thought we could stop for lunch first."

"Noon is fine."

"Great," he said, trying hard to keep the excitement from his voice. "I'll see you then." He turned to leave.

She waited. When he didn't add anything, she asked, "Do you want me to meet you somewhere?"

"What?"

"You said you'd see me. I was wondering where."

"Oh—I'll come by and pick you up."

She started to close the door, then stopped. "What are you doing now?"

He was going to go home and try to get the image of her in that swimming suit out of his head. "Nothing important. Why?"

"I know lying on the beach in the sun isn't all that exciting to someone who lives here year-round, but I thought since it's such a beautiful day you might make this one exception and come with me."

He'd be an idiot to put himself through something like that. "Sure . . . give me a minute to get my suit."

"Do you have a beach towel?"

"No—I don't think I do."

"I'll bring Paul's."

On his way home to get his suit, the same thought rolled through Peter's mind, like the incoming tide, repeatedly pounding its message into his consciousness. He had no more right to sit in the sun with her than he did to haul her off to town with him on some trumped-up excuse to go shopping. It was wrong, and it was stupid.

He was like an alcoholic convinced he could become a social drinker. Night after night he went to bed drunk, only to wake up the next morning positive that this was the day he would succeed in conquering his habit.

At least she didn't ask him to help her apply lotion to her back when they were lying next to each other on the lumpy, hard sand. And he was smart enough not to offer. But then he didn't have to touch her skin to know how soft it was or how it would feel beneath his exploring hands. He was a tactile person; such things were imbedded in his mind. He didn't have to imagine how the almost invisible hairs on her arm would tickle his lip, he knew. Just as he knew the hollow at the base of her throat would smell of flowers and musk.

Katherine rolled to her side, propped her head up with her hand, and studied Peter. "When did you know you wanted to be a painter?"

He shielded his eyes from the sun with his hand and looked up at her. "Always. I can't ever remember not knowing."

"Then when did you know you could make a living at it?"

He smiled. "When someone read the price wrong at the artist's co-op where I was exhibiting and paid ten times my asking price for something I'd always considered a pretty ordinary landscape."

"How do you decide what you're going to paint?"

She'd never asked him about his work before. "It has to interest me . . . or offer a challenge."

"I tried painting once. I was awful."

"I'll bet you weren't as bad as you thought. You probably went into it with unreasonable expectations."

She laughed. "No-o-o-o, I really was awful. But it wasn't a complete waste. I learned to appreciate the people with real talent." Her eyes lit up. "Like you."

"But you've never seen anything of mine."

"Oh, yes, I have. At a gallery in San Francisco. You wouldn't believe the fool I made out of myself. Brandon almost died when I went around telling everyone I knew the artist."

"What would you say if I asked you to pose for me?" he asked, careful to keep it casual.

"Because I interest you, or I offer a challenge?"

"Both."

"I don't know. It seems so narcissistic."

"Not when I do it."

"Don't tell me you're going through a Picasso cubist period."

This time it was his turn to laugh. "Nothing so dramatic. I just paint what I see, warts and all."

"I don't have warts. Just a ton of freckles."

"Well?" He closed his eyes to hide how much her answer meant to him.

"I can't imagine why you'd want to paint someone like me. But if you're serious, I guess it would be okay."

Now he could look at her. "I can start tomorrow. Is that all right with you?"

"Tomorrow's fine. Paul was supposed to come down, but he had his hours changed at the grocery store and has to work."

"What about Brandon?"

"He's not coming, either," she said cryptically.

Peter felt guilty at the incredible rush of pleasure that came with knowing he would have Katherine all to himself for the next few days. If Julia did decide to sell her house, even if he bought it from her and offered to continue the rental agreement with Katherine and her family, there was no guarantee they would take him up on it.

"Is it hard?" she asked. "Sitting still all that time, I mean."

"I don't know," he admitted. "I've never done it."

"What happens if I move?"

"Everything is ruined and I have to start over."

Her eyes widened. "I don't know if I can—"

Laughing, he put his hand on her arm. "I promise you it will be painless."

Damn. He shouldn't have touched her. The ache in his gut was like a giant band, squeezing and turning at the same time. "I'm going swimming," he announced. "Want to come?" *Please say no,* he begged silently. He desperately needed to be alone for a while.

She glanced at her watch. "I think I'll go up and get ready."

He nodded. "I'll see you later, then."

Peter didn't bother taking time to adjust to the chilly water but walked straight in and dove into an incoming wave. Out of the corner of his eye he saw that Katherine stayed for several minutes and watched him swim. He moved through the swells parallel to the shore until his body was numb from the cold. Then he came in.

If only there was a way his mind could be numbed as easily.

CHAPTER

4

Katherine had on a blue-and-yellow sundress, a size too big, with straps that slid off her shoulders whenever she adjusted the napkin on her lap. Peter didn't know whether he was more tempted to reach over to slip the strap back into place or leave it alone, especially when she leaned forward to take another bite of spinach salad and he saw far more than he had any right to see.

She caught him looking.

"I had no idea I'd lost so much weight. I hope the other dresses I brought fit a little better." She pulled up the strap and squared her shoulders. "I've been living in jeans and shorts this summer."

"Nothing special going on at church lately, huh?" It was a safe, if inane question. He shifted in his seat to give the man next to him room to move his chair out of the sun. The sidewalk café on Pacific Avenue where they'd gone for lunch was more crowded than he liked, but it was open

and casual and less like a "date" than if they'd
gone to one of his favorite, more formal restaurants.

"I think this is the first time I've had a
dress on since—" She stopped, as if unsure she
wanted him to hear what she'd been about to
say next. "It's been really hot in the valley.
When I left we were only a couple of days away
from the triple digit record set in the eighties."

He'd quit going to church before he gradu-
ated high school but found it curious that things
had changed so much, the minister's wife could
either stay home from services for months at a
time or attend wearing jeans or shorts. Because
he didn't know what to say, Peter broke off a
piece of the crusty sourdough bread that had
come with his salad and concentrated on spread-
ing the cold butter with a plastic knife.

Finally, to break the awkward silence, he
said, "Going for that kind of record, I can see
why you decided to come down here after all."

"After all?" she asked warily. "I'm not sure
I understand what you mean."

"By yourself—without Brandon and the
boys." Brandon had never spent the entire
month with her at the beach house. At the most
he would come down on Monday, stay a few
days, and then go back home to work on his
sermon for the following Sunday. But the kids
had always come with her, usually accompanied
by a carload of their friends.

Katherine plucked a sunflower seed out of
her salad and surreptitiously tossed it to the

pigeon wandering between the tables. When she glanced up and saw him watching her, she said, "I know I shouldn't do that."

"But . . . ?" he prompted.

"They're such amazing creatures—the ultimate urban survivors, living on dropped scraps of food and spilled water."

He sat back in his chair and stared at her. "You're serious."

She actually blushed, the exposed skin above her sundress turning a deep red. "Don't worry, I know how crazy it sounds. Which is probably why I've never talked about it before."

In the back of his mind he'd harbored a foolish hope that getting to know Katherine better would reveal flaws and that she would become ordinary, freeing him from her spell. Instead, even in the ordinary, she was special. "You're not alone, you know. There are people all over the world who feel the way you do. They save scraps of food all week to feed their favorite flocks of pigeons."

She smiled. "I'm surprised someone hasn't set up a tour."

"How do you know they haven't?"

"Because there are no tour buses outside my apartment."

She lived in an apartment? Somehow Peter had gotten the impression Brandon's church provided a much better living. As a matter of fact, he could swear he'd heard her mention a house before. This, too, he didn't pursue. "Where do you suppose they went after the earthquake?"

"You know, I wonder about things like that, too." She sat back in her chair and stared at the buildings lining both sides of the street. "Looking at this place now, it's hard to believe what a mess it was just a few years ago."

"It was sad to see all those old buildings have to come down."

"Were you home when the quake hit?"

It was a standard California question, one that fell in the category of what someone was doing or where they were when Kennedy or King or Lennon was shot, noteworthy because it gave total strangers a common experience. "I was just outside San Jose, on my way back from a gallery showing in San Francisco. I spent the next five hours listening to reports on the car radio, and the way they made it sound, everything here was leveled."

"It took you five hours to travel thirty-five miles?"

"Only because I decided to take a shortcut."

"Sounds like something I would do. Did you have a lot of damage?"

"A couple of broken windows and cracked walls, but nothing like what happened down here. The houses around the cove really got off pretty easy."

"Michael was thinking about going to San Jose State, but I talked him out of it. Of course I didn't tell him the real reason—he would have told me I was nuts. He thinks real Californians aren't bothered by earthquakes, they just take them in stride. So I convinced him he should go far enough away that he really had a sense of leaving home." She chuckled. "So what did he do? He picked a school in Kansas, right in the middle of tornado alley."

"How does he like college?"

Her face lit up, her eyes filled with wonder and pride, the way they always did when she talked about one of her sons. "I think he felt a little lost in the beginning, but he loves it now. Especially since he decided on his major."

"Is he still considering going into the ministry?"

She took a drink of iced tea before answering. "That was Brandon's idea. Thank goodness Michael had sense enough to go his own way."

"Not suited for the job, huh?"

"No more than I would be." She tossed another seed to the pigeon. This time the action brought a reproving frown from the woman seated at the table next to theirs.

"I would have thought you'd be the perfect candidate for the job."

She blinked in surprise. "My goodness—why?"

He had to be careful how he answered, separating his personal feelings from those of a friend. "You like people—and you're good with them. Your beliefs are as natural as your hair." Way too personal. "What I mean is, you show who you are by what you do rather than what you say. Your parishioners would learn from you by example, not rhetoric."

"How long has it been since you've been inside a church, Peter?"

"A long, long time," he admitted. He'd never tried to hide from her who he was or what he believed or didn't believe.

"It's the rhetoric that brings people in." She paused and smiled. "I'm not sure I'd want anything to do with a congregation that showed up every Sunday just to sit around and watch the preacher be nice."

If she were the preacher, he'd be there every week without fail. He put his hands on his knees and purposely looked her in the eye. "Ready?"

She nodded. "Where to now?"

"The art store. I need to pick up a couple of brushes for the masterpiece I'm starting tomorrow."

It took a second for the "masterpiece" part to sink in. When it did, Katherine blushed. "Does that mean you're going to use fresh paper, too?"

"Absolutely."

When she came around the table he started to reach for her arm but pulled back at the last second. There was no such thing as casual contact for him anymore. He wanted her so badly, he carried the hunger around with him like a backpack that grew heavier every day.

"Would you mind if I went in here first?" She indicated a store called Book Shop Santa Cruz. "I've run out of things to read at home."

"No, go ahead. I'll join you in a couple of minutes. There's something I want to do first."

He found her in the popular fiction aisle.

She was reading the inside teaser of a paperback. As soon as he saw her he knew he'd made a mistake. He should never have given in to the impulse that had sent him to the flower kiosk outside the bookstore. He had no right to buy her flowers, no matter what trumped-up excuse he gave. He started to back away, but she looked up and saw him before he could drop his offering into the garbage can beside the register.

She closed the book, added it to another one she had tucked in her arm, and came toward him. "As soon as I pay for these we can go."

He wandered over to look at an art book on the bargain table while he waited. She'd seen the flowers, so he had no choice but to give them to her. The trick would be to make it look casual, as if it held no more significance than opening a door or holding a chair.

"I am so in awe of people with talent," she said, looking over his shoulder. "Any kind of talent. My next life I think I'll come back as an actor—no, a singer."

"You believe in reincarnation?"

"Not really." She moved to stand next to him. "It's just my way of complaining about my abysmal lack of any but the most ordinary skills."

"What are you talking about? You're the most extraordinary woman I know."

Obviously believing he was teasing her, she made a gracious little bow. "And you're by far the most gallant man of my acquaintance."

Could she really be so blind to her own per-

sonality, to her ability to make people feel good
about themselves because she always saw the
good in them? Was it possible Brandon didn't
realize he was the luckiest man on earth?

Because he was beginning to feel a little silly
hanging on to the dahlias, he handed them to
Katherine.

"These are for me?"

"They match your dress."

She stared at the bright yellow blooms as if
she expected them to disappear at any moment.
"No one has ever given me flowers."

"Never?" She had to mean as a casual gift.

"Not even when I was in the hospital having my babies. Brandon doesn't believe in it."
She brought the flowers to her nose and took a
deep breath. "I mean, he *really* doesn't believe
in it. When Michael and Paul were born he
asked everyone to make donations to the
church's relief association in their names.

"One of the first things he did when he
became pastor at the church"—she smelled the
flowers again—"was to let everyone know how
he felt. We lost a couple of members who were
florists, but the rest of the congregation seemed
to go along with his feelings, especially when he
told them that he felt it bordered on sinful to
spend money on something that would last less
than a week when it could be used to feed a
third world family for a month. You would
have thought the donations to the relief workers
would have gone up, but they didn't."

"How do you feel?" he asked.

She smiled with guilty pleasure. "Special . . . very, very special."

It was such a simple thing. He wondered if Brandon had any idea what his intractable stand had cost him.

CHAPTER

5

Katherine stood in front of the mirrored closet doors and stared at herself. Peter had said to wear something simple, that he was painting her, not her clothes. In the past half hour she'd tried on all four of the dresses she'd packed and wasn't happy with any of them. How could she have lost so much weight without being aware of it?

Had Brandon been right about her getting chunky? Was that why he'd suddenly found her so unattractive?

Agreeing to pose had been an impulse, made without any real thought to the consequences. What if Peter decided to sell the painting and no one wanted to buy it because she was so uninteresting? Models were supposed to be beautiful, or at least distinctive.

She was ordinary at best. Or, if Brandon was to be believed, deadly boring. For some reason Peter didn't see that side of her. Probably because he wasn't around her enough. Even box turtles were interesting at first glance, but no one wanted to be with them all the time.

What if the painting did sell and everyone wanted to know who she was? Worse yet, what if it created the kind of speculation that had surrounded Andrew Wyeth and his pictures of Helga? She'd never be able to explain something like that to Brandon's satisfaction.

Good grief, what kind of paranoid idiot was she turning into? Was she so desperate for a little excitement in her life that she had to make it up?

She sat on the corner of the bed. How had she gone from the girl invited to every party in high school to the woman whose only friends were at the church her husband had asked her to stop attending?

Maybe she was the one-dimensional woman Brandon would have her believe. Sex with him had never been the breathless kind portrayed in books and movies. The times she'd suggested they try something a little different, like making love in the middle of the day or someplace besides the bed, he'd questioned how she'd come up with the idea. The discussion that followed usually killed any desire. With some things she was a slow learner. Sadly, this was one of them. It took several attempts over the years before she finally got it through her head that Brandon liked his sex as predictable as his life.

Or so she'd thought.

If she'd only tried a little harder to discover what he needed, she wouldn't be facing a meeting with a divorce lawyer when she got home. At least that was Brandon's take on their marriage. She didn't know what to think. She was still too stunned by it all. She likened it to going to the doctor to have a wart removed and being told she had six months to live.

She glanced at the clock beside the bed. She had five minutes to make up her mind about what to wear and get out of there.

Peter knew exactly how he wanted to paint Katherine. Over the years he'd sketched her a hundred times from memory, most often with the sea as background. He'd even allowed three of the finished pieces to be displayed in galleries, but always with SOLD signs attached. They were figure pieces rather than portraits, portraying her at a distance, some in repose, others interacting with her family.

In the beginning he'd hoped the exercise would prove cathartic, that he could work her out of his system by using her over and over again as a subject, confident he would grow tired after a while and move on to something or someone else. Only it never happened.

The years of self-inflicted agony finally settled into an acceptance that brought its own form of peace. He loved her. He always would. The sun would rise and set every day, the tide would come in and go out, the cove would have fog in summer, and he would love Katherine—simple, indisputable, inevitable.

She arrived wearing a cerulean blue knit dress that had a round neck and short sleeves. It was fitted to just below her breasts, then fell loose in a soft drape to her ankles. She held out her arms and made a slow circle. "Is it okay?"

"Perfect," he said, his heart in his throat. He'd let himself imagine her opening her arms to him.

"I have a favor to ask."

"Anything." He smiled to lessen the passion of his answer.

"Don't tell the boys I did this. Having your picture painted is something girlfriends do, not moms."

"What about Brandon?"

She hesitated. "I don't think the subject will come up."

"But if it does?"

"Then he would have to be told the truth."

What had he expected, that she would keep a secret that involved him from her own husband? "Would it upset him to know you were posing for me?"

She stuffed her hands in the pockets of her skirt. "Don't worry about it, Peter. Brandon won't be here this summer."

It was inconceivable to him that Brandon could be away from her for a day, let alone an entire month. "Can I get you something before we start?"

"I'd like a glass of water—but I can get it myself." She motioned toward the other end of the house. "It's been so long. . . . Is the kitchen this way?"

"I'll get it for you," he said.

"Please, let me. It makes me uncomfortable to have people wait on me."

When he sent her a questioning look, she shrugged as if the statement were a mystery to her, too. "Can I get you something while I'm there?"

"No thanks. I just had a cup of coffee." He watched her leave, thinking how easily she'd made herself comfortable in his home. It was as if she'd always been there . . . as if she belonged.

He shook himself mentally, releasing his mind from its flight into fanciful thinking. Falling in love with Katherine had been an accident, like getting caught in a riptide. Letting himself imagine things that weren't there, things that could never be, made about as much sense as a swimmer caught in that riptide adding lead weights to his ankles.

Katherine returned with her glass of water. "Where do you want me?"

"On the window seat. I thought we'd try several poses, one profile with you looking out to sea, a couple full face, and maybe one or two looking into the room as if you were talking to someone."

She sat on the loose cushions and naturally brought one leg up to tuck under the other.

"That's good," he said, liking that she showed none of the stiffness he'd expected.

Propping her arm on the oak sill, and her hand on the hidden side of her face, she did as he'd suggested and looked out the mullioned window. The early afternoon sun had just begun its daily invasion into the living room, its rays no farther along than her lap.

The contrast of light and shadow would change throughout the afternoon, giving Peter constantly changing perspectives. To capture the ones he wanted he would have to do quick sketches, going back later to fill in detail. Now it was the light that mattered most, the way it would move across her body, how it would illuminate her hair, how it would give texture to her skin.

His watercolor style was as detailed as if it were done in oils. Using dry brush over washes, gouache paint for small highlights, wax resist, and masking fluid to give him freedom to experiment had offended more than a few purist critics over the years. But he'd never painted to please critics, only himself.

Peter always worked from sketches, never photographs, believing photographs froze movement. Often his sketches would have lengthy notes written on the back to remind him of mood and location.

He would need no reminder today.

Katherine turned to look at him. "Oh—you're working already." She jerked her head back. "I was just going to tell you about the bird on your fence."

"What about it?"

She tried to talk without moving her mouth. "It can wait."

He smiled. "Put your hand in your lap."

She did. "Like this?"

"With the palm facing up." He studied the effect for several seconds before saying, "Don't move. I'll be right back."

Peter went outside and plucked an orange nasturtium. He arranged it in her hand. "You'll never be without a flower again."

Her expression changed, her eyes misty with thought, her mind a place he could not go.

Two hours passed before the yellow light became too harsh to continue. He'd have to wait for the burnt sienna, raw umber, and yellow ocher of sunset to get what he wanted next. "Ready for a break?" he said.

She stretched like a cat waking up from a nap by the fire. "It wasn't near as hard as I thought it would be."

"I'm glad." He laid the sketch he'd been working on facedown on the table with the others. "Maybe you won't mind another session tonight?"

She picked up her glass of water, untouched until then. "What will you do now?"

"With the sketches?"

"With yourself. Are you hungry? I could fix us a snack."

Was that the role she'd assumed in life, the

nurturing provider? "Why don't I fix us something?"

"I don't mind. That way you can relax for a while. You're the one who's done all the work."

Without thinking what he was doing, Peter took her hand, led her into the kitchen, and made her sit at the table while he took a small round of Gouda cheese and grapes out of the refrigerator. He'd broken his rule about touching her. If she were anyone else, taking her hand would have been a casual, even a natural thing to do; but with Katherine it wasn't something he would forget. The feel of her palm resting in his only intensified his hunger for more. Had it been his right to do so, he would have brought her hand up and pressed his lips to the gently curving lifeline that, if the fates had been kinder, would have included him.

He took a cutting board out of a drawer to slice the cheese. "Tell me about the bird."

"It was fairly small—a little bigger than a finch—and had a red head and yellow body."

"Black wings and tail?"

"It was facing me so I couldn't see the tail, but the wings looked black."

"Sounds like a western tanager, but then no one's ever accused me of being an expert. There's a bird book on the shelf in the living room—bottom left-hand side—if you'd like to look it up."

She got up, but instead of leaving, came to stand next to him, picked up the grapes, and took them to the sink to wash. "Sorry, I'm just not used to being waited on."

"How about a glass of wine?" he asked.

"I think I'd like a beer instead, if you have it."

He started for the refrigerator, then caught himself. "It's in there. Glasses are in the freezer."

"Very good, Peter." She patted his arm as she passed.

"Why don't you get one for me, too?"

Now she smiled. "Even better."

"While you're at it, there's some laundry out back. . . ."

That brought a laugh. "Don't push it."

She had a beautiful laugh, spontaneous and free, not the forced, polite kind that left you feeling empty, but the kind that left you eager to hear it again.

She tipped the glass and poured the beer down the side. "Have you always lived alone?"

He was still trying to figure out where the question had come from when she went on.

"Forget I asked that. It's none of my business." She took out a clean dish towel to dry the grapes. "It's just I've never seen you with anyone. You're such a special person, it seems a shame you don't have someone special to share your life with."

How in the hell was he supposed to answer that? "I guess I haven't met the right person yet."

"There's never been"—she struggled for the word—"a significant other?"

Peter's first inclination was to put the strange phrase off to her background, and then it dawned on him what she was really saying.

She thought he was gay.

CHAPTER

6

Peter stalled for time. It was as if the clouds had parted and finally, after all the years of loving Katherine, he understood why she'd allowed him into her life, why she went places with him, why she was in his house now. It wasn't that she was naive or so innocent that she didn't understand how rare pure friendship was between a man and a woman, she trusted him, felt safe with him, because she thought he couldn't possibly be interested in her as a woman.

What a joke.

But was it on her or him?

If he told her the truth, would she pull away? Would it be the end to their friendship? Was he brave enough to risk it?

"I was married once," he said, opting for honesty. "For five years. She wanted children and a man who could give her the financial stability to stay home and raise them. At the time I was working at night doing dead-end jobs in order to leave the days free to paint. We saw each other on weekends and sometimes not even then.

"I've had a couple of relationships since then," he went on, feeling foolish for the need to explain himself, yet unable to stop. "One of them pretty serious, but she was from San Francisco and couldn't take living down here with us provincial types. I still see her when I go to the city, but we're just friends."

"Do you ever get lonely?"

There was something about the way she asked the question that puzzled him, as if it were more general than personal. "I used to. I got over it when I realized being alone is better than being with someone who is just filling space."

She flinched. "I would hate knowing that's how someone thought about me."

"That's not possible, Katherine. You're—" Jesus, what was he doing? "You and Brandon are perfect for each other. Anyone can see that."

"So I've been told." She took a long drink of beer. "I can't believe how thirsty I am."

He took a box of crackers out of the cupboard, dumped them on a plate, and added the cheese and grapes. "Why don't we take this outside?"

She shifted her weight from one foot to the other and back again. "You know, I really think I should go home. I'm sure you have work to do, and you certainly don't need me hanging around getting in your way."

He put the plate back on the counter and

shoved his hands in his pockets. It was the only way he could keep from reaching for her. He'd gambled and lost. Now that she knew he wasn't gay, she figured he wasn't safe to be around anymore. Preachers' wives didn't spend their vacations with other men, no matter how seemingly innocent or platonic the relationship.

"I don't have anything else to do today," he said. "And you aren't in my way."

She put her glass in the sink. "I'm sure you'd find something if I weren't here."

Peter's frustration was like a pill caught in his throat that he could do nothing to dislodge. "Will you come back later so I can finish the sketches?"

"Yes, of course. What time?"

"A little after six?"

"I'll be here." She moved to leave. "Thanks for the beer."

"You're welcome." He followed her to the front door, then watched from the window as she took the path that ran in front of the house next door and eventually to her own, trying desperately to hold on to a sliver of hope that once she had time to get used to him the way he really was, it wouldn't make a difference.

Katherine dug her key out of her pocket and made several unsuccessful stabs at the lock before letting herself inside.

How could she have been so stupid? What

was that old cliché? Those who assume make asses out of you and me? Well, she'd certainly done that. Her only hope was that he hadn't caught on.

Yeah, right, and fish could fly and politicians didn't cheat on their wives.

How was she ever going to go back there and face him? Maybe she could get sick. Nothing serious, just a little stomachache, even a headache would do.

She let out a groan and dropped onto the sofa. What must he think of her? He had to wonder about the dinner invitation, especially with her being there alone. Thank goodness she hadn't told him about Brandon.

She came forward and buried her face in her hands. The worst part, the part she didn't even want to admit to herself, was how much she enjoyed being with Peter. But she couldn't let it go on the way it had. She was married—at least she was for the next couple of months. There were appearances to keep up, proprieties to maintain. Brandon would be devastated if word got back to the congregation that she was seen in the company of another man.

She sounded pathetic, even to herself. She was like a dog left out in the rain, waiting for someone to come to the door and love it enough to let it inside.

Fortunately the phone rang before she'd sunk into a hole of self-recrimination so deep that she couldn't climb out.

It was Michael. "Hey, Mom—how's it goin'?"

"Great. The weather has been beautiful, perfect for surfing. You really ought to try to get down for a couple of days before you have to leave." *Please*, she begged mentally. She needed a distraction, any distraction.

"That's what I called about. It doesn't look as if I'm going to be able to make it down to see you again this summer. The guy I was supposed to room with this year had to drop out of school, so I'm going back early to see if I can find someone else. It's either that or get stuck with someone I don't know."

She had to swallow her disappointment before she could ask, "When are you leaving?"

"Tomorrow."

"So soon? You still have—" She made herself take a deep breath and count to five. "What time?"

"Six-thirty—in the morning. It was the only flight I could get."

"How long have you known?"

"A couple of days."

"I wish you would have called me. I promised Peter I'd help him with something this evening. I won't be able to get out of here until nine, maybe later."

"You don't have to come up. Dad said he'd take me to the airport."

"But I want to see you before you go."

"Come on, Mom. We said good-bye when I was down there last week. You don't need to come all the way up here to say it again."

"You wouldn't care if I wasn't there?"

"I feel like an idiot when people are making a big fuss over me at the airport. It's not like I'm moving away forever. I'll be back for Thanksgiving."

He'd given her logic when she'd wanted emotion. But then she'd led with her chin; she had no right to complain about getting hit. "I love you."

"I love you, too."

"Call me when you're settled in."

"I will."

When she hung up it was with the discomforting feeling that she'd been given a preview of her life to come. In the background of her mind she could hear the ties that bound Michael to his family making a *ping*ing sound as they snapped one by one. But then what could she expect? The nuclear family he'd known all his life was no more.

She couldn't shake the feeling she'd made a mistake coming to the beach house that summer. What had started out a simple need to get away for a while had turned into an abandonment of her family. If Michael had given her the slightest encouragement, she would have gone no matter how inconvenient the trip.

Only knowing he'd meant what he'd said about not wanting anyone at the airport kept her from leaving.

It was hard, this letting-go stuff.

She looked at the clock and wondered if Peter would mind if she came a little early. She needed to be with someone. No, it was more than that. She wanted to be with Peter. He was her friend, and she was in sore need of a friend right now.

Again she said a prayer of thanks that she hadn't told him she and Brandon were separated. It could have ruined everything.

CHAPTER

7

The closer Eric came to Julia's house, the more he realized how anxious he was to see her. He'd been too busy in New York to focus on her the way he had before leaving. What thoughts had broken through the endless meetings and need for immediate decisions had been the kind that left him hungry to share with her all that was happening to him. The feeling was remarkable, one he'd never experienced before. And it was the one thing, he now recognized, that had fatally hurt his and Shelly's relationship.

He'd changed. His trial by fire had turned him into a man who could finally understand and appreciate the happiness that came with real intimacy. He'd never opened himself up to Shelly, never talked about the day-to-day problems or small joys that invariably made him the person he was. Worst of all, he didn't listen when she tried to share the person she was becoming with him. They'd begun their marriage friends and ended strangers.

Now, far more than wanting to tell Julia about his trip, there was a deep-seated need to do so. He was still reeling from the knowledge someone actually wanted to publish his book. The price they were willing to pay was something else. His agent had assured him that there was sound logic behind the insanely inflated offer. By giving him a quarter million more than anyone had ever received for a first novel, the story would be carried by all the print and television media, both when it was announced and when the book actually came out. To try to buy that amount of publicity would cost far more than the advance.

The terrifying part came with the scrutiny the book was sure to come under. His agent and editor were confident the reports would be positive. They insisted the story and the writing were good enough to withstand the harshest critic. But Eric had seen what happened to popular fiction when it was put under the magnifying glass of literary critics. There wasn't enough reassurance on the entire island of Manhattan to convince him the same thing wouldn't happen to him.

What he hadn't decided was whether he cared. The only people who mattered to him were the ones who would put out the twenty-five dollars to buy the book. That was a hell of a lot of money when put up against the cost of milk and bread—though not so much when compared to a night out at a mediocre movie.

Self-doubt was something new to him. He

didn't care for the way it made him feel. Realizing how little control he would have over his book once it was turned over to the publisher had given him real pause. The problem with jumping in the pool with a dive that turned into a belly flop was how hard it would be to go in again without everyone looking.

He wasn't even sure he had another book in him. He'd been so wrapped up with the one he was working on, he hadn't thought that far ahead.

Eric pulled into the driveway at Julia's and stopped beside the intercom to announce his arrival. Filled with an incessant hunger to see her again, he'd considered killing time until she would be home from work but abandoned the idea. He was too tired to wait around without some guarantee she didn't have a meeting or something else that would keep her in the city that night.

Then, as if the long outgoing tide had finally turned in his favor, Julia answered the intercom herself.

"It's me—Eric," he said. "I'm here to get Josi."

"I had a feeling you were coming today." The buzzer sounded and the gate swung open. "We'll be at the door waiting for you."

Could that be the reason she'd stayed home? The thought was like a tossed-back shot of whiskey, stealing his breath and warming his insides at the same time.

He spotted her the instant he rounded the

final curve. She had on jeans and a white shirt with the sleeves rolled up to the elbows. The denim material hugged her hips and thighs as if it had been created with just that in mind. She had an incredible body, her skin a natural, unblemished bronze.

He'd seen hundreds of beautiful women in New York, all sizes, all shapes, but none of them compared with Julia. She'd become the standard for him, leaving all others wanting.

A smile lit her face; Josi filled her arms.

She came over to the car to meet him. "How did it go? I've been dying to hear. Why didn't you call?"

He didn't care whether it was simple curiosity or genuine interest that prompted the questions; she'd cared enough to ask, and that was enough. He got out of the car. "I'm sorry. I guess I thought you wouldn't be interested."

The smiled disappeared and so did the spark in her eyes. "Of course I'm interested. We're friends. Or at least I thought we were."

He tucked his finger under Josi's chin and gave it a quick scratch. She put her head back and purred. "Everything went well. Actually, it went better than well. The book is sold."

"All ready? That's wonderful. Congratulations."

"Thanks. Now all I have to do is finish the thing."

"How long do you think it will take?"

"Three . . . maybe four months." Josi crawled

into his arms and settled over his shoulder, her purr so loud that it blocked all other sounds in that ear.

"We should do something to celebrate." She tucked her hands in her back pockets and rocked back on her heels. "Let me take you to dinner. Better yet, let's stay here and I'll make dinner for us. Connie went shopping before she took off for the day, and said there were lots of things to fix in the refrigerator.

"How does salmon sound?" she went on before he could answer. "I have a killer recipe that will spoil you for eating it any other way. Ken used to say—" She stumbled on the rest but picked up with, "Or if you don't like salmon, I make a pretty good pork roast."

"What did Ken used to say, Julia?"

She stared down at the ground. "It's not important."

He agreed. What mattered was that she couldn't or wouldn't tell him. "We'll save the celebrating for next time," he said. "I've been gone a long time. I should get home and check on things."

"What things?"

The question surprised him. He hadn't expected her to try to keep him there. "I don't know—the usual."

"Is there anything that can't wait?"

"No."

"Then there isn't any real reason you can't stay for dinner."

First he smiled, then he said, "I guess not."

"Good. Now what will it be—salmon or pork?"

"Salmon."

It was her turn to smile. "You'd rather have the pork, wouldn't you?"

He wondered what she would say if he told her that what he wanted had nothing to do with food. An image of her moving beneath him in his bed flashed into his mind. Without taking the time to consider the possible consequences he told her, "I don't care what we eat, Julia. I don't even care if we eat at all. Just being with you tonight is enough."

She chose not to take him seriously. "Wow, if you write like you talk, I can see why everyone wanted to buy your book."

Eric felt Josi tense. She brought her back legs up, preparing to leap from his shoulder. Remembering how quickly she'd gotten away the last time, he tucked her firmly under his arm. She twisted and ducked her head to look around him. Eric turned and saw a squirrel slowly making its way across the yard. Again Josi tensed.

"I think I'd better take her inside," he told Julia.

She looked from Josi to the squirrel and back again. "Do you think she could catch it?"

"There isn't a doubt in my mind." He put his hand over Josi's eyes. She expressed her displeasure with a low growl.

"I'd just as soon not find out," Julia said. She motioned for him to follow her into the house.

As soon as they were inside and the door closed behind them, Eric put Josi down. She immediately wrapped herself around his legs, stopping every few seconds to change directions. "I think she's trying to tell me something."

Julia laughed. "She wants her chance for revenge. You'd understand if you'd been here this past week. The squirrels have been teasing her unmercifully. Every time they see her at the back window, they gather on the deck."

"How do you know that? I thought you went into the office every day."

"I decided to take some time off. It's a little experiment," she said mysteriously. She ran her hand along the back of her neck, lifting her hair off her shoulders. "What can I get you to drink?"

He would have liked something hard and clean, whiskey preferably, but he had a long drive ahead of him that night and it wouldn't take much to tip fatigue into exhaustion. "You have any tomato juice?"

"You want a bloody Mary?"

He smiled. "No Mary, just blood."

"Make yourself comfortable." She directed him to the living room to the right of the foyer. "I'll be right back."

Josi stopped circling as soon as Julia left. She peered up at Eric, gave his shin one last rub, and took off, her tail straight up like an exiting exclamation point.

When Eric had come there to drop Josi off, he'd been in a hurry and hadn't gone any farther inside than the foyer. Even so, he'd come away with a pretty good idea what the rest of the house would be like. As he entered the living room, he saw that he'd been right. While the room was not as ostentatious as he'd expected, what was there bespoke money—lots of it. An eclectic assortment of paintings lined the walls. The spaces on the shelves not filled with books held bronzes, porcelains, and artifacts.

While there were a dozen things that under different circumstances would have drawn his attention, it was the painting over the fireplace that called to Eric. He crossed the room to get a closer look at the man and woman frozen in a moment of poignant intimacy.

So this was Ken Huntington. Handsome, smiling, and obviously deeply in love with the woman he held in his arms—Julia. The artist had captured a magical moment between them.

Or had all of their moments been this magical?

Eric studied the picture. Ken was leaning against the trunk of a large tree. Julia had her arm around his waist, her head resting on his shoulder. His arms were around her shoulders, his head tilted so that his cheek touched her hair. They were dressed casually, as if they'd just returned from a walk in the woods.

"It was a gift from Peter for our eighth wedding anniversary," Julia said as she came into the room carrying a tray. "He's an incredible artist, don't you think?"

"Yes," Eric said.

She handed him his tomato juice. "You ought to have him show you some of the paintings he has sitting around his place." She smiled. "I used to tell him I was going to go through his garbage at night to steal his rejects."

"And what did he say?"

"That I would be wasting my time. He burned what he didn't like."

"Ouch."

"My thoughts exactly." Julia held her glass out to Eric's. "To your book. May it be everything, and accomplish everything, you desire."

"Right now that would be to make the reader feel his or her money was well spent." He took a drink and then licked the thick juice from his upper lip.

Her gaze dropped from his eyes to his lips. Unconsciously she mimicked him and licked her own. "I'll be the first in line to buy a copy. And I'll tell everyone I know to buy a copy, too."

How had he convinced himself he could be patient where she was concerned? He wanted her to be a part of his life now, not a year or month or even a week from then. He set his glass on the mantel, then took hers and put it there, too.

"I've got to get out of here, Julia, before I say something you're not ready to hear." He touched her cheek, then moved his hand to the back of her neck. Slowly he lowered his head and, with a tenderness wrapped in longing, kissed her. Her lips were warm and as soft as a whisper. He closed his eyes and for a blissful second let himself imagine there were no obstacles for them to overcome, no ghosts to battle, only a future to explore. All the good that had happened to him that past week was a cup of water to the ocean compared to this moment.

A soft moan rose from Julia's throat as she responded to his kiss. He could feel a need building in her. Still, seconds later, she put her hands against his chest and gently pushed him away.

"I'm sorry," she said, a confused expression on her face. She looked at the floor, at the picture over the mantel, and finally at Eric. "It's that—"

"It's all right. I just wanted to give you something to think about after I'm gone."

He went to the window and picked up Josi. Before leaving, he stopped to look at Julia one last time. "You know where you can find me. The next move is yours."

Julia fixed the dinner she'd wanted to prepare for Eric that night, mincing fresh spices, opening a bottle of award-winning Chardonnay, lighting the candles on the table. But she couldn't eat and wound up refrigerating everything for Connie's lunch the next day.

Next she tried to put him from her mind by concentrating on a report she'd been given that day on the money the company would save by shifting assembly work to a foreign market. Ken had approved the research even though he'd told everyone repeatedly that he had no intention of doing anything about it.

Then why had he spent what was to her a small fortune sending a team halfway around the world? The question had plagued Julia from the day she'd moved into Ken's office.

She found herself second-guessing him a dozen times a day, trying to do what he would have done without having a clue what that was. While everyone did whatever they could to help her run the place the way they felt Ken would have, no one had offered so much as a nod of encouragement for her to begin making her own decisions.

Ken was an icon, and she was forever cast in the role of his high priestess.

She went to bed but couldn't sleep. After two hours of rolling from side to side in the huge bed, she got up and wandered into the living room, stopping to stand in front of the picture of her and Ken that hung over the fireplace. She closed her eyes and tried to remember what it had felt like to have his arms around her. But it was Eric's arms she felt, his lips she still tasted, and his voice she heard.

Tears came to her eyes as she stared at the picture. "I tried so hard, Ken, but I still let you down. I'm sorry. Please forgive me."

* * *

Julia felt someone pulling her from a place she didn't want to leave. She fought going, but the voice only became more persistent.

"Mrs. Huntington—it's time to get up."

"Connie?" Julia blinked her eyes open. "What are you doing here already?"

"It's almost eight-thirty. You overslept."

She'd fallen asleep on the couch. She sat up and looked at the clock on the mantel. Her heart sank. "Damn—I have a meeting in five minutes."

"Do you want me to call the office and tell them you're going to be late?"

"No, I'll do it." Still groggy, she started toward the bedroom.

"There's something else I need to tell you, Mrs. Huntington."

"Yes?"

"Josi is missing."

Julia heard the concern in her voice. "No, she's not. Eric came home yesterday and stopped by to pick her up after you left."

Instead of relieved, she looked disappointed. "I was hoping he would forget."

It was such an odd thing for her to say, Julia couldn't let it pass. "I didn't know you were a cat person."

"I'm not. I just liked the way she made you smile. You haven't done that a lot this past year." She went to the sofa where Julia had been sleeping and fluffed the pillows. "Maybe you should look into getting a cat of your own."

The suggestion stopped Julia cold. Was

that how Connie saw her—someone who should look to a cat to bring her happiness? "I'll think about it."

She called the office from her bedroom phone, then stripped and headed for the bathroom. As she rounded the bed, she caught the monogram on the pocket of her pajama top out of the corner of her eye. The stylized *H* stood out as if she'd been wearing a brand.

Pat Faith followed Julia into her office. "I managed to reschedule all your appointments except the one with Adam Boehm. He said he would get back to you later when he'd had a chance to check his calendar."

"What about David? Did he turn in the new sketches?"

"Had them here at eight this morning."

"Good." Julia sat at her desk and picked up the phone. On impulse, she put it down again to catch Pat before she left. "Do you have a minute?"

"Of course," Pat said, coming back into the room.

Julia motioned to the chair in front of her. "Do you mind if I ask you a personal question?"

"No. . . ."

Refusing to consider the mistake she could be making opening herself up to someone she really didn't know, Julia shoved her doubts to the back of her mind and plunged ahead. "How are you getting along without Howard?"

Pat settled deeper into the chair. Her husband had died a month before Ken, but even though they'd had such a profound tragedy in common, they'd never talked about it to each other. "It hasn't been as hard for me as it's been for you," she said. "Howard was the best thing that ever happened to me, but he was just an ordinary guy to the rest of the world. With you, it's as if everyone around here thinks Ken's up there sitting at the right hand of God."

Julia felt as if she'd been given an incredible gift. She had someone she could talk to, someone who finally understood.

CHAPTER

8

Peter went into the kitchen, poured himself a cup of coffee, and looked out the window. The blinds were still drawn at Katherine's. He glanced at the clock. Ten to eight. Normally she was up by now.

With the previous night's clear skies, he'd set his alarm for dawn, hoping the fog would hold off and give him the morning light he wanted to finish the painting he'd started the day before.

He'd chosen the pose where Katherine was looking out the window rather than into the room. Her expression, her body language, had an intensity he'd never seen her reveal before. It was as if she were seeing a world on the other side of the glass hidden to all but her, a world that seemed to frighten her, but one that she longed to explore.

He hadn't comprehended what he was seeing at first. It took three attempts to put the clues together, to find the emotion struggling to break through the facade. When he was finally confident he'd captured what she'd tried so hard to keep hidden, he still was no closer to understanding what had produced the emotions than he had been in the beginning.

Would she understand the difference when she saw the finished picture, or would she feel he'd wantonly invaded her privacy?

Their friendship was already on shaky ground. The easy rapport they'd always shared had been dealt a near fatal blow. He almost wished he'd let her go on thinking he was gay. Where was the harm if it was what she needed to feel comfortable around him?

What insane hope drove him? What flaw in his personality let him go on year after year loving a woman who would never, who could never, love him back? Would he one day see in hindsight that he'd wasted what should have been the best years of his life?

If there were a treatment, he would take it. God knew he'd tried to rid himself of her. Unrequited love might seem wonderfully romantic in a song; living it was something else. Kindly put, it was stupid. More honestly, it was sick.

Peter poured the rest of his coffee down the drain and went back to his studio. He stood in the doorway and stared at the half-finished picture of Katherine. Stupid or not, sick or not, he would always love her. It was as useless to deny or try to change as the seasons.

* * *

Katherine grabbed the towel she'd left on a rock and wrapped it around her shoulders. She was half-frozen yet felt wonderfully alive from her swim. Breaking the rules she'd hammered into her children from the first August they'd spent at the beach, she'd not only gone swimming immediately after eating, she'd gone alone.

Now she had goose bumps on top of goose bumps; her teeth were chattering and her skin had turned blue. But she'd watched the sunrise riding a swell and had almost wound up nose to nose with a curious seal. All in all, more than a worthwhile exchange.

Doing something alone was an experience in itself. She couldn't remember ever going to a movie or a restaurant by herself. All her life she'd been attached to someone either by circumstance or by choice. She'd never thought to question the pattern or felt the need to be out on her own. Now that she'd been cut loose, she was discovering a part of herself she'd never known existed.

Simple things astounded her. It was a revelation to realize the world wouldn't come to an end if dinner wasn't on the table at six-thirty. She could eat at five or eight or not at all if she so chose.

Best of all, she could read all night if she wanted and sleep in until eight or even nine without being accused of indolence.

The freedom to do and be whatever she wanted couldn't last, of course. Out of necessity her life would settle into a routine when she went home again. She had Paul to consider and her own class schedule to keep up. But no matter how much she had to do, she would never again let her days become so structured that there was no room for spontaneity.

She was forty-one years old, forty-two in a couple of months. Figuring her family's noted longevity, she could reasonably expect to live another forty or so years. Which meant her life was half over. No, that was something Brandon would say.

She had half her life ahead of her.

Yes, she liked that better.

She managed a smile through half-frozen lips as she headed back to the house. Forty years . . . a lot of adventures could be had in forty years.

Today was a good day to begin. Perhaps she'd even ask Peter to join her. She was still a little disconcerted at the discovery he wasn't gay, but after the initial surprise, she saw no reason their friendship shouldn't go on. The situation obviously didn't bother him, why would she let it bother her? The determining factor had been the thought of losing him as a friend. Just thinking about it had created a profound sense of loss. She liked Peter. He was kind and thoughtful and caring . . . and he made her laugh.

If the day ever came that she considered having someone in her life again, she would want it to be a man like Peter. But that thought hinged on such a big "if," she had trouble imagining it ever happening.

Now that she'd decided to embark on the second part of her life, she was filled with ideas and anxious to get started. Every year she'd added places to go and things to see to her "August" list, spending her winters poring over the new brochures and free newspapers she'd picked up while staying at the beach house the summer before. Then August would come, and despite his promises to the contrary, Brandon would be there only two or three days a week and want to spend them sitting around doing nothing—his idea of a real vacation. Inevitably the kids were more interested in being with their friends at the beach or on the boardwalk in Santa Cruz, and because she'd never be much of a loner—enjoying the sharing as much as the doing—Katherine never went sight-seeing on her own.

Of all her projects the one she most regretted never doing was the search for John Steinbeck's California. She'd spent her winter four years ago reading the books he'd written about the area. By the time August rolled around again, she'd gathered dozens of passages that described real locations, believing it would be both fun and educational to try to find them.

She and Brandon spent their first morning on Fremont Peak wandering through the park. That afternoon they were at the hospital getting medicine for his poison oak. His rash got a lot worse before it got better, and Katherine decided to let the project go for that year.

Her thoughts focused on the past and the

future as she climbed the stairs from the beach, Katherine completely ignored the present. She was almost around the house before she noticed a dark green Taurus parked in front of Andrew's house, taking advantage of the shade provided by a fifty-year-old pine. It was the same kind of car Brandon drove.

Just yesterday she would have been beside herself with hope and anticipation to find him there. Now she wasn't sure what she felt.

"Don't you think it's a little early for a swim?" he said as he came through the garden gate.

Brandon was a clear winner in the genetic dice game; he was hands down the most handsome man she'd ever known. Even after twenty years of marriage she could still be impressed, especially when he smiled. The cotton slacks and golf shirts he favored for everyday wear gave the same effect as a tuxedo on an ordinary man. "What are you doing here?"

He paused, obviously taken aback at the accusatory tone in her voice. "I came to see you."

She adjusted the towel to cover herself better. "Why?"

"Do I need a reason?"

"Yes." She surprised them both at the bluntness of her answer.

"Why don't we go in?" he asked reasonably. "You look half-frozen, and I'd prefer the neighbors didn't see us standing around outside like this."

Had Brandon not gone into the ministry, he would have made a great political consultant. At the worst of times a part of his mind remained focused on the image he presented. Katherine reached inside the bra cup of her swimming suit and unpinned the house key. When they were inside, she dropped the key on the coffee table, turned to Brandon, and repeated coolly, "What are you doing here?"

He avoided looking at her, instead letting his gaze sweep the room. "We need to talk."

Brandon had never lacked self-confidence. It was one of the things that had drawn her to him. He had an incredible power to persuade people to his way of thinking, making them feel the arguments had been theirs all along. It had taken her years to see the mechanics of this manipulative process. When she'd pointed it out to him, he'd asked why she would question his methods when the end justified the means.

"You told me you'd already said everything there was to say," she said.

"I was wrong."

The statement disarmed her. Brandon never admitted he was wrong about anything. She tugged on the towel where it had begun to slip from her shoulder and waited for him to go on.

"I've missed you," he said. "More than I'd expected. These last few months have been really hard on me." He waited. When she still didn't say anything, he made a frustrated sound and put his hands on her arms. "I'm not going to dance around this, Katherine. I want you to come back to me. I see now that our separation was a terrible mistake."

If he'd come a week ago, she would have collapsed in his arms in gratitude that he was willing to give her back her life. Not even a week—three days ago and she would be in the bedroom packing already. "I don't know what to say," she admitted.

He brought her into his arms. "You don't have to say anything. I can see your answer in your eyes. You're as happy to have this behind us as I am."

Finally she found her will. "The only thing behind us is a broken marriage."

He either didn't hear or chose to ignore her statement. He kissed her, his mouth open as he ground his lips into hers. It was the kind of kiss he reserved for telling her he wanted to make love.

Despite the warning voice that told her she would be a fool to give in to him, she felt herself being swept along. It seemed forever since she'd been touched or caressed or even held. She needed what he offered, more than she'd let herself acknowledge. Besides, legally they were still married. After all their years together what harm could it do if they were to bring their relationship to a gentle end by making love this one last time?

"Yes. . . . It's all right," she said on a whispered sigh as he kissed the hollow behind her ear. Shock waves radiated through her midsection. That quickly she was ready for him. *But was it Brandon she really wanted?* The question came from a voice deep inside her mind. She chose not to listen.

He took her hand and started toward the bedroom.

"No," she said. "Make love to me here."

He frowned. "Here? On the sofa?"

"I don't care. The sofa, the floor, it doesn't matter." He'd said he was bored with their love-making. The request should have pleased him. She tugged on his hand to bring him back to her.

"Why would we want to do that when there's a perfectly comfortable bed right down the hall?"

"We always made love in bed." Again she tugged on his hand. "Come on, Brandon, let go. The kids aren't here. No one is going to knock on the door. The phone isn't going to ring."

Still he hesitated. "What's gotten into you?" he asked suspiciously. "Have you started reading trashy romance novels?"

She could feel the mood slipping away, and out of habit or need or simple confusion, she was disappointed. Her lips moved into a pleading smile as her stomach did a slow roll. "Never mind. The bed is fine."

A triumphant gleam shone from his eyes. "I'll be there waiting."

"Waiting?" she repeated inanely.

"While you take your shower. All that sand and salt must be driving you crazy."

They were the exact words she'd needed. He

couldn't have cooled her off more effectively if he'd tossed her back in the ocean. He wanted her, but it had to be the sanitized version. He was no more swept away with desire than Iraq was interested in a good neighbor policy. She purposefully removed her hand from his. "What's going on, Brandon? Why did you really come here today?"

"I told you. I realized how wrong I'd been when—"

"Cut the crap. I'm not buying it anymore."

His demeanor changed. His eyes flashed anger and impatience, emotions he usually managed to keep under tight control. "What's gotten into you, Katherine? When did you start questioning what I tell you?"

Had he always talked to her this way?

As if realizing he'd gone too far, Brandon said, "I didn't mean that the way it sounded. I've been a mess since you left. I can't concentrate, and I haven't been eating properly. My sermons are even beginning to suffer."

"What did you expect? I took care of you morning, noon, and night for twenty years while you were busy taking care of everyone else."

"I don't understand what's happening here," he said. "I thought you wanted to save our marriage, that it was as important to you as it is to me."

"Wait a minute. Just when did our marriage suddenly become important to you? As I recall, when you asked me to move out, you made quite a point of telling me it was the end, that there was no way we could ever get back together."

"Trying to lay blame for our breakup isn't going to get us anywhere," he said in a teacher-to-student voice.

She was cold and uncomfortable and needed time to think. "I'm going to take a shower."

"That's a good idea. I'm sure you'll feel more like talking when you get out." He leaned forward to kiss her cheek and pat her arm. "I'll make coffee."

"How long are you staying?"

He clearly hadn't expected the question. "I guess that depends on you."

If it really was up to her, he would be gone when she got out of the shower. The thought brought her up short. When . . . *how* had she gone from believing he was the source of her happiness to looking forward to a life without him?

CHAPTER

9

Y ou can't do this," Brandon said. "Not after all I've done for you." His expression changed from worried to cajoling. "What is it you need, a little time? I can handle that. I can even understand why you might want to see me suffer a little before you come back. But you have to believe me, Katherine. It may not be obvious, but I've already suffered just as much as you have. I can't begin to tell you the number of nights I've lain awake praying I did the right thing or how much I think about you during the day and how much I miss having you greet me at the door when I come home."

Needing something to do, Katherine reached for her coffee. Her hands were shaking so hard, the hot liquid splashed over the rim and landed on her white slacks, leaving a stain the shape of a lopsided heart. She put the cup down again.

"I'm not going to live a lie for anyone, not even you, Brandon." Knowing the real reason he'd come made everything so much easier. "You should have considered what a divorce would do to your chances to be on the council before you asked me to leave."

She reached for a napkin to blot the stain. "And what about everything I've done for you? You could never have made it as far as you have without me."

"You're right," he said without conviction. "I've never given you enough credit for all that you do, but that's in the past. From now on I promise I'll do better."

She'd never seen him like this. She tried the coffee again and managed to get it to her lips without mishap. A small but noteworthy accomplishment. "Tell me now, Brandon."

"Tell you what?"

"All the things you say you now recognize that I've done for you."

He seemed lost. "You're being unfair. I can't just come up with things. I need time to think." He let out a defeated sigh. "Tell me what it will take to get you to come home with me. I'll do anything you want."

"For how long?"

He recoiled. "Have I ever broken a promise to you?"

"You mean other than 'till death do us part'?"

"Remember, Katherine, you made that same vow before God. You know He would want you to do whatever you can to see it through. Even if it means you have to swallow a little pride."

"Is that what you think this is about?

Pride?" For the first time she raised her voice. "And how dare you use our Lord to try to manipulate me?"

"All right, I admit I made a mistake when I asked you to leave. Now will you forgive me?" He got up to take his cup to the sink, turned, and looked at her. "I've certainly forgiven enough of your mistakes."

Whenever she felt herself beginning to falter, he managed to say something to boost her up again and convince her she was doing the right thing. To go back now would only delay the inevitable. Whatever glue had held them together was gone.

"Wonderful, Brandon—even with all my faults, you're still willing to give me another chance. I can't let you make that sacrifice." She tried but couldn't keep the hurt and anger from her voice.

"After all that you do for everyone else, you deserve to be married to someone who will make you happy—*really* happy. I know that being on the council seems like it would be enough, but in two or three years when the newness wears off, we'd be right back where we are now. I don't want to go through this again. I won't. *I* deserve better."

He shook his head, a mask of compelling sadness on his face. "I never would have believed you could be so vindictive. If you won't come back for me, what about Michael and Paul? Think what it would mean to them to have their parents together again."

"Where was this deep concern for your sons when you told me to move out?"

He sat down again. "What could you possibly hope to gain by punishing me for that now? No, let's get this straight. If you insist on going through with this divorce, it will be Michael and Paul you punish, not me."

A knock on the front door kept her from answering. It was Peter. His timing couldn't have been worse.

"Oh, I'm sorry," he said, looking past Katherine and seeing Brandon standing in the middle of the living room. "I didn't know you were here. I must have missed your car." His discomfort at finding Brandon there was obvious, his words too easily misinterpreted. To Katherine he said, "I just stopped by to see if . . . uh, to see if you needed anything from the store."

"I'm fine," she said quickly. "I went shopping yesterday and picked up everything I needed."

"Then I'll let you get back to what you were doing." He made a small wave to Brandon. "Nice seeing you again."

Brandon didn't say anything right away. He waited several seconds after Peter had gone and then looked her directly in the eye. "Please tell me this is not what it looks like. Have you and Peter—"

"I don't know what you're talking about." She moved to step around him. He blocked her way.

"I wondered why you would want to come

down here all alone this summer. Is Peter the reason you're willing to give up on us so easily?"

"I'm not going to dignify that with an answer."

"I came here willing to do whatever necessary to work things out between us, but I can see now that my prayers are not going to be answered." He ran his hand through his hair. "Perhaps this is God's way of telling me I'm not worthy to sit on the council." He waited. When she didn't say anything, he went on, "I just hope for both of us that it's His hand making the decision, not yours."

"If it's God's plan that you be on the council, He'll show you another way."

Brandon moved toward the door. "I'll tell Roger to get things started as soon as I get home. There's no sense dragging this out any longer."

"You're using Roger for the divorce?" He and his wife, Martha, were the first friends they'd made when they moved to Woodland. She felt as close to them as she did to her own family.

"He seemed the logical choice."

How could Brandon be oblivious of the effect using a mutual friend for their divorce would have on her? How could he be so sensitive to the most minor problem of one of his parishioners and blind to her feelings? "Please find someone else."

He opened the door and stepped outside. "I'll think about it."

She followed him out. "I truly am sorry, Brandon. I just can't go back to the way things were. I don't have it in me."

Katherine stayed in the house the next two days, venturing out only to pick up the newspaper. The dense morning fog reflected her mood, and when sunshine broke through in the afternoons, she closed the blinds.

There had never been a divorce in her family. Her mother and father would take the news hard, as would her brothers and sister. They knew about the separation but had refused to believe she and Brandon wouldn't work things out. All marriages went through rocky times. How could they expect her and Brandon's to be any different? They adored Brandon and talked about him the way parents did when one of their children became a doctor or lawyer. There was no higher calling than to serve God.

Katherine didn't even bother wondering whose side they would be on—especially when they found out he'd asked her to come back and she'd refused. She had no hope they would ever understand her newfound need to discover the woman she was and the woman she wanted to be.

Had she really thought that? Did she honestly believe there would be sides to take? Her prayers changed from asking for strength to see her through the months ahead to being shown a way to keep friends and relatives from feeling they had to champion either her or Brandon over the other.

The third morning of her self-imposed exile, the sun greeted her as she climbed out of bed. She decided it would mark the end of her introspective depression. She'd touched bottom; it was time to get on with her life.

Fresh from her shower, dressed in her yellow terry-cloth bathrobe with a towel wrapped around her head, Katherine was headed for the kitchen for a cup of coffee when she heard a car pull into the driveway.

She went to the window and peeked through the blinds. Surprise hit first, then puzzlement, finally delight. She opened the door. "What are you doing here?"

"I got fired," Paul said, grinning. "Old man Fielding caught me stealing grapes."

"You did not." She put her arms around her youngest son and gave him a longer-than-usual hug, leaving no doubt how glad she was to see him.

"What is it you think I didn't do—get fired or steal grapes?" He had a mischievous twinkle in his eyes.

"Either one." She smiled as she looked past him to the other two boys who'd gotten out of the Mustang. They were Paul's best friends, the bonds established in preschool. "I hope you're planning to stay awhile."

"If it's okay," Tom, the taller of the two, said.

She reached up to adjust the towel on her head as it slipped to one side. "Of course it's okay. Have you had breakfast?"

"We stopped on the way," Charlie told her.

"That was two hours ago," Paul said. "I'm starved. What've you got?"

"Pancakes? Or, if you'd rather, French toast."

"Pancakes," they said in unison.

"Give me a couple of minutes to get dressed, and I'll see what I can do to fill those hollow legs of yours."

The morning turned into the best she'd had in months, filled with teasing and laughter and good-natured roughhousing. The pancakes disappeared as fast as she could make them, followed by the last of the milk and all of the juice. Charlie and Tom threw her and Paul out of the kitchen while they cleared the table and washed the dishes.

Alone on the deck, the ocean breeze directing their voices away from the kitchen window, Katherine asked Paul, "Now why are you really here?"

"I just thought you might like some company."

"And what made you think that?"

He shrugged. "Dad was acting kind of funny when he got back."

She was caught between curiosity and prying. "I like knowing how much you care, Paul, but I don't want you to feel you have to take care of me. What's happening between me and your dad is our problem, not yours."

She thought about what she'd said. "I take that back, it's your problem, too. You had every right to think your dad and I would be together forever. And now you have to deal with your last year of school and getting ready for college and a mother and father who should be there for you but are—"

"Jeez, Mom, if you keep this up, you're going to have me feeling sorry for myself."

She was filled with a love for her son so intense that it brought tears to her eyes. "I must have done something very special to deserve you."

"Just remember that next time I forget to pick up my room."

She laughed and wiped at her eyes. "Forget?"

"All right—postpone."

"What are your plans for this afternoon?"

"Nothing special, maybe hang out here for a while, check out the chicks on the beach."

"*Chicks?*"

He laughed. "You're so easy, Mom."

"Since you don't have anything special planned, how about if the three of you help me make ice cream? I found a machine in the cupboard that looks brand new, and I thought it might be fun to give it a try."

"Yeah, sure," he said, obviously more to please her than out of any real excitement about homemade ice cream. "You want us to go to the store to get the stuff?"

"I'll take care of it." He'd be the rest of the

morning shopping if she sent him with her list. There wasn't enough food in the house to feed three boys another day, let alone a week. The groceries would take a big chunk out of the money she'd budgeted for the rest of the month, but she couldn't think of a better way to spend it.

CHAPTER

10

Katherine looked up from the bed of snapdragons where she was gathering flowers for a bouquet and saw a boy who looked to be eight or nine watching her. "Hi, there," she said, and smiled.

"Hi," he answered without returning the smile.

She sat back on her haunches, keeping herself at his level. "Were you looking for someone?"

"My friends used to live here. But they died."

Now she understood the missing smile. "You must mean Joe and Maggie," she said gently.

He nodded. "Do you live here now?"

"For a little while."

"Do you have any kids?"

"I have two boys, but they're almost grown." She cut a bright red snapdragon and stuck it in the pail of water beside her. "Do you live around here?"

"Me and my sister are staying with my dad over there." He pointed to Andrew's house.

Peter had told her a writer was living in Andrew's house while he was away. He'd been gone when she first arrived and must have returned while she was holed up trying to get her life back in order. "I'm going to make ice cream this afternoon. Would you like to come over and have some? You can bring your sister and Dad, too."

"What kind?"

"Strawberry."

"I like peach," he said softly. "That's what Maggie made."

Her heart went out to him. "I could make peach instead, but I have a feeling it wouldn't be as good as Maggie's."

"That's all right. Me and my sister have to go back to my mom's today anyway." He raised a small hand as he turned to leave. "Bye."

She watched him cross the pathway back to his house. As much as she hated what her and Brandon's divorce would do to Michael and Paul, she was profoundly grateful they'd stayed a family unit long enough to see them through their childhood.

She moved to the giant marigolds that grew beside the gate, looked up, and saw Peter at his mailbox. He noticed her and waved. She waved back. When he returned his mail to the box and headed her way, her heart did a funny skipping beat in anticipation.

She stood and brushed herself off, wishing she'd taken more time with her hair and makeup that morning. Slowly, during the past two and a half weeks, barely more than a fleeting thought at a time, she'd begun to understand how connected Peter was to her feelings about coming to the beach house every year. He was as much a part of her August as listening to the waves, long walks on the beach, and the smell of salt-laden air.

"I haven't seen you around lately," he said, stopping outside the gate. "Is everything all right?"

"Paul showed up with a couple of friends." What was it about Peter that always made her feel special when she was with him? She had a feeling it had a lot to do with the way he actually looked at her when she was talking to him, as if whatever she had to say, no matter how inconsequential, were important. But he didn't just listen, he responded. And he cared. "They've been keeping me pretty busy."

"I meant before that."

She didn't know how to answer him. Their friendship wasn't one of private revelations, and she was afraid to take the chance that things might change if she unloaded her problems on him. "I didn't feel very good for a couple of days after Brandon left."

"You should have called me. I make a great chicken soup."

"I'll remember that." She was tempted to tell him chicken soup was a personal favorite and that she would gladly let him make it for her anytime, but was afraid he would get the wrong impression. "How's the painting coming?"

"It's finished."

The news was both exciting and a little scary. Not only would she be seeing herself through Peter's eyes, so would the rest of the world. "May I see it?"

"Anytime."

"Now?"

"If you'd like."

"Give me a minute to clean up."

"You're fine just the way you are." He held the gate for her.

"I really should wash up a little."

He reached for her hand. "It's not a gallery opening, Katherine, just you and me."

They were halfway to his house before she realized they were still holding hands. "I can't stay long. I told the boys I'd fix them lunch when they got back from swimming."

"How long are they staying?"

"Until Friday. They're going to help me close the house."

He pulled up and looked at her, a stunned expression on his face. "You're leaving Friday? Why so soon? Labor Day's a week and a half away."

The strength of his reaction startled her. She slipped her hand from his and tucked it in her back pocket. "I have to get ready for school. I'm taking some refresher courses for my teaching credential."

"You're going to be a teacher? I thought being a minister's wife was a full-time job."

There it was. She either told him the truth

and spent the little time they had left together talking about her problems or she danced around it and gave herself a few more days of freedom. "I thought it was time I branched out a little," she said simply.

"Did you know Julia was thinking about selling the house?" It was a long shot, but perhaps if Katherine knew, she would change her mind and stay a little longer. He'd thought they would have more time. He'd counted on it. He wasn't ready to have her walk out of his life. He sure as hell wasn't ready to face the possibility of never seeing her again.

"I didn't, but I'm not surprised."

"What will you do—about coming here in August, I mean."

She started walking again. "Most likely, I won't do anything. It was hard justifying renting a three-bedroom house when I knew I would be the only one using it this year. I can't see ever doing it again."

"What if I told you that I was thinking about buying the house from Julia?"

"Why? You already have a—"

"As an investment. August would be yours for as long as you wanted it. At the same price, of course."

"That's crazy, Peter. You could get twice, maybe even three times as much as we're paying."

If he wasn't careful, he was going to trip himself up and she'd know the real reason he was buying the house. She'd never come back then. Hell, she'd probably run home and pack her bags that night. "It's worth it to me to know the place would be taken care of."

They'd come to his front door. "You have no idea how much I wish I could say yes."

"At least tell me you'll think about it." He opened the door for her.

She looked at him and smiled. "That's easy. It's probably all I'll think about while I'm lugging books around campus this winter."

Peter followed her inside. "Can I get you something to drink? A soda? Iced tea?"

She shook her head. "I can't stay long."

A sudden, uncharacteristic nervousness made him hesitate showing her the picture. It had been years since he'd looked to anyone for approval of his work. He painted to satisfy himself. But this was different. He desperately wanted Katherine to like what he'd done.

"It's in here," he said, indicating his studio. When she started that way, it was everything he could do not to stop her. Gaining a semblance of control, he took a deep breath and followed.

She spotted the painting from the doorway. Instead of going in, she stayed where she was and stared, not saying anything. Finally, as if drawn forward by an invisible hand, she moved closer, stopping in the middle of the room directly in front of the portrait.

"This is how you see me?" she asked, her voice barely above a whisper.

There could be no answer but the truth. "Yes."

"But you've made me so beautiful."

"You are beautiful."

She shook her head. "Not like this."

He wasn't looking at the painting but at her when he asked, "Do you like it?"

"It scares me," she said, her confusion reflected in her voice. "But I don't know why." She moved closer still. "How did you know what I was thinking?"

"I painted what I saw."

Finally she looked at him. "How can you see what no one else does?"

"What are you really asking me?"

"I look so lonely. . . ." She turned to the picture. "What am I looking at out that window, Peter? Why do I want it so much?"

Not until that moment did he realize that he'd imagined her looking at him. "You tell me."

"I can't."

He would have given everything he owned to know what to say to her. Gut instinct told him there were words she needed to hear, but that they were in a language he didn't know. "What do you want me to do with the painting?"

"I don't know."

"It's on paper," he said. "Easily destroyed."

"Oh, no. You can't." She put her hand on his arm. "Promise me you won't."

He was stunned to see tears in her eyes. "I never meant to hurt you, Katherine."

"It isn't you, it's me." A tear spilled onto her cheek. She immediately wiped it away with her hand. "I have to go now."

"What can I do?"

"Nothing."

He couldn't let her go. "There must be something."

"It's my problem. I'll work it out."

"Let me help."

She touched the side of his face. "I love the painting." Forcing a smile, she added, "When you sell it, I hope you make lots and lots of money."

"I'm not selling it. The picture isn't mine, Katherine. It's yours."

"You can't . . . I couldn't . . ." She looked at the painting, at him, and then back at the painting again. After an agonizingly long time she said, "Keep it for me." Their eyes met. "Would you?"

It was a connection he hadn't expected. A gift. A promise. A golden cage where he would reside the rest of his life. "For as long as you like," he told her.

The rest of the week Paul and his friends kept Katherine too busy to think, including her in whatever plans they made for the day, even insisting she go to the boardwalk with them, where, against her better judgment, she let them talk her into going on the roller coaster. She ate cotton candy, a candied apple, and a questionable-looking hot dog she was still burping six hours later.

Friday arrived with a thick roll of fog sitting offshore, a breeze to keep the heat from being oppressive, and a sky so blue that it begged to be filled with brightly colored kites. Because it seemed a crime not to take advantage of their last day of vacation, Katherine insisted the boys go swimming while she packed. After lunch they stripped the beds, cleaned the bathrooms, and loaded the car.

Paul made an endearingly sincere offer to ride back with her, but she convinced him that she was looking forward to the quiet of making the trip alone. The boys took off at four, hoping to get home in time for a party that night. She stood in the driveway and watched them leave, then went inside to finish cleaning.

As she worked her way through the remaining rooms, caught up in the mindless process of dusting, polishing, and vacuuming, her thoughts wandered in a dozen directions. Inevitably, no matter how circuitous the route, she wound up thinking about Peter. For days she'd looked for him whenever she was outside, but hadn't seen him since he'd shown her the painting. It was almost as if he were purposely avoiding her.

A glorious sunset chastised her for being inside when she looked out the window after finishing the kitchen floor, the job she'd left for last. She made one final inspection, then went outside, a reward for all her hard work. As she walked around the house, she checked to see if Peter's car was in the driveway. Finally he was home.

Smelling like pine cleaner and bleach, her hair in a careless knot on top of her head, her makeup a fleeting memory, she headed for his house, afraid to take the chance he might leave again if she took the time to clean herself up.

He answered her knock so quickly, it was almost as if he'd been standing on the other side of the door waiting for her.

"Hi," she said, suddenly, acutely, aware how disheveled she looked.

"I thought you were gone already," he said.

"The boys left around four."

"Would you like to come in?"

She glanced down at herself. "I didn't come to visit."

He waited and then asked, "Why did you come, then?"

How could she have rehearsed what she wanted to tell him the whole time she was cleaning and have forgotten it now? "About the painting . . . I love it, Peter. It's important that you know that."

"But you still don't want it."

She had a hundred reasons, but only one that mattered. He'd exposed something she didn't want anyone who knew her to see. "Maybe someday," she said. "But not now."

"Thanks for stopping by."

She nodded and took a step backward. "I should go now. I've got a long drive ahead of me."

He didn't say anything, just watched her leave.

The walk back to the house seemed impossibly long. She went inside to check the locks on the doors and windows, then stood on the deck to watch the last bit of sun disappear. Reason told her it was time to leave, but sentiment made it almost impossible. She'd already lost so much, it was hard to see this, too, end.

Finally it was the cold that got her to move. Resisting the temptation to make one last walk through the house, she crossed the living room and went out the front door.

She drove by Peter's house slowly, hoping he would be outside or standing at a window and that she could wave a final good-bye. He wasn't either place. Having anticipated that she would feel loss, she wasn't surprised when it came. What she hadn't expected was that it would be so powerful or be accompanied by a haunting sense that she'd left something undone.

Ten minutes later she was on the highway when she glanced up and saw the sign for the last exit to Santa Cruz. Another half mile and she would be headed inland on 17, the ocean a memory.

More on reflex than conscious thought, she left the highway and turned around, not sure why, only that she couldn't leave until she'd seen Peter one last time.

He didn't answer her knock. She tried again and waited. Still no answer.

Then, almost as if he'd left her a note, it came to her where he was. She headed for the beach, stopping at the top of the stairs to look for him. A three-quarter moon reflected off the water, drawing her eye to a solitary figure on the shore.

Peter looked up and saw someone walking across the soft sand in his direction. He stopped and stared and mentally dismissed the idea that it was Katherine. He continued to refuse to let himself believe she'd come back until she was standing so close that he had only to reach out to touch her.

Katherine looked intently into his eyes. "Tell me about the painting. I want to hear it in your words."

Peter's heart did a roll and then slammed against his ribs. "What is it you want to know?"

The words didn't come easily. She started and then stopped, then started again. "What was I looking at so longingly?"

"Me. . . ." The declaration was like opening a door to his prison. He was free of the secret that had kept him there all these years. Now there was no going back, no possibility of resuming their old friendship, no more dreaming of what could never be.

"How long have you felt this way?"

He gave her a rueful smile. "I think it was from the first day I saw you."

"I didn't know. I never even suspected." She frowned. "But I must have. At least on some level. If you hadn't been here, Peter, I think I would have stopped wanting to come a long time ago."

He'd never felt more alive or more on the outside. The confession didn't unlock any doors or open any windows that would let him into her life. It was nothing more than a confession. It gave him no rights, it solved no problems. "Funny how things turn out, huh? Now you're probably thinking it's a good thing that you're not coming back."

She didn't say anything for a long time, and then, "Brandon and I are separated. We're getting a divorce."

He couldn't breathe.

"I'm seeing a lawyer as soon as I get home."

"Is this what you came back to tell me?" he asked carefully.

"Yes."

"Why now?"

"I don't know. I think maybe I was afraid I'd lose you as a friend if I told you before."

So much rested on the answer, he hesitated asking the question. "And now?"

She swayed toward him. "I know you'll always be my friend." She added softly, "No matter what happens."

He put his hands on the sides of her face and slowly brought her to him. Their lips touched in a tentative kiss. The second kiss was more confident. Their tongues met, their breath mingled. Then came a sigh, and then a deep-throated groan, as Peter put his arms around her and lifted her off her feet, turning in a slow circle.

When he put her down again, Katherine broke the kiss and looked at him. "This is happening so fast. I need time to think, Peter."

He'd had years of practice letting her go, it shouldn't be hard to do it again. But that was before. "I understand," he said with great effort.

She laid her head on his shoulder. "Please wait for me."

He held her close, oblivious of the sounds of the ocean echoing off the cliffs, the waves lapping at their feet, the cold wind swirling around them. "If it takes forever, I will be here," he said softly.

PART FIVE

SEPTEMBER

CHAPTER

I

Josi uncurled from her sleeping position on top of Eric's manuscript, rolled over, and stretched her full length, knocking a pencil holder to the floor. Eric leaned forward in his chair, picked up the oft dropped pencils, and put them back on the desk. He absently scratched Josi's chin and noted the loud, rumbling purr of response, his sole sense of satisfaction at something well done that morning.

Certainly the chapter wasn't going as well. But then none of them had since he'd returned from New York. It seemed there was nothing like a couple of million dollars' advance to instill a crippling case of writer's block. Before the book sold he'd been writing for himself. If a sentence or paragraph or chapter pleased him, that was all that counted. Now he found himself trying to please an entire publishing house by second-guessing what they had liked in the first half of the book.

Eric leaned back in his chair as Josi shifted

position again, her tail taking possession of the letter he'd received that morning from Charlie Stephens. Charlie had written to thank Eric for putting him in touch with Chris, whom he'd talked into helping out at the South Los Angeles Athletic Center coaching a freestyle wrestling team. Chris came whenever he had time off from his preproduction responsibilities for the movie. Almost as an aside, Charlie had ended by mentioning casually that he and Chris's mother also happened to be seeing a lot of each other and that there would be an update in his next letter.

As always when Eric allowed his thoughts to drift from the book, they found their way to Julia. He hadn't seen or heard from her since the day he'd stopped by to pick up Josi, a little over a month ago. He'd had her number half-dialed a dozen times but always changed his mind at the last minute. When he'd told her the next move was hers, he'd had no idea she would take so long. The wait was damn near killing him.

At least he'd heard about her from Peter and knew she was doing okay. She'd gone through with her plans to sell the beach house to him, and from what Eric had seen since, it appeared Peter still intended to use it as a rental, at least temporarily. That past week the woman who'd been there in August had come back for several days. Eric had run into her and Peter on the beach a couple of times, but they'd been so focused on each other that they'd walked right by without noticing him.

Planting his feet on the floor and rolling his chair back, Eric got up and went to the kitchen to pour his fifth cup of coffee that morning. Unsurprisingly, it tasted the way it smelled, burned and bitter. He poured it down the sink. Grabbing a soda from the refrigerator, he walked around for several minutes, rolling his shoulders and stretching his back before sitting at the computer again.

A half hour later he was still staring at the blinking cursor at the top of an empty page, his hands planted on the arms of his chair, when Josi opened one eye and swiveled an ear toward the front door. She stayed that way for several seconds before she opened the other eye and raised her head.

Eric listened but, as usual, heard nothing.

When she rose to a sitting position, he pushed back his chair and stood. He'd stopped questioning Josi's psychic connection to the FedEx truck weeks ago.

Which was why it took his mind a full five seconds to register that it wasn't someone from FedEx standing on his front porch, but Julia. She was wearing a full-skirted, navy-blue-and-yellow dress that had narrow straps over the shoulders and buttons down the front. Her hair was loose and a bit wild, as if she'd been driving with the window rolled down and had been in too big a hurry to bother with repairs.

This was not the Julia Huntington he'd come to know, but he found the changes exciting—and promising.

"What are you doing here?" he asked.

"I imagined a lot of greetings on the trip down, but that wasn't one of them."

"Let me try again." He folded his arms and leaned against the door frame, making every effort to hide how seeing her again made him feel. "You look—" His gaze swept her. There was no getting around it. "There's only one word, incredible."

"Thank you. I feel pretty incredible, too." When she smiled, her eyes hinted at more surprises to come.

"Am I to assume you came all this way just to see me?"

"I hope you don't have a problem with that."

Finally he returned the smile. "The only problem I have is, what took you so long?"

"I had some things I had to do first. If you'll ask me in, I'll tell you about them."

He moved out of the doorway and was hit with a heady fragrance as she passed. He'd never noticed that she wore perfume. Had she put it on today especially for him?

"Is she your muse?" Julia asked, spotting Josi and going over to give her an affectionate scratch.

"If she is, it's time I traded her in for one that works." He couldn't believe Julia was actually there. Nothing had prepared him. It had been a perfectly ordinary morning; the sun hadn't shone any brighter, the ocean had been its usual blue.

She turned to look at him. "The book isn't going well?"

"It'll keep. I want to hear about you first."

"So much has happened I don't know where to begin."

He held up his hand. "Wait. Before you say anything more, there's something I think we need to get out of the way." He put his hands on her arms and brought her to him. He took a minute to study her face, to note the sparkle lighting her eyes, her slightly parted mouth, before he came forward slowly and brushed his lips against hers. But one chaste, welcoming kiss wasn't enough. It never would be for them. He kissed her again and then again.

She put her arms around his waist and with a sigh said, "Wow—just like I remembered."

"I love you, Julia." There it was, unplanned, unexpected, and impossible to take back. "I know it's too soon, that we have a hundred things to learn about each other, and that the odds are against us. But nothing can change the way I feel about you, and I guess a part of me figured it was time you knew."

"You're right. It is too soon, and we do have a lot to learn about each other, but I'm pretty sure I love you, too. No, I'm very sure." She tilted her head back to look at him. "How would you feel if I moved in next door for a couple of months? I think it would help if we were a little closer while we're trying to work things out, don't you?"

"I thought Peter told me you'd sold him the house."

"I did, but he let me back out of the deal at the last minute. He said he didn't need another house anyway. It seems Katherine is going to be staying at his place when she visits from now on."

"What about work?"

"Mine?" she said innocently.

"Yes, Julia—yours."

"That's all taken care of, too. I put the company up for sale three weeks ago and sold it to the highest bidder two days later. There's a ton of paperwork that still has to be done, but basically it's a fait accompli."

He was dumbfounded at the news. "I don't understand. You were so worried about what would happen to the employees if you sold. How did that change?"

"Well, it didn't actually. I just arranged things so it didn't matter whether they lost their jobs or not."

"Okay, I'll bite. How did you manage that?"

Her excitement spilled over into an ear-to-ear grin. "I gave them half the money from the sale. Now they can keep working or take a couple of years off or even take an early retirement. They have the same freedom I do."

He couldn't believe he'd heard her right. "You did what?"

She laughed. "It was so obvious. I don't know why I didn't think of it before."

Eric hated bringing in a cloud to mar her

brilliantly blue sky, but it had to be asked. "What about it being Ken's business that you sold?"

"That's absolutely amazing. You never met Ken and yet you talk about him with the same deference that everyone else does, as if he were still alive. Do you have any idea how that makes me feel?"

She was right, they did have things to work out. More than he realized. "I didn't mean it the way it sounded. I know what losing him meant to you. It was just my clumsy way of asking if you'd found peace with your feelings."

"A part of me will always love Ken." She fixed her gaze on the front of Eric's shirt as she talked about the man she'd once believed she couldn't live without. "Can you understand that? I guess what's more important, can you live with it?"

"I learned a long time ago that love isn't something you turn on and off, Julia. I know that Ken will always be an important part of your life."

"There's more." She hesitated telling him what came next, then just plunged ahead. "Do you have any idea what you're up against with my friends—with everyone who knew Ken?"

"If the hostility Peter has shown me since you and I became friends is any example, I have a pretty good idea."

She gave him a wry smile. "Actually, Peter is beginning to show signs of coming around. He said he no longer thinks it's impossible for me to find someone who could make me happy."

"How kind of him."

"His attitude is precisely the kind of thing I'm talking about. It's what you'll be going up against with everyone who knew Ken. There isn't one of his friends who thinks there's anyone who can take his place. They might forgive my reaching out in my loneliness, but they'll never forgive you for thinking you're good enough for me."

She wasn't looking for an easy answer or casual reassurance. What they were facing was a real problem and had to be acknowledged. No matter how bigoted her friends might be toward him, they were the people who had stood by her and helped her through the most devastating period of her life. They were important to her; therefore they had to be important to him.

"I can take it, Julia. The people who know and love you—and that includes me—only want one thing, and that's for you to be happy. When your friends see that happening, they'll come around."

"I really do love you," she said as she touched the side of his face. "I never thought I'd hear myself say that again."

"So, when will you be moving in?"

"My bags are in the car."

The trust she'd put in him stole his breath. She'd walked away from the only life she knew, the only emotional security she had, to take a chance with him. "I promise that you'll never look back and question what you did today."

"I came here because loving you is something I want, not something I need." She looked at him long and hard. "Do you understand what I'm trying to say?"

"That you love me with your mind as well as your heart?"

"Well put." She snuggled closer. "But then you are the writer of the family." Looking up, she added, "Now that we have that out of the way, I think we should do something to celebrate."

"Make love?"

She smiled. "That, too."

"But first?"

"It can be put off for second," she said in a husky, inviting voice.

This time when they made love it was unhurried and tender. Eric slowly and purposefully explored Julia's body, imprinting her feel and look in his hands and mind.

When he entered her she was warm and wet and eager, lifting her hips to match his thrusts, wrapping her legs around his waist, calling his name as he reached between them and brought her to an explosive climax.

Afterward, his hand resting on her belly, her head nestled on his shoulder, he asked, "I don't want you to get the idea we're through with this celebration," he said, his lips touching her temple, his breath caressing her flushed skin. "But why don't you tell me what you had in mind for us to do next."

"I want to meet Jason and Susie—and Shelly. I was hoping she would let the kids stay with us a couple of weeks so we could get to know each other."

He would have sworn nothing could make him happier that day. He'd been wrong. "Jason's in a year-round school and has a break coming up next month, I'm sure we could work something out with Shelly to take them then."

"Do you think they'll like me?"

She wasn't looking for an easy answer about this, either. "Susie will be easy. She loves everyone and sees no reason they shouldn't love her back. Jason's lost too many people in his short life. He's slower to trust people. But he'll come around. And when he does, the two of you will be terrific together."

She propped herself up on her elbow and looked at him. "I want us to have children, too, Eric. I'm tired of empty rooms in empty houses."

"Was this a project you wanted to get started on right away?"

She laughed. "I think it can wait a while—but not too long."

He put his hand on the back of her neck and brought her to him for a kiss. No matter how many books he wound up writing in his lifetime, he would never be able to come up with a better ending.

But their story wasn't an ending—it was a beginning.

America's #1 Bestselling Female Writer

Janet Dailey

Over 300 million copies of her books have been sold, in 98 countries!

NOTORIOUS

In rugged northern Nevada, Eden Rossiter fights to protect her family's ranch. But Eden's strong will weakens when a handsome stranger takes up her cause and captures her heart. **"The novel succeeds on the strength of Dailey's well-paced plot and emotion-packed ending."—*Publishers Weekly***

ILLUSIONS

The glitz and glamour of Colorado ski country is the setting for this spellbinding story about a beautiful security expert, Delaney Wescott, who is drawn into a high-profile murder case while protecting a handsome movie idol.

And a must-have for the millions of Janet Dailey fans...

THE JANET DAILEY COMPANION

by Sonja Massie and Martin H. Greenberg

A comprehensive guide to the life and the novels of Janet Dailey, one of the world's bestselling authors. Includes in-depth interviews and profiles of many of her books.

National Bestselling Author
ERIN PIZZEY

For the Love of a Stranger

Anna Kearney and Mary Rose Buchanan are as opposite as best friends can be. Beautiful Anna is blessed with the gift of empathy, allowing her to look deep inside the hearts of of strangers. Selfish, decadent, and wickedly sexy Mary Rose vows to share her heart with no man–but her body with many. From the serene Irish countryside to the glittering nightclubs of New York, these two women share tumultuous roads, and the pains and joys of love and friendship.

Swimming with Dolphins

There's something special about the Caribbean Island of Little Egg that makes Pandora feel that she might be able to escape the pains caused by her tyrannical mother and a series of abusive husbands. On Little Egg, Pandora finds refuge, understanding, and the gentle love of a man that helps banish the ghosts of her past and may finally lead her to happiness.

Read all of Erin Pizzey's Glorious Novels of Women Coping with the Challenges of Life and Love

Kisses
In the Shadow of the Castle
Morningstar
Other Lovers
The Consul General's Daughter

All Available from HarperPaperbacks

HarperPaperbacks *By Mail*

To complete your Barbara Delinsky collection, check off the titles you're missing and order today!